HUNTER'S ORANGE

WILLIAM DIETER

AVON
PUBLISHERS OF BARD, CAMELOT, DISCUS AND FLARE BOOKS

AVON BOOKS
A division of
The Hearst Corporation
1790 Broadway
New York, New York 10019

The Atheneum Publishers edition contains the following Library of Congress Cataloging in Publication Data:

Dieter, William,—
Hunter's orange.
I. Title.
PS3554.I36H8   1983   813'.54   82-73280

First Avon Printing, December, 1984

For my wife B E T S

I have brought her home, my love, my only friend. There is none like her . . . none.

TENNYSON

> . . . He threw down the beast
> And knelt above it with a knife. On the instant
> It vanished like a shadow, and a cry
> So mournful that it seemed the cry of one
> Who had lost some unimaginable treasure
> Wandered between the blue and the green leaf
> And climbed into the air, crumbling away . . .
> Til all had seemed a shadow or a vision
> But for the trodden ground . . . the pool of blood. . . .

WILLIAM BUTLER YEATS

HUNTER'S ORANGE

CHAPTER 1

The Great Light came into the cave and woke him and he opened his eyes. He lay without moving for several minutes and then he got up and moved to the fire. It was dead. He poked at the coals and retrieved a scrap of tendon from the ashes and chewed it for several minutes and then put it in the hide pouch he wore at his waist. He drank some water from the stone but the bone dipper scraped the side and the noise woke the Woman. She stirred against the layout of hides and watched him in the growing light but she did not get up. Beside her one of the Children whimpered in its sleep and clutched at its stomach. He removed the scrap of tendon from the pouch and dropped it beside the Woman. He bent down and laid his hand against her eyes and then he left the cave, taking with him both his long throwing spear and the short stabbing spear and a few flint blades and a flesher, which he put into the pouch at his waist. The tall hunter who had arrived just after the remove and the shorter one with the scar on his face joined him when he emerged from the cave. The three of them loped easily down the slope and headed toward the Great Light that lay at the bottom of the sky as if in a pool of its own blood. Below them, in the green narrow place where the waters ran, a white fog was rising from the trees.

3

The three motor homes left Salt Lake City at the exact time the plans called for, just as they did every year. The departure was without incident except that during the predawn breakfast at the Kimballs' house they got into their annual flap over terminology. Two of the couples maintained that three motor homes driving in line were a "caravan" while the third couple insisted that "convoy" was correct. "No way is it a convoy," Red Taddish argued. His wife, Dorothy, explained that the word "convoy" held too much of a military connotation. The Wallaces agreed. "It makes you think of maneuvers, of getting into position for an attack," they said. "And that can't be true because we are totally nonviolent. Right?"

"Right, we are nonviolent."

"Therefore we are a caravan."

Nothing was settled, as usual, except that the argument was assured of a continuance until the following year. But as the three motor homes wound their way out of the neighborhood there *was* that sense of the predawn convoy, the ponderous creep of coupled vehicles through the darkness, the rumble of gears. It was secretive somehow, furtive, portentous.

They drove out onto Redwood Boulevard and then turned south on City Bypass 215 toward its junction with Interstate 15, three couples in three motor homes, each towing an off-road vehicle. In the lead were Bike and Karen Kimball, towing a Bronco. Next came Von and Sandy Wallace, pulling their Jimmy. In the rear of the line was a customized blue-and-orange Blazer hitched to the motor home that belonged to Red and Dorothy Taddish. They were going hunting, the same as every year, the only difference being that this year the game was buffalo. They had applied six years ago for the special permits and their names had finally come up and now they were on their way. Not without expense however; the three permits

4

had cost two hundred dollars each. "Don't think about the money," Bike Kimball admonished his wife the day the permits arrived in the mail from the Utah State Division of Wildlife Resources. "The important thing is that we finally got them. They're here and we're going! We're going for *buffalo!*" and he grabbed Karen around the waist and danced her across the living room and down the hall and into the kitchen where the wall phone was, and from there they called the good news to the other two couples.

The plans this morning of departure called for a stop at the Big Buck Cafe in Provo to eat breakfast and then to continue on Interstate 15 until they reached the village of Scipio, where they would take highway 50 southeast to Salina. At Salina they would stop and powwow on which route to take from there to Hanksville. They were taking the trip as they had planned it, in segments, cutting them out of the day like pieces of cold fudge from a plate, enjoying each one, having fun. They'd always had fun. They'd always been friends, ever since high school fourteen years earlier. The Taddishes and the Wallaces lived in the suburb of Granger where Red and Von worked at the copper smelter. The Kimballs had their home in Granger too and Bike was employed by the Utah Department of Highways, Planning Division. All six of them had been in the class of '66 at Granger High School and all of them were thirty-two years old except for Sandy Wallace, who wouldn't be thirty-two until the first week in December, which was five weeks away. All three couples bowled in the same league at the Deseret Lanes on Redwood Boulevard and there wasn't ten points difference in their average score after four years of bowling. None of them had ever bowled a three-hundred game. All of them belonged to the Third Ward Church of Jesus Christ of Latter-day Saints, Granger Stake. None of them had been married in the temple—for *time and eternity* the church called it—and only Bike Kimball among their number had ever been on mission. They were godparents to each other's children. Each couple had two children except for Red and Dorothy, who had had only one and they had lost her six years earlier in an accident. None of the wives worked outside the home. As the bishop said, they had the finest careers they could hope to have, the careers they were best suited for—home and family. Sandy Wallace had actually worked part of one year in a clerical position at Palmer Elementary in Granger and she had liked it at first, but then she quit.

Their progress on the highway now in this black time before dawn seemed an eerie thing to Sandy. Not frightening, just eerie. It wasn't the darkness that did it but the light, the light their headlamps threw forward onto the pavement, always the same length, always the same diameter and the same circumference as though the vehicle they rode in and the light it projected were all one thing, a capsule hurtling down the highway with the darkness collapsing in behind it like black sand. They seemed forever on the verge of piercing the darkness, of shattering it, of forcing it to open to them.

The caravan had approximately ten miles to travel on City 215 before it reached Interstate 15 proper, but before they had gone five miles Red Taddish pulled out from the tail of the line and passed the other two rigs, his horn blaring and his headlamps flashing, and took the lead. "I knew he was going to do that," Sandy Wallace exclaimed. It was part acceptance and part disgust. "I knew Macho Man couldn't stand to be last in line for very long."

"Maybe he thinks he's got to run interference for me like he used to in high school," Von offered.

"No, he's just got to be in front. He's got to be first. Can you imagine it being that important?"

They never did pierce the darkness. They seemed close to breaking through many times but all that happened was that the darkness began to leach out, to pull back from the highway and slink away across the fields so that when dawn finally came it wasn't a sudden startling thing at all. It was just there, coming

6

like fog rather than like an explosion, showing up as a timid glow on a newly visible line far ahead of them that turned out to be the horizon. As they watched the glow it became more a color than a light, first pink and then rose and finally crimson. Then it was a whole flower growing out of the earth directly in front of them, a soft unfolding flower in many shades of red. Sandy made a reverent whispering. "How beautiful it is." And Von answered simply, "Yes," for it was true, the dawn was awesome in its beauty.

The highway still paralleled the Jordan River and as the daylight spread it threw into relief the great benches of the valley—long flat-topped terraces that led like giant levees down to where an ancient river once had run. "Just think," Sandy said, "some of the original Indians of North America might have lived in this valley. They could have run along these same benches on a morning like this. Maybe starting out on a hunt, looking for food. They had to find their own, God knows. There wasn't any Big Buck Cafe for them." Beside her in the seat Von searched the shadowy benches for the ghosts of those early runners. Sandy was right, they could have moved through here. The earth was certainly no less huge and empty now than on that long ago day. But there were no runners, there were no forms, nothing swarmed or intruded. This day was its own, it was being born and was new, commanding its own attention.

The dawn came on and came on and the flower wilted and the petals blew away, passing over their speeding caravan into the west.

When the caravan reached Provo it exited the Interstate and pulled into the Big Buck parking lot and everyone got out. They stretched or rubbed or yawned, whatever they had to do to come fully awake, and they all put on their jackets. All except Karen Kimball. She had on a sweater and a pair of tight jeans—she owned no other kind—and walking behind her across the lot Red Taddish made a clucking noise in his mouth.

7

"Must be jelly," he said, watching her hips sway, " 'cause jam don't shake like that."

Everyone chuckled, Karen perhaps more loudly than the others, and as they climbed the steps of the restaurant Red repeated the remark and someone said, "Oh, Red, you're such a clown!"

But Red Taddish wasn't a clown, not really. Some men are natural clowns, they're born to it. Other men can learn it, learn how to grin but never actually laugh, learn how to pretend not to care about the attention their antics earn them when in truth they seek it constantly, even desperately. Red could learn things —he had learned to dance, for example—but not this, he couldn't grasp the clown skills. Another problem was his appearance; he didn't look the part. Intrinsically, clowns own no sharp features. There are no lean sinister-looking clowns, not even under the costumes and the paint. What they are is bland. Average. They are neither unusually short nor exceptionally tall, never distinctive in any physical way. That's what ruined Red Taddish for clownship. His face was acceptably forgettable but his body wasn't. He was too big, too hulking, too Eric-the-Red to be a successful clown. It kept him from exuding the helplessness and vulnerability that a genuine clown has innately. Oh, Red could be funny at times and do funny foolish things, but he wasn't a clown. He *wanted* to be, but he wasn't. Another deterrent was his personality. His quirks and his preferences governed him too much. He was too one-track; there was no impartiality in him. To the true clown a trick cigar is no more hilarious than a simple hot foot, but Red Taddish would disdain the hot foot and absolutely double up over a trick cigar. He'd giggle in that high thin voice he had and slap his thigh and carry on outrageously. Clowns don't do that. People would say, "Oh, Red, you're such a clown!" But it wasn't true.

The cafe was well lighted and smelled early-morning warm. Mounted in a line against one wall stood the heads of a half-dozen trophy bucks. On one rack of antlers directly behind the

8

cash register hung a hunter's orange cap, much faded now by a sun that was as destined to shine in every day on that same spot as the rheumy eyes of the bucks were to gaze out forever upon that particular arrangement of booths and tables. The six travelers took one of the front tables and a busboy came out from somewhere in the back and gave them water. When the waitress came everyone ordered an omelet, hash browns, juice, a plate of silver dollar pancakes in lieu of toast, and Red asked for a side of biscuits and gravy. "I figured you for biscuits," the waitress mumbled. But she didn't look up from her pad, she didn't look at anyone. It was her standard let's-test-this-group approach, the one that went for the quick laugh, much harder to pull off on the breakfast shift. But it worked. She got the laugh. Everyone at the table laughed, although they didn't look at her when they did. They didn't look at anything except the menus she had thrust into their hands, which meant that she could look at them now. It was part of the approach. She had established a position she was comfortable in, she could handle them, she had followed the rules and the rules were explicit: Don't laugh first or look first but quietly pick one guy out of the bunch and work through him. The biggest guy, the moose, was always the best. Handle the moose in the group and you've got the group, that was the rule. She had this one. "So you figured me for a side of biscuits and gravy, huh?" Red asked archly, looking at her now, playing right into it. "How come you to figure that?"

But he knew the answer. The whole group knew the answer. The waitress knew it when she watched them come through the door and sit down. "Guy as big as you," she said to him, making it complete now, "a guy as big as you had to go for biscuits and gravy. That's what we call a lead pipe cinch." The group laughed again and she let them, but not too long. Too much laughter at this point was not good either. "Coffee?" she asked quickly. It was almost urgent. "Coffee for the cobwebs?" They quit laughing, they had to, they had to answer her and

"God, yes," was what they said. "That's what I need, hot coffee. Can you bring the pot?" She left the table and when she came back carrying the pot *they* got a chance to study *her*. They saw a lot of miles on the face, hard miles, some puff and some sag too, a lot of lines that were beginning to etch in. Much more obvious was the fact that her dentures were badly worn and had gradually collapsed her lips into a thin nervous cut that would never heal no matter how much she licked at it. She had a lot of hair that didn't minimize her face, as she had hoped, but rather framed it. Her hair was a loose fluffy pile of auburn. Too loose, too fluffy, too auburn. She poured coffee all around and the game resumed. "I see you three bucks brought your better halves with you," she said with that arrogance of one who knows, who has always known, what to say to men.

"Hell yes," Red said, and Bike answered that they brought them every year. But it was Von who made the remark Auburn Hair had been waiting for. "No fun without the girls," he said. Auburn looked directly at Von and said, "I know what kind of fun you're talking about, buster." It worked, of course, it always worked in a mixed group. One of the guys was certain to mention the word "fun" and when he did she had the punch line ready for them like a completed dinner check. The group was certain to laugh and this one was no exception. It laughed explosively, almost gratefully, and each of its members stared at the dupe who had spoken the magic words and was blushing now, making the others laugh even harder. It was perfect exit music for Auburn, and she took the coffeepot with her.

She did a silent refill ten minutes later when all six eaters were deep in their plates and then came back ten minutes after that to fill again. This last fill was the important one, the one the tip rode on. She liked a folksy close—warm, familiar, sincere. "How far you folks going?"

"Hanksville," Bike Kimball answered. "In that general area. We're going hunting."

"I figured that," Auburn said; she wanted to add *you dumb ass* but she didn't, it wasn't the time for it although she could have said it if it had been all guys at the table. "My brother and his wife left this morning for the high Uintas," she went on to Bike. It was always the *high* Uintas the way it was always the *deep* sea, the *low* flats, the *burning* sands.

"That so? We've been up in the Uintas lots of times. Good spot."

"Good for mule deer," Auburn said. "You folks going for mule deer?" It was nonchalant, almost a throwaway.

"We're not going for muleys," Bike answered, and it came in a brief quiet interlude where there were no spoons and saucers clattering and it sort of hung there. Auburn didn't trust hanging remarks. They were dangerous things like a late glass of water or a forgotten dessert or a kid in a highchair yanking on your boobs if you got too close; any one of them could cut the hell out of a tip. She looked at the speaker and then at the big red-haired moose. If the moose didn't offer an answer now she'd have to ask and she didn't especially want to. The moose caught her looking and glanced at the other guys and then back at her and said, "We're going for something a lot bigger than muleys."

Auburn stopped filling and set the coffeepot down. The moose obviously wasn't going to help, in fact, he had gathered his audience and was going to play it against her. She could do Twenty Questions with him and eventually get an answer but it would take too long. And it could kill the tip. She took a last chance and tried this: "Bigger than deer? You guys looking for elephant?"

It didn't work. They didn't even laugh, let alone fall for the trick and reveal the name of the animal. She looked away from Red and picked up the pot and slipped immediately into another role. "Gosh," she minced, "I really don't know animals. I've never been hunting myself. There's no way I could kill one of those poor defenseless little—"

"Give a guess," Red commanded. "Take a stab at it. Bigger than a deer. Heavier. Two, three times heavier."

"Golly . . ."

"Might even go a ton."

"A ton? Gosh, that's what, two thousand pounds? Are you kidding me? What weighs a ton? What kind of animal?"

"Horns," Red hinted. "No rack. No antlers. Just horns. And big ones." He bunched his shoulders and drew them for her with his hands.

"Horns?" Auburn scanned the circle of faces for help. "Elk? Moose? What?"

Red loved it but he glowered at the group around him, defying them to reveal the name. "Elk and moose has got antlers, woman!" he exclaimed in a whine of exasperation. "God, you don't know game for squat, do you?"

"Gosh . . ."

"Give up?" one of the women offered in a fit of pity.

"Golly . . ."

Bike Kimball opened his mouth to speak but Red silenced him with a glance. Nothing more came from Auburn and then Red held her down with his eyes and revealed the secret. "Buffalo."

Auburn's mouth dropped and she forgot herself. "No . . . *shit?* Buffalo?"

"You got it."

But she still wasn't absolutely sure, and she wanted to be. She wanted to play the jokes, not be played on. She eyed Red warily and said, "Like what used to be on the nickel? That buffalo?"

"Right."

"Here in Utah?"

"Right here in Utah. The genuine article. The real McCoy. Real American buffalo."

"Bison," Dorothy put in. "Their real name, the scientific one, is *bison bison.*"

"Well, thank you thank you," Red cracked, and laughed uproariously. So did Karen.

"I should have known," Auburn said, directing a self-effacing

12

glance at Red. "When you said it weighed a ton and had horns I should have known what the animal was."

"You should have," Red said, accepting her confession. "What else has got horns and weighs that much?"

"Right," Auburn said, "what else?" but there was an abrupt indifference in it. "How in hell did you ever get a license?"

"You wait, that's how!" Bike broke in. It was a pounce. "Six years we waited."

"God Almighty," Auburn drawled, letting go completely now of the sensitive little girl who didn't like hunting and never used bad language. "I'll bet it cost a bundle too."

"A leg, an arm and two puppies," Karen said, and Auburn ignored her completely.

"It cost a thousand dollars for one license," Red announced importantly, holding up one finger. "One thousand big ones."

"I'll be dipped," Auburn said.

"Actually," Bike put in guiltily, "that's the fee for out-of-state. Residents pay only—"

"That's a lot of oatmeal cookies," Auburn said to Red, and Red said back, "If you're a Utah resident you pay a little less than that, of course."

"Seems only fair," Auburn said. "And just wait till I tell my brother and his wife that I seen some buffalo hunters. They won't believe it. They'll think I was out back smoking one of those loco sticks." She laughed at her own colorful terminology, and then she said, "Will you be coming back this way?"

"Oh, yes. We live in Granger so we've got to come back through Provo."

"Maybe you'll show me your kill," Auburn said to Red. "I never seen a buffalo. They were extinct for a long time, I know that. But I'm glad they've come back."

There was a perfect silence and Dorothy Taddish coughed weakly in the exact middle of it. "I am," Auburn repeated, pushing at the sudden awkwardness, misreading it. "I'm glad."

Bike sat forward and shoved his coffee cup back from his

13

plate in that officious way he had, as if to proclaim the conversation ended. Auburn picked up on it and left the whole bunch of them there at the table looking at Bike. He said, "What did we decide on the expenses for this trip? Didn't we make a plan for these meals?"

"I pay for all the meals," reported Dorothy, who was in charge of finances. "On my Visa card. When we get back home I add up all the slips and split the total three ways. Three families, three ways. That was our plan."

Bike said, "I knew we'd made a plan."

"You couldn't operate any other way, could you, Bike?" Von said.

"And the tips?" Karen asked. "What do we do about the tips?"

Bike began something on the tips but Dorothy interrupted. "They go on the Visa slip along with the meals. That way everything's in one total."

"Sounds good to me," Red said, and handed Dorothy the guest check Auburn had given him. Dorothy left the table and walked up to the cash register, and while she waited for the cashier a man sitting at the counter glanced at Dorothy and then at his plate and then back at Dorothy. The double take was not unusual. Dorothy was different looking. She was thin and small and extremely pale-skinned, white almost, but that wasn't the main difference. It was the eyes. Dorothy had eye wells that were set deep in her skull. In addition to being deep they were dark, as if she had brushed the eyelids with a cosmetic that was too dense, or perhaps excessive. But it wasn't cosmetics, it was her skin and the way her eye sockets were shaped. It gave her eyes an uninvolved look; they seemed removed from her. Sometimes when she was speaking her eyes sat back in their dark wells and looked out as though the words weren't hers at all and she was trying to listen to them. It made for two Dorothy Taddishes much of the time, the one speaking and the one watching. Her voice was nice enough, a trifle husky from the cigarettes perhaps, and she never spoke fast or with any real harshness, even when she was drunk. And despite every attempt to do otherwise, she stayed thin. Red kidded constantly about fattening her up, at least in front of company, saying that the only butt she had on her was the one she'd borrowed from the little neighbor boy. Dorothy would counter with things like "the closer the bone the sweeter the meat," or "a thin board never rots in the middle." But Red would persist; he had some pretty good lines worked out for himself. "I like some meat with my potatoes," was one, but his favorite for company went, "I need some handles to hang on to when I get my monthly ride." Dorothy would laugh real hard when he said it but her eyes wouldn't. They just watched.

While Dorothy was paying the check Karen suggested pit stops for everyone, and when they had finished and left the restaurant Auburn went immediately to the cash register to check the Visa charge slip. The check had come to $18.35 and the tiny woman with the weird eyes had paid it, not the moose. And she had added only a five-percent tip. "God save us from buffalo hunters!" Auburn exploded. "The cheap bastards!"

The morning warmed steadily. As they drove south from Provo past Spanish Fork and Santaquin and Nephi, toward Scipio and the junction, Dorothy had to keep adjusting the heater in the Pace Arrow, sliding the knob away from HOT and into COLD. Finally she went to OFF altogether. They had all worried about the weather for the trip. When you wait fifty weeks for just two, and those two come in late October, you worry about the weather. They needn't have. The sky was mostly clear and what clouds there were looked like the fluff that children pick out of milkweed pods and toss up into the air. The fluff had risen and enlarged and then stopped high in the sky, wispy and soft and white. The air was actually too light to hold much else. Dorothy could feel it. She said to Red, while her thoughts were on it, that there was a fondness in poets

15

and other writers to say that the air in autumn was so crisp and dry that it sometimes tingled.

Red gave a little snort.

"You can actually feel it tingle in your nostrils when you breathe."

"Fuck that," Red said.

"Do you have to use that kind of language?"

"The only tingle I'm going to get is when I drop my bull buffalo. I'll tingle all the way down to my balls."

For a big man he didn't have a big voice and that had always bothered Dorothy.

"Or maybe I'll shoot a cow," he went on. "According to that book you brought home from the library a cow don't look much different than a bull." He glanced at her. "I'm thinking of a mount now. The horns and the head are so near alike who would know it wasn't a bull? I mean it, Dorothy, who would know?"

Dorothy didn't agree or disagree. She didn't answer because she wasn't listening. She was looking up through the tinted part of the huge windshield at the clouds, at what the children had tossed there, the harmless white fluff from the fields of milkweed they played in.

CHAPTER 2

He ran easily in the soft black ash of the ridge. He could not hear his two companions but he had only to turn his head to see them, the scarred one several spear lengths behind on one side and the tall hunter double that distance on the other. He could tell from the position of the Great Light that they had run a long while since leaving the caves. They had made good time and he was not surprised. He had always been a good runner, setting a strong pace, forcing the others to keep up, and that's what his father had named him—Good Runner. It didn't mean that he never got tired. Most of the time when he ran his chest got noisy from the air pumping in and out so fast, and his mouth felt like it had filled up with the fur of hares and he kept wanting to spit it out. But that was normal and as long as he didn't hurt anywhere he would be all right. He knew that his legs were strong, as strong as his arms when he had to throw the long spear at the beasts.

When the Great Light was almost overhead Good Runner knew that they were nearing the place where the beasts could be found. Down the edge of this ridge and across the valley where the trees grew and where you could begin to hear the sound of the waters falling is where the beasts should be. He hoped they would still be there. Many of the beast herds had been disappearing lately, running away from the Great Light and its burning heat, shaking the land in their going. Without the beasts there would be only the hares and the strange birds that lived among the trees. There was almost no meat on the birds, and very little more on the hares. Without meat the band would be forced to live on berries and roots and the wild plants they gathered. Without meat the People would become weak and their bones would begin to show and their eyes would bulge out. The Children's bellies would swell and they would no longer play and jump and laugh around the fires.

The ridge ended and Good Runner started his descent into the valley. The soft ash gave way to a hard-packed dirt and the small flat-topped trees began to appear. The leaves had been stripped from the trees and he could see the black ugly birds huddled in the branches. After a while stones started to protrude from the dirt and there were thorn bushes growing beside the path. He glanced over his shoulder as he ran and searched for the two hunters, but they had fallen back.

He ran on without slowing and the air in his chest became louder. His legs still did not hurt but he knew he had to be careful. If he staggered into the thorn bushes by mistake or if he ran too long where the stones were sharp, his feet would swell and bleed and he would not be able to go on. He would be forced to stop and his two companions would go on without him. He would never see the caves again, would not drink the sweet water from the stone nor play with the Children nor enjoy the Woman. The Great Light would pass across the sky and then disappear, and then rise up, and pass, and disappear again. There would be nothing to eat and with his feet broken he could not move to hunt. From where he lay on the dirt he could never rise again. His chest would stop taking in the air and his body would go stiff and the Great Light in its endless passages across the sky would shrivel him up like it did the hides.

18

The town of Scipio sat at the junction of Interstate 15 and US 50 like an old man who had been set down there and instructed —perhaps in jest but certainly to keep him out of the way—to watch over the junction of the two highways and report any strange movement. He obeyed, he sat down, but he fell asleep watching and the Granger people drove their caravan right by and he never saw them. He never even woke up.

It didn't matter. US 50 stretched with scarcely a bend from the Nevada state line east across Utah until it reached the Wasatch Mountains, where it had to twist around and make a new path in order to cross them, they were that high and barrierlike. Scipio just happened to be located at the spot where the twist started. Dorothy Taddish said the name must have come from one of those Roman emperors because it certainly wasn't one of the Mormon prophets. In any event, there was no good reason for the town or anybody in it to be awake and watching that particular morning. The highway entered and left Scipio with equal unconcern, angling generally southeast and assuming no self-importance whatsoever about being the only mountain pass road in that part of Utah's longest mountain range.

But Salina, the town that highway 50 had climbed and twisted thirty miles to reach, was not asleep. It was a much larger town than Scipio and never slept at all, mainly because it was the western terminus of new Interstate 70 which shot westward all the way from Colorado. And this morning Salina was the designated powwow place, planned so by Bike Kimball, who was in charge of travel, and the Granger caravan stopped at the Stag Inn on the curve at the south edge of town. They took a table in the bar and decided to have a round of drinks rather than coffee. "Isn't this a little early for drinks?" Sandy asked.

"I don't think it's too early," Dorothy Taddish said, and they all agreed with that assessment, so Von Wallace went to the bar to order. The order never varied, it was always the same—five Coors and a Slops. *Slops* was Von's acronym for State Liquor on Premise Sales, a system under which the customer could buy his booze in a bottle and his mix in a bottle, but never the two together in a glass. According to Von it could happen only in Utah. Only Utah could decree that its citizens weren't adult enough to walk into a bar and order and consume a glass of wine or a mixed drink. Beer they could drink to the utmost limits of stupidity, but not a highball. And it wasn't true, Von further expounded, that each new generation was brighter and more enlightened than the preceding one, for as the generations came successively into being they continued to legislate state-controlled liquor stores as the only place where liquor and wine could be legally purchased. But to show it was not *totally* un-modern, the state allowed many of its restaurants to include on their premises a separate package store that offered for sale a limited selection of alcoholic beverages. Dorothy Taddish's selection was always Smirnoff vodka, always the 1.6-ounce miniature. At home the Taddishes kept on hand a considerable inventory of vodka minis and in their motor home there were sacks and boxes and cartons of these tiny bottles. Dorothy Taddish, obviously, did not like beer. That's why the order was always the same—five Coors and a Slops.

The bartender was a bushy-haired young man who looked at Von's orange cap instead of his face. "Going out after them, huh?" he asked, not caring really, just making conversation because that's what the boss wanted.

Von answered that, yes, he was right, they were going out after them.

"What's open? Deer, elk, what?"

"Deer and elk season ended yesterday."

"I didn't know that." The bartender set five bottles of Coors on a tray. "We don't have cans, is bottles okay?"

"Bottles are fine."

The bartender turned to the back bar for the vodka. "So what are you after then?"

"Buffalo," Von said.

The bartender turned and looked Von in the face for the first time. "What?"

"Buffalo."

"I'll be go to hell," the bartender exclaimed, and he stared at Von as if there were a special set of signs that would confirm *buffalo* and one of them might be on Von's face. Or might not be. Either way he made some kind of decision and started with several things at once. "I heard one time there was a season on buffalo in this state. I'm not from this state actually, I'm from Colorado. But a restricted season, you know, that sort of thing. A restricted hunt where not everybody—" He stopped and the original half-smile of disbelief came back into his face. "I'll be go to hell. Buffalo!"

"What do I owe you?" Von said.

"I was going to say I never knew anyone who had bagged a buffalo but come to think of it my dad knew a guy who got one. Guy he worked with. Came back from somewhere with a buffalo. I think it was a buffalo. I didn't know him myself, he was my dad's friend. Real good friend. Grew up together." He stopped his chatter abruptly and zeroed in on Von's face. "Jesus Christ, what do you shoot a buffalo with?"

"You shoot him with a bullet."

"Just any bullet? I mean . . . a regular one?"

"A big one. The bullet's got to be big enough to penetrate and kill the animal quickly. That's the important thing." He held out some money. "What do I owe you for the round?"

The bartender reached under the bar and brought up a glass of soda with ice cubes in it and set it on the tray with the bottles. The stir stick had a knob at the end in the shape of a stag. "That'll be five-fifty," he said. Von handed him six one-dollar bills and waited for the change. When he got back to the table they were arguing about the best route to take to Hanksville. Von set the tray down and they all grabbed their drinks. "I ordered a goddamned can," Red said.

"They don't have cans. Just bottles."

"We'll let Von settle it," Karen was saying. "We'll let him pick the best way to Hanksville."

"Screw that," Red said.

"Bike's in charge of travel," Sandy put in. "Travel is his responsibility, he should be the one to decide. He should know the best route. After all, he works for the Highway Department."

"I'm with Red on this," Karen put in. "If he wants to go south from here to Richfield I see nothing wrong with that. What difference does it make?"

"The road from here to Richfield is Junks Élysées," Sandy said.

Red banged his bottle of Coors down on the table. "Junks what?"

"Junks Élysées."

"It's 89," Dorothy broke in. "The road to Richfield is US highway 89." She turned to Bike. "Isn't it?"

"We don't go as far as Richfield," Bike said. "We turn off at Sigurd onto state 24 and that takes us to Hanksville."

Dorothy said, "I never heard of Sigurd." She held her Slops protectively in both hands. It was already half gone. "Sigurd sounds like an Ingmar Bergman movie."

"I want to know what the hell Junks Élysées is," Red said, having trouble with the word this time.

"It's from Champs Élysées," Dorothy answered him. "It's a famous boulevard in Paris."

"I'm asking Sandy. It's her word. I want to know what the Junks part of it is?"

"Richfield is the Junks part of it," Sandy said. "The road through Richfield is Junks Highway. Can you understand Junks Highway? It's a highway that runs through everybody's junk.

Junk cars. Junk sheds. Junk antler piles. Every do-it-yourself Jack Mormon in the state of Utah has his own personal junkyard facing on that highway."

"Easy now," Red said. "My old man lives in Richfield."

"Is his yard full of junk?" Sandy asked him.

Red shot her a look. "Hey, back off! Just because a guy can't afford a big fancy house with three bathrooms and a double—"

"Is his yard full of junk?" Sandy asked again, her voice rising.

"Let's be nice," Bike broke in. "Besides, we don't go through Richfield. No matter how we get to Hanksville we don't go through Richfield."

"You decide how we should go, Bike," Dorothy urged. "That's your responsibility. You're in charge of travel."

"The shortest way is state 24," Bike explained. "You head south from here and turn off at Sigurd, like I said. You go through Capitol Reef National Park and that way. It's the shortest route but it's not the best one."

"The Interstate is best," Von said. "Interstate 70."

Bike agreed. "Physically, yes, it is. It's new, it should be. They were working on it in a few places but I think they're finished now."

"You hear that?" It was Karen. "Didn't I tell you it was the best road?"

"I thought you were the one who wanted to go to Richfield with Red," Dorothy remarked.

"The problem," Bike put in, "is that the Interstate is seventy miles longer. You actually wind up coming into Hanksville from the far side, from the east."

"Then that's out," Red exclaimed. "We can't go that way, it's too far."

"Who says we can't?" It was Dorothy this time. "I'll bet the Interstate's a great road. I'll bet it goes through some of the most beautiful country in the state."

"If you like wasteland, yes," Karen said.

Sandy said, "It's back to you, Bike. You're in charge of travel. You pick the route."

"Does that mean he'll buy the extra gas for all three rigs if we go the long way?" Red wanted to know. But while Bike was getting an answer ready two strangers approached the table, breaking up everybody's best argument. The two men looked like they had just waded up from a duck blind. One of them had a face like the Marlboro man and the other one resembled him strongly, although he was older. "We were just talking to the bartender," the older man began with a smile. "He tells us you folks are going for buffalo."

"That's right," Red said. "We're going for buffalo." It sounded more like a dare than an answer.

The younger man grinned and showed all his teeth. "Where do you get that kind of luck?" he said, and you could tell now from the grins that the two were related.

"It's not exactly luck," Bike said in that gracious way he had with new people.

"I'm sure of that," the older man came back, trying to make it sound wise. Then he asked Bike when the season opened.

"Day after tomorrow. Saturday. The first of November."

"And it closes?"

"The eighteenth of November."

"That's a long season, considering what the game is."

Red Taddish said loudly, "You two do some hunting, do you?"

"We do," the older man answered. "Bird mostly. We just got back from our blind up on the Sevier Bridge Reservoir. It's a membership deal. You buy in, you always have a spot in the blind, that sort of thing."

"How'd you do?" Von asked him.

"We filled up," the younger man answered, smiling. "We generally do. But a duck's not a buffalo."

"No shit," Red said.

"We've never been lucky enough to get a crack at buffalo,"

24

the young man went on. "In fact, I've never known anyone to get a permit." He eyed all of them at the table, looking for a spokesman. "What system do they use, a lottery?"

"Not exactly," Red said. It sounded knowing and the two duck hunters waited for him, but it was Bike who finally answered. "One permit, one animal, is the way they work it," he said.

"Is it buck only?" asked the younger man, and then he caught himself. "I suppose it's bull, not buck," and he blushed a little and would not look at his father. "Is it either sex?"

"Hunter's choice we call it," Bike said with a little laugh. "Same thing."

The young man nodded and then he asked Bike what he thought the kill ratio would be. "Eighty percent?" He watched Bike's face. "Seventy-five?"

"A hundred," Bike said. "It's historically a hundred."

The young man whistled in admiration. "That's incredible. It really is. What I wouldn't give—"

"There's only a couple dozen permits issued each year," Bike told him.

"That's what you call exclusive," the older man broke in. "I'd like to be one of the exclusive ones. Or get lucky." He made it sound anxious. "Or know someone," he added, eyeing each of them.

"I know what you mean," Red said, staring back.

After what seemed a long time the man said to Red, "Do you know someone?"

Red picked a spot in the center of the table to stare at, a clear spot among the ashtrays and the bottles. "I might," he said.

"Does that someone have a name?" asked the older man.

"It's possible," Red answered, and with his thumb he rubbed off part of the label on his bottle of beer.

The older man had been standing with one rubber boot propped up on an empty chair and he immediately dropped it to the floor and stood erect. "Listen, what are you folks drinking here?" and his whole manner became expansive. He glanced at the bar and snapped his fingers. "Give these folks here another round," he called to the bartender, "whatever they're drinking."

"Right," the bartender called back, and in the emptiness of the bar the word sounded hollow. The older man was concentrating now on his success, scanning the circle of faces at the table, smiling paternally. "I see you boys brought your better halves with you."

"We always do," Bike said.

"I like to see that. I like to see wives do things like this with their husbands. Sport things."

"Do you ladies shoot?" the younger man asked, looking at them. "Do you have licenses?"

"No," Dorothy answered simply.

"But they're great bed warmers," Red put in.

"You bet they are," the older man laughed. "Good for these cold nights. Better than whiskey." He winked. "And no hangover."

While they were laughing the drinks came and they all thanked the older man. "You are most welcome," he answered effusively. "When you're on a hunt you should enjoy yourselves," and when he trailed the bartender back to the bar to pay for the round he glanced back and Red got up from the table and followed him. At the bar, Red accepted a piece of paper from the bartender and wrote something on it and gave it to the older man. They kept nodding their heads in a kind of exaggerated politeness while they talked and then they returned to the table and Red sat down again, but the older man did not. "It was a pleasure meeting you good folks," he smiled. "I hope you get your animals." His son added pretty much the same thought and together the two of them returned to their original seats at the bar.

Red's grin was almost a noise, so smug was it. "What the

hell's going on?" Von asked him. "What did you give that guy?"

Red took a big gulp of beer. "I gave him a name."

"Whose name?" Bike wanted to know.

"The name I've heard you mention. Barnes. The guy in charge of the Big Game Department office there in Salt Lake. Where you got the permits."

"What's Barnes going to do for this guy?"

"The same as he did for us," Red answered lazily. "He's going to put his name on a list."

"Where on the list?"

It was pure enjoyment for Red; his face was almost obscene. He was going to answer when he got ready, you could see that, but Karen started to push him. "It's not at the top of the list, is it?" She had even picked up Red's smirk. "The man thinks it's the top but it's not, right? It's really on the bottom. It's where our names went six years ago. Right?"

Red looked like he wanted to yawn. "You're getting warm," he said.

"And you told the man that Barnes would take care of him, didn't you?" Karen kept on. " 'See Barnes,' you said. 'He'll take care of you.' You repeated it several times."

"I believe that pretty well covers the way the conversation went."

"You fox!" Karen burst out at last, for it had been building in her. "You absolute fox!" And Red himself let out the whoop of triumph he'd been holding in. He waved his beer in the air and then chugged it.

"I think that's deceitful," Dorothy said.

"Deceitful, my ass," Red belched. "The man was asking for it."

"But you led him on."

"I led him where he was headed. He wanted to buy somebody. He thought he'd spotted the right man and he made his move."

"That doesn't speak very well for you."

"Red's right," Bike broke in. "That's the way the guy operates. You can see it. He's probably bragging to that son of his right now that that's the way you get things done in this life. Know the right man and then get to him. Buy him if you have to." He eyed the group, seeking confirmation of his insight. "That guy will take a checkbook into the coffin with him."

Red Taddish laughed outright, and at someone else's remark, a rare thing for him. "Maybe he'll buy the devil a drink. I wonder what a round costs down there?"

"Oh, Red, you clown!" Karen laughed. They all laughed. The smoothness of Red's deceit persisted and it was fun. The drinks were fun, especially the free ones, and they ordered another round, a quickie, one for the ditch. After all, it was the first day of vacation with a whole thirteen to go. Thirteen and a half actually. They finished the last round and left the bar. Outside, at the bottom of the steps, they linked up and hooked arms and on Karen's command the six of them scooted across the parking lot in a knee-bent crouched-forward lockstep exactly like Groucho Marx used to do it. At the Kimballs' vehicle they broke apart with a yelp of self-congratulation and someone took that moment to announce that they would take state route 24 to Hanksville. "Maybe we'll go Interstate 70 on the way back."

"Right!"

"Maybe stop in Green River and whoop it up."

"Right!"

"Maybe the weather will turn bad while we're there, a blizzard or something, and we'll get snowbound and have to hole up for several days."

"How terrible for us!"

"What route has the most taverns?" Dorothy demanded.

"The Interstate doesn't have any."

"I hate the Interstate. I have always hated it."

"What's the first town after we turn onto 24?"

"Loa," Bike answered.

"Sounds like a pineapple."

"Does Loa have a tavern?"

"Does the LDS church have stakes and wards? Loa has six taverns! Plus a tabernacle for those who want to sing!"

"Then why in hell are we standing out here in the middle of this dried-up parking lot?"

They all piled into their rigs and wheeled out of the lot onto the highway. Red Taddish took the lead and in the first quarter mile he had popped the exhaust of his Pace Arrow a good half dozen times.

When Karen stepped up into the cab of the Huntsman, Bike glanced at her rear end and said, "Did I hear something rip?" Karen reached back and felt along the seam of her jeans, and Bike said, "If those things get any tighter you really will rip out."

"It'll be jelly that spills," she laughed. "That's what Red says it is."

"Red says a lot of things. It's part of his learning to talk."

"Wasn't that clever," Karen asked when they were out on the highway, "how Red snookered that guy in the bar into buying a round of drinks?"

"Well, it wasn't illegal."

"That guy thought he was buying something big, didn't he?"

"The man has to buy his way. It's a compulsion. I was right about him."

"You're right about everything, Bishop." She occasionally called him Bishop, had since the first year out of high school when they were married, which was immediately after he had returned from six months of missionary work in Chicago. He hadn't come off mission voluntarily; he loved the discipline of religion, the evangelism of it, the regimen. But his father had died unexpectedly and his mother had called him home. But Karen didn't want to think about that now. "The old duck hunter in the bar thought he could cut a little time off waiting in line, didn't he?" she said.

"I'd like to see the guy's face when Barnes tells him that the two-hundred-dollar fee is up front, without interest, and that the line starts at the bottom and works up. Slowly."

"Old Lumpjaw had that duck shooter snapping at the bait like a carp at bad cheese."

"There's no law against it, that's for sure. It got us a drink."

The day climbed steadily toward noon and the sun, weak and distant as it was, still had not surrendered the sky to the gloom that Von always suspected was waiting just over the horizon in November. But it wasn't there this time. "It's almost like we were assigned the good weather along with the permits," he said to Sandy.

But Sandy said, "Wasn't that something the way Red tricked that man in the tavern into buying us a drink?"

"It's like Red. Real slippery."

"I wasn't thinking slippery exactly. More . . . clever. After all, I did laugh at what Bike said about it afterwards, about the checkbook in the coffin."

"Slippery, clever, same thing. Red set the trap and then teased the man into it."

Sandy glanced at him. "You sound like it bothered you."

Von glanced back. "It didn't bother me. It's your standard Red Taddish. It's what he does. It's the way he thinks. I mean, who would have thought to pull a stunt like that, steering a friendly conversation into a con for free drinks?"

"Red did it for a gag," she said. "Don't take it so seriously." The words had some scold in them, and just a trace of surprise. "After all, Red's on vacation."

"Or he's bowling. Or he's in the lunchroom at work. Or he's back in high school playing football."

"What do you mean?"

"This is old stuff for Taddish. We'll be at the bar in the

bowling alley and he'll get some guy going with a bunch of talk-talk and the next thing you know we've got a freebie round stacked in front of us."

"I don't see—"

"He was doing that in high school, pulling his little con jobs. He was always getting us extra soap or towels after a game. He'd manage it somehow. He'd think of a way to beat the system. That's Red. That's how his mind works. To tell you the truth I'm surprised Red didn't try to bribe Barnes himself six years ago. He would have, except he wasn't the one who dealt with Barnes. Bike did."

"Well," Sandy said, "no harm done."

Von glanced at her. "Is that the criterion, Sandy? The degree of harm we'll accept before we call a thing what it really is?"

"Oh boy," she laughed, shrinking down into the seat. "Am I sorry I brought this up? Go ahead, ask me. Am I sorry?"

She was sitting close to him, as she had been at dawn, and Von put his hand on her knee. "Are you sorry you brought this up, Sandy?"

"Not a bit. It's nice to get a rise out of you."

They rode in silence and Sandy studied Von's hand on her knee and marveled anew at the amount of hair that grew on it. Von was hairy everywhere; his chest was a mat of thick black coils made soft and cushiony by the sheer mass of them. And he was dark-skinned, which only served to heighten the effect. Mother Wallace said her son looked like George Raft with a few inches on him. Von did have a certain patent-leather look, a sort of square-jawed slicked-down mien. Sandy remembered that her father had called him Dick Tracy when she and Von were first courting. Von's family had come from Roosevelt on his father's side and from Duchesne on his mother's, red dust towns in northeastern Utah where the bridges were narrow green Erector Set structures straddling rivers that were just as narrow and that never ran very fast and were always the color of bad strawberries. Father Wallace had packed up his family and moved to Granger during Von's first year of high school. Von's first name was LaVon but only one grandmother ever called him that. When Sandy first met Von in their freshman year she had been intrigued by how much older he looked than the other boys. She assumed it was the dark looks, all the hair. Now, fourteen years later, he looked pretty much the same and it was the other guys who seemed to have grown older. Von hadn't changed much inside either, she thought, although he could occasionally withdraw into himself and become what she called dreamy. He laughed so quietly that she often had to look to see if he was really laughing. He was easygoing and very patient, sometimes almost ploddy, but his mind was quick. He grabbed hold of new things easily and he was a magician at arithmetic. In the bowling league he could extend line scores in his head long before anyone could even begin to write them down. He was a ballistics wizard and had his own reloading press; he could read ballistics tables just once and recite them forever after. And he was absolutely the best shot with a rifle in the state of Utah. He had accumulated dozens of trophies and awards since high school. Sometimes Sandy called him Sergeant York and it seemed she was forever scouting up old catalogs and telephone directories for him to box up and fire into when he was testing the shot pattern of his hand loads. But most of all, Von was the kind of man who prevailed. He was a steady constant wind that blew across her life and she thought sometimes that he should have picked up and blown hard occasionally, but he didn't. She had expected, as the years passed, to witness an eruption of anger from Von at least once, to see the breaking and smashing of released violence, the tears of a choked speechless fury. But it never came.

CHAPTER 3

He crossed the valley floor and reached the trees and ran among them as silently as he could, the two hunters running directly beside him now. The bony long-tailed birds huddling in the branches blew upward in a startled flutter as the men passed underneath, but they did not stop to stone the birds. They kept running, picking the soft matted places for their feet when they could, searching the low branches of the trees for crouching animals, watching everywhere, everything.

They heard the water long before they reached it. It was a rumbling sound like the smoking mountains made sometimes just before they coughed smoke and cinders. It was a sound that made the earth tremble under their feet just as it did when the beasts ran in ropy black herds across the yellow grasses.

They finally reached the place where the water fell and they stopped in the wet thunder to watch it. It tumbled over the edge of a cliff and fell into a boil of spray that flew back up with a great roar. There were times when the spray caught all the different colors of the Great Light and held them above the water in a giant arch. When their ears grew numb from the noise of the falling water they turned away and circled around toward the back of it, for Good Runner had led here in other hunts and knew that up above the falls, long before the water fell into the canyon, it lay very flat and wide and still upon the land. It lay in the shape of a beast's heart where the beasts would gather to drink and where tall green rushes stood to mark the shores of it. The three hunters ran toward that lake now, hearing the rumble of the falling water move slowly behind them and then finally fade out altogether.

When they spotted the lake in the distance they ran faster, but before they reached it they stopped and studied the edges of the water where the rushes grew. The rushes were brown and brittle now and the lake was much smaller. Good Runner ordered the scar-marked hunter to move out to one side and the tall hunter to move an equal distance to the other so they could scan the rushes from different angles, the same as if there were more of them and they had more eyes. When they were in position Good Runner picked up a stone and heaved it into the rushes. He waited, and then he threw another. He ran forward and stopped and threw more stones into different spots, and listened as hard as he could, and on either side of him his two companions did the same. Nothing moved within the rushes, no beast or lurking Other, nothing that could harm them, and he signaled the two hunters to return to him so they could enter the rushes together and reach the water.

The rushes were tall, almost as tall as he, and they cracked noisily as he crept forward. He knew he had to be careful in a place like this. When the beasts came to drink and brought their small ones with them they could be savage. They would snarl and toss their heads and pound the earth with their hooves if they were surprised, and they would stand in front of their little ones and would not be turned away. At other times the beasts hid in the exact places where the hunters themselves liked to hide, and more times than once Good Runner had parted the reeds and a beast had loomed up before him—the fierce horns, the eyes red and glaring, the ragged jaws. But there was nothing hidden here now and when Good Runner reached the water he motioned the two other hunters to drink *while he stood guard. They fell forward onto their bellies and thrust their faces into the water and drank. Good Runner watched the shore across from him and the slope of the small hill beyond, and he listened for the sound of movement in the rushes at his back. There was nothing. When the two hunters had finished drinking, Good Runner took their place, lying flat in the hard mud with his mouth in the water. The water washed the fur away and returned the feeling to his tongue. It was good to drink water again. It gave pleasure like eating hot meat or enjoying the Woman or lying down to sleep on soft hides in the cave after a hunt. But he knew he had to be careful. Strange Others could come if the three of them drank together without a guard. He remembered a hunt from long ago when a group of his father's band had come upon a pair of Others with their faces in a pool of water, drinking. His group had hidden in the reeds and then jumped out, shouting and waving rocks, and they had stoned the startled Others, had crushed their heads there in the tall reeds by the quiet water.*

She was Sandy Johnson first, before Von. Von figured there were several dozen Sandy Johnsons scattered throughout the state of Utah. Not his Sandy, but Johnson girls with that name. It was because the state was heavily Scandinavian and those dozen other Sandys carried that same Nordic look—the turquoise eyes and the wide unboned faces and the hair that was not light tan and not white but blond, true blond. Brigham Young hair, Von called it, somewhat thick and never worn long nor especially wavy, and if it was worn with a touch of bangs then a kind of Dutchy look was added to the faces. When you looked at a Utah Sandy you thought *summer sky, porcelain,* without ever reaching too hard for those descriptions. And the

35

girls weren't just handsome faces, they were also handsome bodies. They had wide shoulders and good breasts, and hips that big healthy babies came out of, repeatedly. Driving now beyond Sigurd while Sandy napped, Von knew that he could turn the El Dorado around and go back to Scipio and from there turn north or south or west, no matter, and go to all the high schools in all the towns in Utah and see again the same physical Sandy Johnson he had first seen. But not this one, thank God, not the Sandy Wallace who dozed now in the front seat with her head in his lap and her feet propped against the armrest on the door. There was no replica of this Sandy anywhere, no replacement. She was a month shy of being thirty-two years old and two healthy male children had been pushed into life by those strong hips, and if she had changed physically at all it was those two new lives that had done it, not the years. Sandy had "nested in," as her mother would say. Von had brought home the twigs and the down and the pieces of string and Sandy had fashioned a nest for the four of them, protective, warm, as clean and untainted as the builder herself. And only once had she wanted to test her wings again. It was when the boys were still small, in the first and second grades respectively. A position had come open in the local school system— assistant to the budget director in the superintendent's office— and Sandy had applied for it. She'd been accepted. It was her first adult job (she had carhopped at a Dee's Drive-In over on 33d South while still in high school) and she gave it the excitement and the attention first jobs always get. Transportation to this new job was no problem and neither were the hours. She liked the office people and her boss, and she got a chance to use her innate organizational skills. But well into the intricacies of the job and mastering them completely, she quit. She resigned at the end of work one Friday afternoon and never went back. What she tried to explain to Von was that she had suddenly seen the job as a race she'd never gotten in shape for. She wasn't tearful about it. "I can't win that race," she told him. "I can run in it but I can't win. I've missed too many workouts."

"Workouts? What do you mean?"

"You hear people say that a change in their lives or a certain move they made opened a new door for them. They use that term a lot—*opened a door*. But for me it's *two* doors. One is you and the kids and keeping our house, and the other is the job and the possibility of really moving up. It splits me right down the middle."

"Sandy, you know I've been behind anything you ever wanted to do—"

"Oh, hon, I'm not talking about that. It's the preparation. I haven't practiced right. My whole life has been spent doing the wrong kind of exercises. Since I was a little girl they put a doll in my arms and guided me toward preparing for a husband and kids and a home of my own. It's a wonderful calling, a wonderful job and I love it. Then this thing at the school opens up. Another great job. Another door. I'm not afraid of two doors but I can't walk through both of them at the same time. Not and do the job I want to do. I want to succeed and be the very best but I don't think I can. Not at the school. For me it's a race that's been . . . fixed. Not in an evil way by evil people, but just . . . by tradition."

Von wanted to understand; he genuinely tried to. What he said to her was, "Do what the little voice tells you, Sandy. That's the honest way. That's the one we have to live with."

She stayed home. Their new house was finally completed and she nested it into shape with that same effortless certainty she had applied to the first one. The bowling league started and she signed them up. She joined Pioneer Daughters at the church and got involved in PTA. She enrolled in a ceramics class and bought a secondhand kiln and fired it up and painted wood dove pairs and mallard ducks and pheasant males, and gave them as presents. She cooked and cleaned house for Karen when Karen was recovering from a hysterectomy, and when the Taddishes' little girl drowned in the swimming pool Sandy held

37

Dorothy in her arms for hours, week after week. The accident had happened at early evening in the Taddishes' own backyard pool, a new one. Red had killed two six-packs and fallen asleep in his deck chair while Dorothy was in the house preparing a meal, and the little girl had slipped under the water. "I should have stayed with her," Dorothy sobbed over and over. "I shouldn't have left her."

Year after year the men took their vacations together in October or November, depending on what season was open and what they wanted to go for. They all owned four-wheel drive vehicles, but in the spring of 1972 Bike got a promotion at the Highway Department and he and Karen bought the first motor home in the group, a Huntsman. For the next three years Von and Sandy went with them in the Huntsman on the hunting trips, with Red and Dorothy trailing along in their old pickup. In the fall of '75 Von and Sandy bought their own motor home, the El Dorado. Red couldn't stand it any longer and bought a new Blazer pickup, which he immediately customized, and right after that he bought a motor home too, a Pace Arrow, a rig much larger and more plush than either Bike's or Von's. In the years that followed the three couples did the caravan thing in their motor homes when hunting season came, towing their offroad vehicles behind. The game was plentiful everywhere they went and they'd make their kills early, usually in the first twelve hours. They'd dress out the carcasses and hang them on tree limbs near where they parked, and then they'd spend the remaining time in the Pace Arrow playing pinochle and drinking Coors (Slops for Dorothy) and listening to the old high school records they always brought along: the Dave Clark Five, the Supremes, Junior Walker and the All Stars.

They took a lot of animals over the years. A place in South Salt Lake did their head mounts and the guys had the best of them on their den walls, but eventually they had to rent a garage to hold them all. The three families chipped in on the cost of a frozen-food locker and had their meat cut up and

38

packaged there. Most years at Christmas they would donate the meat to Deseret Industries, which was LDS affiliated and was a kind of work-if-you-want-welfare program that the church had initiated to help the needy. The Mormons didn't believe in gravy trains and free riders. Sandy had been involved in that particular area of church activities through her work with the Young Couples section of Pioneer Daughters, and that was how she came to suggest giving Deseret some of the deer and the elk and the antelope venison, there was so much of it. They all agreed it was a wonderful idea, very unselfish, very civic-minded. Then, too, there was a prescribed shelf life on frozen game and several of the packages were pushing at the dates.

Sandy was sensible. Von supposed he respected that quality in her more than any other. She had come from a small family whose wants had been filled competently, with nothing friv-olous or lavish getting in the way, and it had smoothed off in her what might otherwise have become the sharp corners of her life. She was not impulsive, not at all, but she was gutsy, she wouldn't back down. And she was intensely passionate, al-though she held that part of her in a fierce privacy that only Von shared. Von studied her now as she lay relaxed and de-fenseless against the seat. Her hair had darkened slightly; it wasn't a difference you could see exactly, you had to remember what her hair had looked like before. In color her eyes were unchanged but in size they seemed smaller somehow, perhaps because she saw more now, concentrated more, or maybe the muscles at the outer edge had simply begun their inevitable gather. The wide face, the skin color, the mouth, they were all the same. No cavities in the teeth, not even a hint of wattle under that marvelous chin. And her breasts, my God, how wonderful her breasts were. How big really, how settled and full, not the high hard athletic knobs that the high school Sandy's had thought were the perfect manifestation of their womanness. The girls didn't know then what a woman was; they could look at their mother or aunts and even their older

39

married sisters and still not know. It was only when they had married and climaxed repeatedly under their husband's body in the hushed safety of their own bedroom, long silent-scream whole-body orgasms that shuddered and shook them, that they knew what it was to be a physical woman.

Von reached down and without pressure laid his right hand on Sandy's breasts. He knew her breasts without seeing them under the sweater. They were not exact globes, not the un-tipped schoolboy fantasy breasts but imperfect rather, not knowing total roundness. Upon their front lay aureoles so large they seemed to be costume pasties, chocolate rings of skin that seemed to hold swollenness in place and keep it from bursting, like exotic washers. At their center were nipples incredibly long, an inch perhaps, protruding provocatively as if they were yet another piece of the erotic costuming. There were times at home when Von would sit down and stand a naked Sandy directly in front of him and tongue the breasts that loomed before his face, suck on the candy-stick nipples until they grew hard and springy against his tongue. Then he would turn her body to the side and reach down and stroke the final piece of the costume, that secret hidden part that the eyes from the very beginning had known they would seek out, the inverted triangle in the nest of the thighs that was darker in color than the other body hair, matted and curl-soft and waiting for his touch.

Remembering that private feel of her, Von cupped one breast in his hand and squeezed it gently. Sandy stirred sleepily on the seat. He slid his hand to the other breast and repeated the pressure and he saw her eyes open, and her hand came up and touched his and her eyes closed again. "Pull your sweater up," he whispered. She lay still for a moment as if in a delayed hearing and then she arched her back and pulled her sweater up to her neck. "Your bra," he whispered. "Unhook your bra." Sleepily she did his bidding, undoing the garment with a deft movement and folding it away to the sides like exquisite wrapping paper from a gift of pink-tipped alabaster roses. He rubbed his hand over them slowly, tracing the rich lower arcs, kneading the full bulbs, feeling the breasts wholely, thumbing the nipples until they quivered. Sandy's breathing quickened and Von moved his hand downward and with his thumb rubbed a circular spot in the crotch of her jeans. The denim felt coarse and obtrusive. "Slip them down," he whispered to her. "Panties too."

She did, and the white belly and the tawny secret hair of her lay naked before him. He covered the softly mounded mat with his hand and felt it open magically to his touch. He stroked her there, firmly and then gently, outside and then inside, softly, rubbing his thumb in a slight motion at the top of that mysterious cleft and then moving it down the full warm opening length of her, and then back, and across, and then down again, steadily, insistently. Her hips began to writhe and she grabbed his arm with both her hands. "Oh, Von, I'm going to . . ."

He stayed with her, keeping exactly to the rhythm they had jointly assumed, and her hips ground into the seat and then thrust up against his hand in quick frantic jabs. "Oh, God . . ." she moaned, and then her whole body locked, frozen upon some peak he had lifted her to but could not remove her from, not now. Her eyes were clamped shut and her face was turned to one side and her mouth was open slightly as if it wanted to cramp, to twist downward with some agonized unbidden cry. As her body gradually unlocked itself and her hips sagged back into the seat he did not remove his hand but cupped it into a kind of vessel for her, for her wetness and her nakedness and for her unspoken but familiar need to be covered by him at that moment. He watched her relax everywhere, the cords of her inner thigh, the column of muscle in her belly, the thickly curved scimitar of her breasts. It wasn't until he felt the wheels of the El Dorado slip onto the shoulder of the road that he took his hand away and concentrated on regaining the lane.

Slowly, almost absently, Sandy restored her clothing and sat up in the seat, wetting her lips and pushing weakly at her hair. "Aaahh," she whispered huskily, "you got me, babe. You put me away," and she looked at him for the first time.

He thought that her eyes at that moment were the purest softness he had ever seen. "You're really something stretched out on the seat like that," he said to her. "I couldn't keep my hands off you."

"I'm glad," and her smile was limp and rubbery and her eyes were far away. "I love you, Von," she said simply.

He squeezed her hand.

"I can say that now. I don't like to say it when I'm . . . when I'm *there*. It sounds too phony, too . . . backseat."

He winked puckishly. "We never did do it in the backseat, did we?" and Sandy was in the act of replying to that when the siren sounded, when they actually heard the sound well enough to recognize it as a siren. They both cried out, "What's that?" knowing what it was by then but getting the knowledge mixed up with the curiosity, and they began searching for it at the same time, craning and twisting to locate in the sideview mirrors the flashing red light that they knew was bound to accompany the siren.

But they never saw the flashing red light. There was none. There was no familiar black-and-white state patrol vehicle zooming up beside them, insistent, menacing in the way that unsummoned authority can be menacing. There was only a motor home alongside them, massive, blocky, cream-colored. Red Taddish's Pace Arrow motor home. "It's the Joker," Von announced in a mix of disgust and relief. "We bought it again," and he pulled over onto the shoulder of the highway and cut the engine and rolled his window down.

In the Pace Arrow, Dorothy Taddish was rolling the window down on her side and Red was leaning across her, waiting for her to finish, so that for a moment their faces were close together, hanging there in the window like disembodied masks in a frame. Then the window was down and Dorothy's face receded and Red's swelled to the forefront. "You there in the recreation vehicle!" he called. "Where you from?"

"Utah," Von answered, going along.

"I should have known. You Utah people aren't used to motor vehicles yet."

"What are you going to charge me with?"

"I'd get you on a 409," Red shouted, "but that's a household cleanser." At that point he abandoned his role. "Goddamn," he said, "you guys were all over the road back there. What did you do, eat too many of them beer sandwiches?"

"I thought you were in front of us," Von said.

"I was. But I saw you weaving around in my rearview and thought you were in trouble so I pulled off into a turnout so you could see me and stop." He spat through the window. "Hell, you went by me like Brigham Young went by Omaha."

Von said, "I'd forgotten you had that siren rigged up."

"I pulled Bike over a couple years back up in Wyoming when we were on that One Shot Antelope. You remember that? Scared the hell out of Bike."

"Bike scares easy. He's a law abider."

"He's a lot more fun than you are, Wallace."

"Why don't you take your toy siren and go scare him then?" Sandy shouted through the window.

Red laughed and pulled back from the window and got out and started to walk around to them. Apart from his size and his red hair, Red Taddish was basically nondescript. Like many big men he did not have a baby face so much as he had a neutral one. There was a certain ruddy aspect to his skin at times but it wasn't inborn, it was more what wind or sun or cold did to it on occasion, and sometimes it was the flush that exertion gave it when he pushed the great bulk of his body too hard. He came up to Von's window and bent down. "I stopped Bike back there on the highway," he said. "I waved him over when I passed him to come after you. I'll go back because I need to talk to him. There's a junction up ahead somewhere and if I remember

43

right there's a cafe sits on one corner. I thought we'd stop and grab a bite. I used to go down that other road with my brother Dee. Years ago. Down to Otter Creek, to the Reservoir. Dee hunted down there a lot."

"Right."

"If the cafe is still at the junction what do you say we stop? Can you stand something to eat?"

"I can stand anything. I'm on vacation."

Red had remembered correctly. At the junction of state highways 24 and 62 sat a cafe and attached gas station. The cafe was called the Antlers. *Closed Sundays. Waitress Wanted Inquire Within.* The first thing they saw when they walked in the door was a poorly done six-point buck mounted on the back wall. One of the buck's tines was badly discolored and its right eye was about to fall out and expose itself for the cheap marble it was. They took a table and ordered cheeseburgers and chili all around, and beer, except Dorothy, who substituted a hamburger for the cheeseburger. "I can't eat cheese when I'm traveling," she said to Sandy. "It binds me up. Makes me uncomfortable. I can't stand being uncomfortable on vacation."

While they were waiting for their order to arrive Sandy kept studying Red's cap and finally she said, "I'll give you ten dollars for that cap."

"Shit," Red snorted.

"I like the color. The competition orange."

"It isn't competition orange," Dorothy said.

"Looks like competition to me," said Karen.

"Actually," Bike put in, "the only requirement for the hunting orange is that it be fluorescent. The color shade is unimportant. It must be orange and it must be fluorescent, that's what the regulation calls out."

"I'll give you fifteen dollars," Sandy said to Red.

"Shit," Red drawled, and he wouldn't look at her.

"That cap cost twice that much," Dorothy exclaimed. "It's guaranteed waterproof. It's got special ribbing and it's ven-

44

tilated. And it has super earflaps, all lined and everything." She looked at Red. "Show them, honey." She said *honey* as unconsciously as young girls scream.

"Screw that," Red said.

Dorothy grabbed the cap from his head and folded the earflaps down and held it up for their inspection.

"Good-looking cap," said Bike.

"Twenty dollars," Sandy said.

"I won't go hunting without a good cap," Red declared, taking it from Dorothy and putting it back on his head, looking only at Bike.

"And it's got to be the right cap," Bike said. "That's important."

"Red didn't want to wear his old cap for this hunt," Dorothy explained. "Not for buffalo. He said the buffalo trip was a special thing for him. He'd waited a long time for this hunt."

"We all have," Bike said.

"Right," Dorothy said. "But a good cap is not that easy to find. We looked all over town for the darned thing."

"I can believe that," Karen put in.

"And new boots too," Dorothy went on. "Red wanted new hunting boots. We looked all over Salt Lake County for something that was right for the money. My lord," she frowned, "the prices they're asking these days."

"That's for sure," Karen said.

"We finally found a pair in a store in Sugar House. They were Stalwarts. Waterproof, reinforced toe, steel shank. We looked at a pair of Wolverines that were nice."

"They had a deluxe leather top I liked," Red said.

"The Stalwarts?"

"No, the Wolverines."

"We got the Stalwarts," Dorothy said. "The Wolverines didn't have the steel shank."

"Steel shank makes the boot," Bike said.

"How much did you pay?"

Dorothy said, "Would you believe sixty-five dollars?"

"I'd believe it."

"I'm not going hunting without a good pair of boots," Red declared.

"Absolutely," Bike said. "And they've got to be the right boots too. That's important."

"Guess who else got new boots," Karen said, and everyone looked at Bike.

"What kind did you get, Bike?"

"Western."

"What kind?"

"Tony Lamas."

"Ooooooohhh," and it was like a little chorus. "Money, money!"

"That's a real boss boot," Karen explained. "Hand-crafted leather. Twelve-inch scallops. Hell of a walking heel on 'em."

"I had Dan Posts once," Red broke in. "Boots before last. Good boot."

"You've got to have a good boot when you're in the field," Bike declared. "Lot of walking involved. Lot of standing. You need that support under you."

"What did *you* get, Von?" Dorothy asked, including him now, for he had been quiet.

"I got a permit to shoot another animal," he said, but then the big Indian woman in the tennis shoes who had shuffled out from the kitchen to take their order and had also cooked it was now ready to serve it, carrying it out to them on a tray that she held against her belly like she would a washtub. It was good food. The chili was a bit fiery but it had plenty of meat and beans in it. "What's the meat in this chili?" Bike asked the Indian woman, and she answered that it was elk.

"I knew it," Bike said. "You can't fool me on elk."

"Good chow," Karen declared later when they were near to finishing. "Damned good," Bike said, drinking his coffee and studying the cafe. It was small and bare and smelled of sour furniture polish. "Not much to look at but damned good food," he said to Red. "How come you know about this place?"

Red was only halfway through his chili, taking his time with it, drinking a lot of water. "I was telling Von and Sandy," he began, "my little brother Dee used to hunt down this way." He broke off and cast a quick glance at Dorothy. "You remember Dee," he said to her, and then he went on with it. "Dee had a big thing for bow and arrow a few years back. Really got into it. The state has got regular seasons for that kind of hunting—"

"Primitive weapons seasons," Bike broke in. "Archery tackle and muzzleloaders are considered primitive weapons."

Red chewed a spoonful of chili and swallowed it and then continued. "Dee couldn't wait for that archery season to start every year. I believe it was the last half of August. Anyway, he liked to go down into the Otter Creek area. It was a good spot. Still is. My old man said he used to hunt down there before there were roads in. But with a .338. He wouldn't be caught dead with archery tackle." He stared at them indignantly. "Me neither. I ain't gonna drop no deer with a dammed arrow. I ain't Hiawatha." Someone at the table snickered and he waited for that to develop but it didn't, so he went on. "Dee had this really far-out gear. A big quiver with braided leather thongs dangling from it. All kinds of shiny arrows. A bow that pulled right close to forty pounds at the draw. The whole palooka. Must have cost him a bundle." He waited for the Indian woman to pour coffee all around and leave the table and then he went on. "The only thing is, Dee didn't use it much. After the first year he put the whole damned outfit away in one of the old man's sheds and never touched it again. What he went to," he said, delaying a little, sucking a fragment of food from a back tooth, "what that little shit went to was a goddamned crossbow! Big wicked-looking hummer with a great huge stock and a trigger—"

"Absolutely illegal," Bike broke in. "Forbidden in any part of the state you want to name. *Any type of crossbow shall be*

47

illegal," he intoned. "*Arrows with chemically treated or explosive arrowheads, and any mechanical device for cocking, releasing or holding the bow at draw shall be illegal.*"

"Dee had this old pickup truck," Red went on, "and he'd built a false bottom in the bed. Hard to spot with the dirt and all. He kept that damned crossbow hidden in that false bottom." He took a drink of beer. "I didn't know about the new crossbow at the time. I thought he was still using the original rig. But he kept carting home all this game, all this meat, and I asked him one time how in hell he could do it with that little old cigar store bow and arrow? Cigar store my ass, he'd say, you want to come with me I'll show you. Well, after hearing that half a dozen times I finally went with him. And sure enough, here he comes dragging that crossbow out of that phony truck bed and into the woods with us. His first kill was always a buck because it was always Buck Only down there at Otter and that buck was for the warden in case Dee got stopped at a checkpoint." He paused and eyed the crowd. "After all, both Dee and I are famous for bagging those special deer that got eight quarters of meat on them but only one head." He laughed at his joke and went on. "Dee would flush up an animal and draw down on it with that big Robin Hood shooter and *thang* that goddamned arrow would be sticking out of the animal's gut before the bow string had ever quit humming. I never seen anything like it. Those arrows were thick and stubby and had those steel tips on them that looked like they'd come off a hay mower. Those babies could go through three fence posts and never splinter the wood. *Thang* they'd go. *Thang!*"

"Man, is that illegal," Bike exclaimed, wiggling in his seat. "That is so illegal that I'm surprised—"

"Baby brother could crank that arrow back and touch that trigger and kill anything that walked on four feet. There was never any rifle noise to scare the animals off, you see. They'd just stand there and look around and Dee would stick 'em. Then he'd gut 'em out and chop off the legs and the head and

48

pull the hide and throw that whole works into a gulley. He'd quarter up right there and stow the meat in that fake truck bed. Lord, how he'd bring back the meat! No wonder I'd been so impressed. He had half a dozen freezers full. He sold enough meat over on the Ouray reservation to pay for his crossbow ten times over. Those Indians just scarfed it up."

"If he'd ever got nabbed selling meat they'd have thrown the book at him," Bike declared. "The regulation spells that out very clearly. *It shall be unlawful for anyone to sell or offer for sale any game meat taken by the seller within the state of Utah.*"

Red shook his head in a kind of surrogate insolence. "The little shit never did get caught. He was always one step ahead of everybody." There was a certain finality in the way Red spoke the words and it was obvious the story was over. A silence fell. "That's really something," Karen said. Dorothy said, "That Dee always was a damned fool." Red took that moment to let go with a wicked belch. "I think some of Dee's old meat found its way into that chili," he said.

They all laughed. "It was probably our Indian waitress who bought it from him," Karen put in, and they laughed again. Von snorted and almost spilled his water and Red tilted his cap down over his eyes, way down, and laughed like Ed the Talking Horse used to laugh on TV.

"Twenty-five," Sandy said. "Twenty-five for the cap, that's my last offer."

It got a little silly then and when it all died down Dorothy went up to the counter to pay the check and the big Indian waitress told her she couldn't take MasterCard.

"This is Visa," Dorothy told her.

"Don't take Visa."

Dorothy paid the check out of a twenty-dollar bill and didn't take a tip back to the table.

"What were you doing up there so long," Sandy said to her, "applying for the waitress job?"

49

"That aborigine," Dorothy muttered.

"The job would probably provide all the chili you could eat. No money, of course, but lots of chili."

"Couple hours from now I'm gonna be thirsty!" Red called from the middle of the parking lot, and they all shouted back, "Would you believe an hour and a half?"

The Pace Arrow took the lead followed by the El Dorado, with Bike and Karen bringing up the rear in the Huntsman. As soon as they were out on the highway and up to speed Karen said to Bike, "You should have gone to work for the state Attorney General's Office instead of Highways."

Bike didn't respond immediately, which was typical of him, but Karen saw that the remark had surprised him because his eyebrows squeezed in a little. "What do you mean?" he said finally.

"I wish you could have heard yourself back there in that cafe."

"I heard myself. What are you talking about?"

"Red's telling a funny story and you're sitting there making a list of the rules that were broken."

Bike waited much longer this time but she wouldn't speak before he did, she wouldn't break the pattern. Without any emotion he said, "That was a funny story?"

"I thought it was. So did the others. They all laughed."

He looked at Karen this time. "Did you ever see a crossbow, Karen?"

"I know what a crossbow is."

"But have you ever seen one? Have you held one in your hands? Have you seen the damage they can do?" He waited and she knew from experience that his voice would go up when he started again. "Karen, a crossbow is barbaric. It's medieval. It's one of the most vicious weapons a hunter can use. Outlawed in every state in the union."

"But you aren't the only one who knows that, Bishop. Do you believe for a second there was anybody at that table who didn't know Dee Taddish was breaking the rules? That was the *story*, for Christ's sake! The story was *about* breaking rules. And why pick on Dee Taddish? Do you think he's the first hunter to ever cheat? The first hunter to take more than the limit with a weapon that some guy sitting in an office somewhere decides is illegal?"

"Karen," Bike began patiently, "you're invoking the rules yourself at this very moment. You're identifying weapons and limits and the standards that rules of hunting are based on."

"It's because I *know* the limits. I know weapons. I know seasons. I've lived around hunters all my life. I know the exact difference between a muzzleloader and a bolt action. And so do the others. That's my point, Bike! Why do you feel that you're the one who's got to remind everyone of the regulations? Of every rule violation? You come across like some self-appointed watchdog for the Utah Big Game Department instead of a guy who works for Highways and is on a hunting trip with his buddies. For Christ's sake, how do you think you sounded to the people at the table?"

"How did Red sound?" and his voice had lost all pretense at patience. "Was anybody *really* listening to what he was saying? Here's his own brother killing everything he sees—buck, doe, fawn, everything—with an illegal weapon. Out of season. Selling the meat. Spitting all over the rules." He lowered his voice but his face stayed tight. "Karen, the rules are important. Driving twenty miles an hour in a school zone. No passing on hills. No smoking around explosives. Those are rules and they were made to protect us. Hunter's rules are no different. They are what the whole society of hunters wanted."

Karen said, "Oh, for Christ's sake," and she threw up her hands and let them drop in her lap as though she had been carrying them a long time and was tired. "You should have been a game warden, Bishop. You could flash your badge at people and read them the rules all day long."

"Hunting's a sport, Karen, and sport is a business today. A

big business. If a hunter is going to claim the right of recreation then he must assume responsibility for the animals he kills. He's got to concern himself with their welfare and their protection. And it isn't just the *animal's* protection. It's ours too. Our safety."

"A perfect world, huh?"

"It's not impossible. Conformance. Obedience. Good sense. Those are the ways. We could provide sport for man and survival for our wild herds. We could eliminate accidents—"

"Oh, for Christ's sake."

"But without rules it's impossible."

"You're going to eliminate hunting accidents, is that what you're saying?"

"We've got to try. It's really only a matter of education."

"No," Karen said emphatically, settling back into the seat, tapping her knee, wanting the victory of this final point. "It's a matter of individuals. As long as you have individual hunters with guns in their possession you're going to have accidents. Your precious rules will never change that. They'll never eliminate pure assholes like that one down by Pinto Little a few years back. You remember him, Bike? The one who killed those two boys? Two young boys riding home from school on their bicycles, right in their own lane behind this cut bank, and he blows them both away. They're wearing brown jackets and white stocking caps that their mother had knitted for them. White caps with big white tassels and this guy kills them both with two shots. Right in their own lane. He told the investigating officer he thought they were muleys. Do you remember, Bike? Are your sanctimonious rules going to eliminate *him*?"

CHAPTER 4

The Great Light burned a fiery path across the sky. As he crouched in the thick airless reeds the sweat ran out of Good Runner's hair and down onto his face and into his eyes. The inside of his mouth seemed stuck with fur again. He thought of the water lying just beyond the reeds and how it would feel on his body if he leaped up and ran to the edge and jumped in, how it would course through the tangle of his hair, how the drops would spray a circle in the hot dry air when he shook it from his head, how like the beasts it would be when he blew streamers of water from his mouth. The huge woolly beasts with the twin tusks and the long snouts did that; they clumped into the water's edge and sucked up water and sprayed it over their bodies with shrill trumpetings of enjoyment. It had always puzzled Good Runner how such immense beasts could be so playful. They liked mud, they would burrow in it, roll in it, they would lie in mud for hours. Yet they were dangerous, he knew that too. He thought back to the days when he had lived with his father and hunted in his band. It was in the long ago times beyond the smoking mountains where there was snow part of the year, and many many hunters. They had hunted such beasts then and Good Runner thought now of the ways they had taken to stalk them. Sometimes they had hidden in the trees, usually two hunt-

53

ers together, pressing themselves flat against the lower branches as if they were part of the tree. When the beasts came to strip bark and pluck leaves from the branches with their snouts the hunters would leap up and thrust their spears into the beasts' necks. The beasts would scream in fright and lumber away from the trees and the hunters would run alongside and stab at them with their short spears, trying to turn the beasts and keep them circling within the killing ground. There was much danger in this. Good Runner had seen many hunters stumble and fall beneath the huge hammers of the beasts' feet. He had seen them yanked from the ground by those strange snouts and flung aside, or hurled to the ground and trampled until they were no longer recognizable. Sometimes the beasts could not be headed and would run away into the grasses with a speed none of the hunters could match. At other times the beasts would stand and fight. Some of them managed to withstand the attack and others would topple almost immediately into the dirt, the spears having found the magic place within their bodies. Sometimes a rush of blood would follow the spear out of the beast's body and at other times there would be only a bubble of red at the mouth before the animal crashed to the earth. It was a strange thing. Some hunters preferred stabbing the creatures between the hind legs, hoping to penetrate the huge sack of waters that lay inside and thus poison the animal into a slower less dangerous death. Good Runner remembered hunting the other beasts too, the ones with the massive hump on their shoulders and the sharp horns. In the land of his father's band there were many canyons, and many cliffs rimming them, and the hunting ways varied. The hunters would sometimes split into two groups, one to frighten the beasts and stampede them over the edge of a cliff, and the other to wait at the bottom and club to death those beasts who survived the fall. At other times, when there were many hunters on a trip, they would form a noisy circle around a herd of the beasts and gradually tighten it, shouting and waving hides and stick figures at those beasts who tried to break through the ring and escape. By slowly shrinking the circle the hunters could spear the panicky creatures easily when they became a single knotted mass at the center. Or on another kill the hunters might fit their bodies with the heads and the hides of the very beasts they stalked and would creep up on them through the grass, pretending to graze just as the beasts themselves grazed, and then jump up when they were close and hurl their spears. Good Runner remembered the snows that came when he was young and how the hunting parties dressed head to foot in the warm heavy hides and did the special dances and painted the shape of the beasts on the cave walls and in the drifts of snow outside. Sometimes the shaman would pile old beast skulls in a prominent place in the snow in the hope that the living beasts would see them and seek to join their white-faced companions. More often the hunt would take the form of an ambush. The hunters would stomp out long courses in the snow leading to suitable depressions and then fashion slick ramps down which they would drive the frightened beasts by shouting and waving hides and blowing bone whistles. Floundering in the deep snow, unable to escape up the icy ramps, the beasts could be destroyed one by one.

But no matter what the hunt or the ways of it, regardless of the place or the distance or the time, the band never sought more meat than it could carry back to the People in the caves. Good Runner could remember the butchering lines they would set up after a big kill with each section of the line responsible for a separate task. After the chief hunters had eaten the tongues and the livers of the slain beasts in the ceremony of obedience and gratitude to the Beast God, the butchering would begin. In the times of snow his father would order hides tied together to make a huge sled that the butchers would pile high with red wet meat and the hunters in a long line would drag back to the caves across the snow. In warmer times some of the hunters would accompany the hunt not carrying spears or clubs but only a special rack of antlers that they had made up. By notching the tines in certain spots and tying the antlers together with rawhide thongs pressed into the notches, they were able to assemble large racks which they fitted down over their shoulders. In that way a single carrier could tote huge quantities of meat back to the caves. Good Runner could remember a particularly successful kill when there was so much meat that several of the carriers ran round trips that covered many days. Because they used the tusks and the horns and some of the larger bones for weapons and for tools, these too were carried home.

And oh, he remembered the feasts in the caves when the hunters came back—the ceremonies and the dances and the smell of cooking liquids and roasting meat. Only after Good Runner's father, the leader, had eaten could the hunters and the People eat. That was the rule. The Women built long fires in the cave of the towering ceiling where your voice would bounce back to you. The Men sang the chants and heated the bones in pouches of boiling water and shaped them into new weapons. The young Women scraped hides and soaked them in vats of water and ashes and beast brains; they cracked open the larger bones and scooped out the marrow and piled it in stone bowls. The old Women stuffed gut casing with a mixture of pounded berries and hot fat, and they hung thin strips of meat on racks to dry there was so much of it. The buds of cactus were boiled down into a thick bitter broth that the Men drank before they danced. There were roots and seeds and huge crisp fronds to munch on and then all the People together, in noisy chattering circles, would roast chunks of meat on their sticks and eat until their belly skin tightened and their eyes sagged shut and they fell into sleep on the soft hide layouts beside the dying fires.

There had never been any of the helpless fluttering wraith about Karen Kimball. Raised on a farm west of Granger, she had done her share of chores and raised her animals and been active in church programs and the county 4H clubs. The walls of her bedroom had been plastered with Certificates of Excellence and Achiever badges and a host of blue and red ribbons. At Granger High School she had starred in girls' volleyball and been three years a cheerleader. She had married the year of her graduation when Bike was called home from mission for his father's funeral, and in the ensuing fourteen years two nine-pound baby boys had thickened her waist just a bit, and her knees had chubbied a little, and her upper arms had filled out more. She wasn't fat by any definition but nobody hoisted Karen Kimball above his head and twirled her either. Not anymore. One year at a casino in Wendover on the Nevada state line a drunk had tried to hunch her in a hallway outside the restrooms and she had bounced the guy up against the wall and cracked his front teeth with a punch. "If a whole high school full of boys couldn't get my bra and panties off what did this poor asshole think *he* was going to do?" she kept repeating to the casino manager. Karen had brown eyes and brown hair and big hands and a marvelously seductive voice that seemed like it should have belonged to a more fragile woman. Her facial features weren't big exactly but they gave the impression that they might be slightly swollen, or had been, or that she had awakened from a hard sleep just minutes before. Her language was somewhat earthy; it had never been what her mother's generation would have called ladylike. She said shit and damn and hell quite often, and sometimes fuck when she was alone, but none of it in front of her sons or her parents or her four older brothers, and she had a way of saying *Oh, for Christ's sake!* that was unforgettable once you'd heard it a few times. It wasn't necessarily an expression of anger, although she was often angry when she said it, but mostly one of disgust. It was a disgust that must have tasted bitter, for when she spoke the words she

57

spewed them out as though they had spoiled in her mouth. Her eyes would flare slightly and her jaw would sag a little and out they would come—*Oh, for Christ's sake!*

Karen pressed back into the corner of the front seat and let the high meadow country slip past the speeding camper without much notice. She wanted to savor for a moment what she considered her victory over Bike. It had to do with the Pinto Little story, the one about the two boys being shot off their bicycles. Bike had always considered it *his* story, the dreadful example he invariably cited when expounding on hunting accidents, which he did often and at length. Preventing hunting accidents was a righteous cause to Bike Kimball, allowing them was moral laxness, committing them was the unforgivable sin. As gruesome as the Pinto Little example was, he loved to use it. It answered his need completely, it was his Lot's wife. This story of what could happen with careless inattentive hunters in the field was for Bike his summing-up position. He applied it to the end of his preachments like a coup de grace. Only this time Karen had told the story, had used it on its own author, and she sat now in a corner of the seat and chewed quietly on the satisfaction. She said nothing to Bike. She wasn't pushing the victory. She didn't particularly want to argue in case it came to that, although she knew that all couples argued at one time or another. Perhaps argue wasn't the best word but whatever you called it you knew for damned sure when it was happening. Your voice started to rise and your words came faster and your hands began to rap the air as though you had a gavel and were seeking attention. But you never actually lost control, not after you'd been married for a while. There was a line to arguments and you had to know how close you were getting to that line. And you never crossed it. You could feel your back tighten and the heat start to climb up from your neck but you stopped before it reached your eyes. You came to learn that it wasn't wise to go any further, that the anger should stop at that point, that if you went ahead and smashed across the line then what lay beyond was screaming and breaking things and crying and stomping off, and maybe hitting or even worse. She wondered if Von and Sandy ever argued. Sandy was the type that wouldn't say shit if it came in tubes and she brushed her teeth with it, and Von probably deserved her because he was the kind who kept his own silence in things. She wondered about Dorothy and Red. They probably didn't argue at all because Red was such a lummox and Dorothy reminded Karen of the tiny asp that was hidden in the basket of fruit in that Shakespeare play they had made her read in high school. Any argument between those two would be a total mismatch and there was no way Red could win. Of course if you didn't argue then you couldn't make up, and making up was the time when getting some was the best of all, full of heat and squeezes and those deep hungry give-it-to-me kisses. She wondered if Red was any good in bed. Did he actually climb on top of that little Dorothy or did he set her on top? Could you really spin around on a man's thing? If the man would let you do the moving you could probably make it. But would it be any good that way? Could you come big? If you sat up there just right maybe you could put the man where you wanted him, where it felt best, and you could be just as selfish as you wanted to be. She wondered how big Red Taddish was. How long? How big around? What was it one of the girls in the bowling league had said—big man big cock, little man *all* cock? Von Wallace was a smaller man than Red so did that mean he was bigger between the legs? When Von got hard could you climb it with your hands like boys did on a baseball bat when they were picking which team would get first bats? Sandy never discussed Von in that way. Dorothy would talk occasionally but it was never complimentary; she always referred to Red as Captain Quick. Karen supposed it didn't really matter what size a cock was, although the guy in her special dream had a long one with a big red-purple head on it. How did the old saying go? It ain't what you got it's the way that you use it? She wasn't sure about Dorothy but Sandy seemed well taken care of.

She never acted horny or hard up, she never made remarks, never cracked wise at the bowling alley like some of the gals about grabbing some guy in the shorts. Perhaps she didn't really care about sex. Maybe, Karen thought, Sandy Wallace was one of those frigid women.

She left that subject and turned to looking out the window. The road was climbing into a pass and Karen noticed that pinyon pine were beginning to show up on the hillsides. It was harvesttime for the pinyon nut and she remembered as she watched the trees slide past the window that as a child she and her brothers had gathered bushel baskets full of the nuts, shaking them from the tree onto blankets spread underneath. They would take the nuts home and pick them over and wash them and soak them briefly in soy sauce, and then roast them in the oven. Their parents would bring in bags of jerky from the shed and carry up jugs of apple juice from the root cellar and they would have a feast on Saturday nights, or sometimes in the backyard on Sunday after church if the weather was good. She leaned her head back and closed her eyes and remembered the pungent smell of the roasted nuts and how the taste would stay on her tongue for hours afterward. She remembered her four brothers and her parents in the house with the huge lawn and the gardens, and the fruit orchards beyond. She had been the only girl and there had been disappointment in that for her. She had planted so many garden seeds and hoed so many rows and picked and harvested so many times that she came to think of herself as an Indian maiden learning to be a squaw. At other times she saw herself as the child in the paintings of the Pilgrims' first Thanksgiving, helping the women in the kitchen, keeping the cats out from underfoot and washing the wooden ladles and laying out dry aprons and carrying away empty baskets. But never among the men and the boys, she never saw herself there. Not among the hunters with their britches and buckles and coned hats marching into the woods that were always there at the edge of the painting, carrying muskets and axes on their shoulders and trailed by Indians who were always wrapped in blankets. When the hunting parties returned—this was in another painting—she was still with the women, jammed in the doorway of the cabin that always stood at one end of the clearing, drying her hands on her apron and waving welcome, the kittens underfoot and great pots of food steaming on the stoves. The hunters would be laden now, muskets shouldered, carrying huge ostrich-sized turkeys and balancing freshly cut saplings from which hung rabbit and deer and sometimes a wild pig. The boys were always there too but trailing slightly, laughing excitedly, waving richly feathered garlands of pheasant and duck at the waiting women and followed by the tall flat-haired Indians with their arms folded benevolently under their blankets. And the woods were forever deep and dark beyond, all in a land where everyone laughed and the wind never blew and it never got cold and the snow didn't pile up and trap everyone in the cabin.

She had always hated being stuck with the women. Women were forever waving hello or crying good-by. They never went, they stayed. They were not getters, they were receivers. "I don't want to be a girl," she remembered sobbing to her mother. "I want to be a boy. I want to go hunting with Daddy and the boys."

She never did. She was always the one in the doorway when the hunters left on their trip every fall, standing with her mother and many times her aunt, who came and stayed at their house until the hunters came back with their kill. But getting ready for the hunt was always fun; there was a flurry to it, a concentration like when Christmas was near. Her aunt and uncle usually came out from town late in the afternoon of the day before and that was exciting—the different sound of their pickup and the headlights sweeping up the lane and the hugs and the handshakes and the big meal in the dining room on the good tablecloth. Afterward, while the men and the boys sat around the table rubbing their rifles into shiny black sticks, Karen would stack the boxes of cartridges and restack them and then stack them again, they were so much fun to handle. Her father made his own bullets and there was the sweet smell of the powder and the old-penny smell of the casings, and the thick stiff new-shoes feel of the cartridge belt he wore. Her brothers usually got new longjohns and boots and jackets to replace what they'd outgrown from the year before, and they'd wear them around the house that last night. Karen hated that. And she was never allowed to sharpen the knives, the boys did that. The boys did everything. "It isn't fair. I never get to do anything!" she remembered complaining to her father so many times. "Someday," he'd say to her then, "someday we'll go hunting, just you and I. We'll go for rabbits or squirrels or something. Just the two of us."

They never did.

Later that evening, in the living room, the men would show the women the maps and go over the routes they would be taking to the hunt area, and they'd say, "Golly, it's too bad you gals can't go with us," when all the time you knew they didn't mean it, like asking the postman every day how he was getting along. Her mother and Aunt Della would pack up a cooler full of sandwiches and cookies and fruit, and get the thermos bottles out and fill them with hot water overnight so the coffee would stay hotter when they filled them in the morning. "Someday I'll go hunting by myself," she would scream at her brothers, "and I *won't . . . take . . . you!*" They would just laugh at her and go to bed early like Daddy told them to, except they wouldn't sleep. She could hear them in their room down the hall, talking all at the same time and just quiet enough so the sound wouldn't carry downstairs so Daddy would hear.

In the morning they'd be gone. The house would be empty and still and the radio would not be on. Karen would run to the kitchen window and verify the pickups' not being in the lane, and then go to the front window to check the fields for the light skiff of snow that Daddy always hoped would fall so the tracking would be easier. Her mother would phone the school to tell them that the boys had the flu and wouldn't be in for several days, and Karen would have to walk to school by herself, vowing every year to go directly to the principal's office and tell the secretary that her mother had lied, that the boys weren't sick with the flu but had gone hunting with her father and her Uncle Willis.

She never did. She hated the boys enough to do it, but she always chickened out when the time came. "It isn't fair being a girl," she told her aunt. "Girls don't get to do fun things. I hope they don't even *see* a deer. Except Daddy. And Uncle Willis of course. I hope *they* shoot a deer."

The days dragged unbearably. They would go some nights to visit other women her mother knew whose husbands were also gone hunting but it didn't help the time go faster. No matter whose house it was it was always too quiet. You could hear things in it you ordinarily didn't hear, a clock striking somewhere or the sound of the furnace blower going on. But all the days eventually came down to one, the last one, the day the hunters came home. It was usually during the night that they arrived. A crack of light would knife into the bedroom and her mother would be there on the bed pulling her blankets down and shaking her. "Karen. Karen, Daddy's home. Daddy and the boys are home." Karen would throw herself out of bed and run out of the room and down the stairs into the awful stinging glare of the kitchen light. " Here she is," her father would say. "Here's my baby," and he would drop to one knee and hold out his arms and she would throw herself into them. He smelled exactly the same every year. The coldness of the night air would be on his jacket but there was always the other odor, the one she remembered best, the mysterious mix of cigarettes and wood smoke and gunpowder and the sweet-sharp smell of dried blood and hides. In the morning the animal heads would stare at her from the beds of the pickups, the horns looking like an unpainted trellis with the vines gone, the eyes open but looking fake, the lips like stiff black rubber and the mouths open just enough to show the unbelievably small teeth. "Which one's yours, Daddy? Where's the one you shot?" After breakfast the men would hang the carcasses on hooks in a shed for the aging, and the dogs would whine and drag their rear ends and beg the boys for some of the meat. Each year Karen asked her father if she learned to shoot a rifle could she go with them the next time? "Can I, Dad, please? Will you take me even though I'm a girl?"

He never did.

Karen woke up when Bike turned off the highway and crunched gravel on a tavern lot at the west end of Torrey, swearing to him that she hadn't really dozed but had been listening to the sound the mud-and-snows made on the highway and thinking of the buffalo, wondering where they would first see them.

"For an hour, Karen?"

"My God, I fell asleep," she confessed to Dorothy as they walked toward the door of the tavern. "I was sitting there thinking about things and bang!"

"Lucky you," Dorothy came back. "I can't sleep in a car. Never could. Ever since I was a little girl."

The name of the tavern was the Bull Yard and it was totally deserted. They had two rounds of drinks and played six quarters in the jukebox and then left when Red started to get into it with two insurance salesmen who came in later but wouldn't be hustled into buying a round.

Once inside the cab of the Huntsman Von settled back in the seat and let Sandy drive. They were the last rig in the caravan and were quickly away from the little town of Torrey with its mammoth cottonwood trees making an incongruous boulevard of the main street. The highway climbed once and dipped once and then entered the devastated world of Capitol Reef National Park.

It was as if some artist had worked in a giant earth studio there and had gone mad from the solitude and broken the earth into pillars and arches and obelisks and domes and then dumped vermilion paint over it. He had suffered a few trees to remain intact—juniper and tamarisk and pine—but they didn't really belong; they were too innocent and too brilliantly green for that carnage. Some of the canyon walls had managed to wear clean over the years, looking smooth and shiny as the face of a spade, but the rest of the rocks were still splashed with the dull varnish of the original attack.

The highway eventually climbed out of the tortured arroyos and onto a plateau, a hard broken land that had managed to get a little beauty for itself, but no grace. The only gentle thing that had ever touched it was rain, and if that fell too fast or too hard then it turned abusive too. Get nothing, give nothing. The land was all jut and edge, a geometry of lines shearing and beveling every which way, and it was strangely disquieting. Perhaps it was the time of day, and the light. The light was dying. It was draining from the earth, isolating the knobs and ridges of the Reef, holding up the last of the day to the travelers crossing there, the last of life and color before the darkness rose from below and engulfed them forever. Von wondered why he found autumn sunsets so mournful, why they troubled his sight, why they touched so many of the sad lost things in him. The other seasons were not like autumn, they were never mournful. Winter was asleep and spring began things, autumn ended them. It was the time of husks and shells. He remembered the bird nests in the huge silver maples in the yard of the house in Roosevelt when he was a boy, how naked and forgotten the nests looked in the branches after the leaves had fallen. He supposed there was something in boys that couldn't tolerate reminders, for he and his brother Orin couldn't wait until they had climbed into the leafless trees and tumbled the nests onto the yard below, itself a dead brown thing. Yards in the fall were the little cemeteries of the town, they existed solely to accumulate things that were dead. Only when the hunters came back was there any life in those yards. Von's father and his two grandfathers always went hunting in the fall and they'd never missed a single year that he could remember. They left Von and his brother and their mother and grandmothers there at the house with instructions to *take care of things*. Von guessed they did all right. The women used the time to can, he remembered. *Put up* is what they called it; they would put up six quarts of plums (Brigham Young had insisted that the Mormon pioneers plant fruit trees) and put up four quarts of chowchow and put up two pints of piccalilli, and more jars of green beans than anyone could count. The Wallaces had always been a family that "saved jars."

Von and Orin, his brother, usually managed to avoid the sour steam of the kitchen and would play in the leaf piles in the yard. Unlike in spring there was no juice to the earth in autumn; the dry stiffening rust was everywhere, giving sound to things that ordinarily had none, such as sunflower stalks when the wind blew and milk-cart wheels and gates that wouldn't latch. The gardens beyond the house lost their color even as they had lost their manna; they looked like old throw rugs that had lain too many years under a south window. There was only one color ever present in the fall and that was the hunter's orange his father and his grandfathers wore when they finally returned home with their pickups full of carcasses, and they would set up the butchering stations on the lawn. They would hang the carcasses on the bottom limbs of the maples, but it was never for aging. The game could age in the field after being gutted or to hell with it, that's what Von's father always said. An animal hanging too long in an aging shed could give up five percent of its meat real easy; a small animal such as an antelope with a field-dressed weight of eighty pounds could surrender as much as ten percent. Shrinkage was too high a price to pay, his father insisted, for the bit of extra tenderness that aging was supposed to provide. Nor did his father ever use the services of a professional butcher at a locker plant. It would have been the supreme

66

insult. "Hell," he'd growl to the boys, "I'm already a better butcher than they'll ever be. Besides, the more you learn about an animal's body the better hunter you'll be."

The men would set the sawhorses under the maples and lay the scrubbed-white cutting boards across them to make the tables. At each table they'd lay out the knives and the whetstones and the butcher saws, and the freezer paper and the freezer tape and the marking pens. They placed the meat grinder on a separate table for the sausage making, along with the plastic bags or suet they'd removed from one of the freezers in the cellar. In the area just behind the tables they'd set the big square washtubs—some for bones and meat scraps, some for stew meat, others for ground meat or jerky.

With the carcasses hanging by their hocks from the maple limbs the men would start the butchering. Making their cuts at the neck and around each leg above the hoof and then up the inside of the legs to the gutting cut they'd made in the field, they'd strip the hide from the carcass. The head was removed by cutting through the muscles between the skull and the first neck vertebra, and then twisting it off. The lower legs contained no meat and could be twisted off as well; they went into the scrap tub. Once removed from the body, the feet seemed insignificant and without function, bending in the stiff inanimate way of dolls' feet. Looking like soggy mittens with the thumbs gone, the tongues were cut out and tossed into a special bucket. The brains got scooped out and plopped into pans for feeding to the dogs. The eyes too. There was a thing about the eyes that Von remembered. His brother one year had decided he wanted to save the eyes; he'd come up with a plan to sell them to a taxidermist there in town. "That's stupid," his father said. "Taxidermists don't use the animal's real eyes. They use glass eyes. Glazed glass. Much more real looking." But Orin envisioned riches in animal eyes, the kind of riches he had actually enjoyed one year when a pair of front mole feet brought in a whole fifteen cents at the Co-op. Their father turned out to be

67

right, which was disappointment enough—the taxidermist didn't want the eyes. Nobody did. They dried into shrunken discolored nodules even the pet weasel wouldn't eat.

The antlers were saved too. One of Von's grandfathers cemented them into a wishing well in his backyard and the other grandfather used the antlers, along with chunks of petrified wood from around Delta, to build a wall across the front of his yard. The need fell off after all the possible combinations of walls and wishing wells got built, and the antlers began to pile up, filling one shed and then part of another, all tangled and locked together, growing whiter and somehow more pure and ceremonial every year like the Elk God totem Von had seen once in an Ogden museum. Or was it the Moose God?

What was left on the carcasses hanging under the maples was good meat and the men moved among the tables like holiday butchers outfitted in festive orange jackets. The smells became part of the celebration as well—raw meat and fresh hides, the soapy-waxy odor of the bone marrow, the dried blood. Often there was an argument about how the meat was to be used. One grandfather wanted all the meat cut off the skeleton and ground up indiscriminately for hamburger and sausage, while the other wanted the boneless meat saved for stew. Von's father liked to cut up a big game carcass the way he would a beef, making several kinds of roasts and steaks as well as ribs and hamburger, and it was he who made the decision that ended the argument between the grandfathers. "We got lots of tables and lots of saws," he announced one year. "Each man is going to butcher his own carcass the way he wants it butchered. That way, if he shot up his animal real bad in the field it's his own meat he ruined."

Von's father had a way of cutting up a carcass that guaranteed him a maximum yield. He'd start by completely removing one front leg and shoulder from the rib cage. He'd separate the muscle of the shoulder into whatever decent steak or roast he could get out of it, and he'd either grind the shank meat or cut it

68

up for stews. Then he'd repeat the process for the other front leg and shoulder. Next he'd trim as much meat as possible from the neck; neck meat was excellent for making mincemeat. The flank was boneless and he'd remove that by cutting along the last rib down to the loin and then along the loin to the leg, then down again. This meat usually went into the jerky tub. On a larger animal like a bull elk he'd get some steaks out of that portion, thin but good. If he was cutting on a small muley or a pronghorn he'd butterfly those steaks. The real prime steak came from the loin, however, and that was next. His father would carve each loin free of the backbone with the same care he took in clipping hair out of his nose, and then he'd cut off the loosely attached meat near the neck end and pop it into the stew tub. He knew exactly where that dividing line was. "That end meat will savor your stew," he'd say, "but it'll toughen your steak every time. If I want a tough steak I'll go to the super-market."

A lot of people didn't like wild ribs but that didn't include the Wallace family. They believed that barbecued ribs, if taken properly from a decent-sized elk, were a blue-ribbon offering. "Better'n Texas chili," his father would boast, and he'd saw the ribs into pieces eight inches long and four ribs wide, and smack his lips while doing it. Then it was on to the roasts, which were Von's mother's favorite. When his father got done cutting those rump and sirloin roasts out of the animal they looked like plump red footballs he had promised the boys they could play with when the work was done.

But jerky was the real treat for Von and Orin in those days. After trimming off the gristle and fat, their father would quick-freeze the selected chunk of flank until it was firm and then slice it into perfect strips a quarter-inch thick and usually one inch wide and ten inches long. Then he'd lay the strips on his cutting board and flatten them good with a rolling pin and rub them soundly with a mixture of salt and garlic and onion and crushed bay leaves, and the boys would rush the strips to the house where their mother would spread them in a warm oven and crack the door for good circulation and not take them out until twenty-four hours had passed. "Jerky wants the proper brittleness," she would explain. "They should bend like a green stick but never snap like a dry one. The key to it is that full day in the low heat." She was right, just like their father was right. If not enough moisture had been removed in the oven you could open a container of jerky at Christmastime and a wild green mold would be dancing all over that meat.

So what you had after all the carving and sawing and chopping and slicing was an animal spine hanging from a tree limb. There was no way to tell what the animal had been at that point, except in those cases where the head had been left on, and then it looked not so much like an animal destroyed as like some new one started. The tubs were full by then however and the spine with a few ribs clinging to it was yanked down and cleavered into lengths of soup bone, or else ground along with some gristle into dog food, but only after the suet had been tossed into the chopped meat so that the sausage could be made. Undaunted, the dogs stayed to the end, whining and begging piteously. There was very little left for them. There were no fat dogs on the Wallace place in Roosevelt.

Sometimes there were rabbits to clean and dress out. They didn't arrive in the back of pickup trucks but usually in gunnysacks slung over a shoulder on a weekend afternoon. There were no ceremonial tables or tubs set up for the rabbits, and the orange costumes were missing from the yards. There was no sense of grandness or drama with rabbits; they were too small. Chopping the head off was the first thing to be done; no one looked at dead rabbits much until then, no one wanted to see that big-eyed ears-up lip-nibbling look of innocent surprise that a rabbit had. It was too much Peter Cottontail and Br'er Rabbit and Bugs Bunny for most people to handle. Von came to believe that a rabbit was never meant to be killed but the word hadn't got out to the hunters in time and it was all a tragic mistake.

70

Once the head was chopped off you nailed the carcass to the wall of a shed and made the necessary cuts and peeled the hide down. There was a certain expertise involved in doing that. You could handle the entire job with a jackknife if it was big enough and had a sharp blade. Ideally, the rabbit's feet would be severed without injury so they could be washed and dried and drilled later with little chains and sold as key rings or lucky charms in the drugstore. That was another of Orin's ideas. It didn't work out but Von remembered that it was the stench of the two dozen rabbits' feet in Orin's dresser drawer that had finally gained Von his own room.

Once divested of the feet the whole rabbit hide could be easily peeled back. It was like the procedure Von had seen telephone linemen perform when they'd strip the thick rind of insulation away from the skinny wires inside. That's what a rabbit looked like with his pelt removed, bony and naked and exposed. You couldn't get a feel then for the stupendous leaps you had seen it make in a field, the incredible turns at speed along a line fence.

With the tip of a good jackknife you could easily pry the shot from the rabbit's body, leaving the tiny depressions in the flesh like strange blue-pink bruises. You had to be careful with a jackknife; if you didn't wipe the blood off when you were done the little bits of gray-white fur would stick to the blade and you had a mess. All in all the whole business with the rabbits had seemed a waste to Von. "They're so little when they're dressed out," he remembered telling his father. "It makes you wonder why people shoot rabbits in the first place." His father had answered solemnly that people had always hunted rabbit, from the Pilgrims on down. Maybe before that. "But it's best with fresh snow on the ground," he'd explained. "Better tracking. I remember when I was a boy to home we'd go for rabbit every Sunday afternoon in the wintertime. There was this brushy country a mile or so from the house. We'd walk those draws out and flush up a bunch of cottontails every time. They love that kind of cover to live in."

71

"To get shot in too, huh, Dad?" Von had answered, and he remembered that his father had gotten very angry.

The years were like hoops, Von thought, they would roll away unobtrusively one by one and then without meaning to you'd come on a bunch of them one day, all piled up somewhere, faded and broken and looking a little sad, and you'd stand there and remember them for a while. He remembered the Roosevelt autumns, the vivid incongruent orange in the lifeless yards. He remembered the Roosevelt house after he was married, with himself and Sandy sitting in the kitchen one Saturday morning in winter. Like all farm kitchens in winter it rocked with heat; it was the hot isolated core of a house that in all its other parts was drafty and cold. Orin, home for the weekend to hunt, came in from outside flushed with the cold and fierce-eyed with a secret excitement. "Come outside," he said, "I want to show you something."

"What?"

"Come on out."

"It's cold out there."

"Come on. This is really something."

In the bed of the pickup parked in the lane lay two dead foxes. The suddenness of seeing them was a shock, Von remembered, and he drew back, if not physically at least mentally, with a feeling akin to embarrassment as though he had interrupted someone's privacy. "I been watching them every weekend," Orin was saying in a triumphant voice, "running in the early morning. I been waiting for them."

What they were now, after his waiting, was a pair of rich cinnamon carcasses lying in their own blood as if it were a glue to stick them to the truck bed so they couldn't move. And they didn't. There was no tremor to them anywhere, no pulse in the neck and no flutter in the ears. There was no rise and fall to their bodies, not the least sound of air about them. They seemed unmarked. Freshly dead, their fur had not yet surrendered that silky sheen that had belonged to their life. Their

72

faces were the tiny chiseled kitlike masks peculiar to the fox—baby faces on adult bodies. There was only the slightest grinning at the mouths and the moistness on the black buckle of the noses had only recently dried. The eyes, being open, seemed to look out but it was an appearance only; like the windows of a deserted cabin they did not look back at those who watched. The tails were marvelous, Von remembered, full and thick and luxuriant like rust-colored dusters lying there against the impersonal metal, exotic gifts his brother had called him from the house to see. . . .

Sandy's hand on his knee woke him, and her voice saying, "Von. Von. Wake up."

He sat forward and opened his eyes. "Are we there?"

"Honey, you were asleep and you were talking."

"Where are we?"

"You were talking in your sleep, Von. It was very plain. You said, 'Don't kill them.' "

"What?"

" 'Turn them loose,' you said. It was plain as day. 'Don't kill them. Turn them loose and let them run.' "

Hanksville was a small town that had thought a lot about growing bigger and more important but hadn't really done much about it. There was this vast wasteland surrounding the town, full of majesty and spectacle and extraordinary color, and it's likely that the town had become so awed by all that splendor that it just sat there spellbound year after year, missing its best chances to grow and become more important as it had thought so often of doing.

But Hanksville had a campground, a good one, a KOA, and while Red Taddish was in the office paying the hookup charges Dorothy waited for him in the front seat of the Pace Arrow. The day was nearly done, it was almost dark but not quite; the vehicle was facing west and Dorothy could see the light beyond the horizon, sunken beyond color now. She hated this bridge between the end of day and the beginning of night. At home she wouldn't even look into the west; she pulled the shades so she couldn't see the sunset light. It wasn't that the light faded but that it died, and with its death came all manner of others—the clouds, the sky, the safety of visible distances. It seemed to Dorothy that the matters of day were known things, that they could be held in one's hand and be measured and identified, but at night they fell out and couldn't be recovered. They were lost in darkness. She hated the coming of that darkness; an urge to escape would seize her then, a need to break loose and fly after the light until she could see it fully again, reclaim it, until it could envelop her once more and make her safe. At those times her body seemed physically to rise into the air and begin to race westward. There was terror in the voyage for her— skimming the earth so swiftly, speeding now at treetop level and now at mountain, feeling the land plunge suddenly away into pits of shadow and black wind, seeing mountain peaks loom disastrously and then veer miraculously aside. And always the light receded before her, sad and beckoning and wanting not to die but to be saved and she must hurry to save it, to hold it and keep it forever against the darkness. Backward she would race along the silver sluice of highway, beyond the ranges tipped with light into basins already drained of it, past Salina and Scipio, Spanish Fork and Orem, along the benches below the city, onto Redwood Boulevard and into 33d South and off diagonally from there to the white-with-green-trim house where even now the darkness was gathering under the eaves, and upstairs and down the hall to a small room struggling to hold the light, to a drawer in a dresser and a little girl in a picture there, red-blond hair, kitty-cat face and the eyes brightly green and deepset and . . . *aaahhhhh* . . . too late, too late, the horizon had sped away faster than she could follow and she had lost the light, lost it all to darkness in that closed-up house, lost the elfin green-eyed girl forever. . . .

She pushed open the car door and jumped out onto the pavement and someone was standing directly in front of her, blocking her, someone, Sandy, Sandy Wallace . . . "I should never have left her, Sandy . . . I should have stayed. . . ."

Sandy reached out and gathered her in and spoke her name softly, and just as softly held her, shielding her face from the faraway west and the light that had been born so long ago in a pearl and crimson morning, and had finally died.

CHAPTER 5

They waited at the lake for hours but the beasts never came.

Good Runner rose then from the rushes and signaled the two hunters to come to him. The beasts had gone away, he told them, they must not wait any longer for their return. There was another place some distance away where he had hunted in times before. A number of much smaller ponds lay upon the earth and the beasts would sometimes come there to drink and to lie in the cool mud. He had seen them. They would go now to these ponds and make a kill there.

But first Good Runner got down on his belly one last time and drank from the water and then splashed it over his head and the upper part of his body. When the others had done the same he unfolded the small pouch that had been fashioned from the lining of a beast's stomach and filled it with the water and tied it shut and secured it to his waist, and then they left.

The Great Light was a ball of ocher sinking below the rim of the earth as they ran. A line of low ragged hills stood on the left and shadows crept out from them like strange misshapen Others who had come to investigate the runners as they trotted past.

They reached the ponds after a short time but there were no

beasts in sight. There was no spoor anywhere, nor were there signs of birds. The three hunters shouted and rapped their spears together and beat the edges of the short grass with their feet but no hares nor other small animals leaped out. There was a clump of trees standing in the rear of the ponds but the light was failing swiftly now and the hunters did not enter. It was not wise to search for beasts in the darkness; the big cats would be lurking there. They would have to wait until the Great Light reappeared on the opposite edge of the earth before they resumed their hunt. They knelt at one of the ponds but the water was scummy and smelled bad and they drank the water from Good Runner's pouch instead.

The stars began to show in the sky overhead, brightening one by one, and the three hunters retreated to a flat rock that stood by itself in the grass some distance from the clump of trees. They sat on the top of the rock with their backs touching, looking out. The moon rose into the sky and the air grew chill. There were many stars now, glittering whitely, drifting steadily before the moon. In the pale light Good Runner could see the great cats prowling in the edge of the trees with their fire eyes and shadow bodies and their fierce silver claws.

———————

They had trouble making plans for the evening; they were hopelessly split. Some of them wanted to go out. "Hell, this is our vacation," Red whined in that little boy tone big men sometimes use to get their way. "If we'd wanted to eat off home stores and drink up our inventory we'd have stayed in Granger. Let's go out!"

"Right," Dorothy agreed. "We can nod off by the fire later. Much later."

"We need a change, man," Red went on, getting to his feet.

77

"We been cooped up in that RV all day. We need a couple yuks. We need to see some neon."

"If we're going to do that then why did we bring all that food?" Bike wanted to know, not getting up. They were sitting in the leatherette chairs in the KOA clubroom. "When we planned for this trip didn't we agree we could cut a lot of bucks off the total bill by packing in our own grub? Freezer meats, canned goods, taters and maters. Didn't we say that?" He waited, searching the circle of faces. Red sat down again.

"That may have been one of the things we looked at," Dorothy put in limply.

"We did more than look, Dot. We decided on it."

But no one seconded Bike. There was a dead moment. Karen started something and then stopped and it seemed to prod Bike's impatience. "I mean it, guys," he said. "Are our rigs full of food or aren't they?" The higher his voice rose the more erect he sat; he had completely lost that casual slump he usually affected. "Did we make a food plan before we left home or did old Bike Kimball just get paroled from the puzzle factory?"

"I knew you were puzzled," Sandy said, "but I didn't know you were old."

Bike ignored her. "Am I right on this or am I wrong?" he said, and he was indignant now.

"It's not a matter of right or wrong," Von put in, but he wasn't sure of his backing and the uncertainty weakened his voice. "It's more a question of do we want to stay in or do we want to go out."

"That's right," someone agreed, but it seemed far away.

"Hold it," Bike said, and his eyes were raw and his voice wasn't high now, it was flat. "You're sandbagging me and I don't like to get sandbagged. Everybody here knows we made a decision on food. We said that on the road we'd do Visa and keep the slips and split the total when we got back. And when we were parked and in place," he went on, "we said we'd eat in. Now was that the plan or wasn't it?"

"There's a new problem, actually," Sandy said. "Far more serious. I'm not sure Hanksville even stays lit after dark."

"Silly girl," Von scoffed. "Hanksville is known throughout the state as Las Vegas East."

"Damn it!" Bike flared. "I want an answer! Did we make a food plan or didn't we?"

"Hey," Von said quietly. "Hey, ease up, huh?" He reached out and popped Bike playfully on the upper arm. "You're right about the plan, okay? We said we were going to bring food and we brought it. None of us have forgotten that. But what we've got now is a change, Bike. A possible *new* plan, at least for tonight. Am I right?" and he turned to the others.

"Right," came the chorus, and there was some relief in it.

"What we could do is eat in and then go out," Sandy suggested. "Kind of a compromise. A plan B."

"No way, Jose," Red put in gruffly. "We do all of it or none of it."

"I like Sandy's idea," Von said. "It sort of splits the evening. Half in, half out," and he looked at Sandy.

But Sandy was looking at Red. "What do you mean we have to do all of it or none of it?" she demanded. "That sounds like an ultimatum. I don't like ultimatums."

Red glared at her.

"Maybe the rest of us don't want to do all of it," she went on testily. "Maybe what we want to do is a little of both."

Red broke off the stare. "Make up your minds," he shrugged, and they could tell he had taken himself out of it.

"I like plan B," Bike put in, and his voice was so back to normal that everyone looked at him.

"All right!" Karen exclaimed. "Now we're moving again. Each couple can bring something in the food line and the girls can fix it. And while that's going on the guys can break out the hootch."

"Right."

"And after that we can hit the sidewalk!"

"Right!"

"And if they don't have a sidewalk?"

"Then we hit the street."

"And if they don't have a street?"

"We call mother."

"You know what I want!" Karen cried, shooting to her feet and taking a stance in front of them, her hands on her hips. "Give me a G!" They did. "Give me a Ranger!" They did. "That's *Granger*, you idiots! Now let's hear it right!" and they gave her a *Granger*! that rocked the clubroom.

"Crazy!" Karen shrieked. "We're still the best there is!"

"Wait a minute, wait a minute!" someone cried. "We forgot something. Where do we eat? Whose place?"

Von removed his cap and held it out. "I want to see three sets of keys in this cap," he commanded. He removed his own keys from his jacket pocket and dropped them in, and when the other two sets followed he folded the cap over and shook it elaborately and held it out to Bike. "Close your eyes and pick a set," he told him, and when Bike lifted the keys out Dorothy's hands flew up. "They're ours," she squealed. "They're the Pace Arrow keys."

"Then that's where we go," Von announced grandly. "The Pace Arrow. The palatial vacation home of the Robert Taddishes of suburban Salt Lake City."

Sandy broke into the laughter and wanted to know if there was some preference on what food to bring, and if not, would hamburger and fries be acceptable? Dorothy didn't care and Karen said she didn't give a good rat's ass but Bike had something: "No chili, please. My stomach still wants revenge for that batch I gave it this noon at the junction." They all burst out again and Bike took Karen's arm and started to leave the clubroom. "We'll shower and shave and meet everyone at the Pace in one hour, how's that?"

"You go ahead and do what you want," Sandy said dryly. "But me, I'm not going to shave."

"Funny, funny."

"Just a smartass at heart," Karen cried, and they left the clubroom, but back at the Huntsman she flipped on the light over the sink and made no move to wash and peel the potatoes she had agreed to bring. She turned instead to Bike, who was lathering his face. "You love to make a scene, don't you, Bishop?" she snapped. "You actually delight in embarrassing me."

His face didn't start to knot up with surprise this time. "I just don't like to get sandbagged," he said.

"No one was even close to sandbagging you. I don't think it ever crossed their minds. They were too shocked by the federal case you were trying to make out of it."

"If we plan to do a thing we should do it," Bike said, straightening at the sink and stopping with the lather, looking straight at her. "What's the sense of making plans and assigning responsibility if we don't follow through?"

"Red wanted to change the plan. It's that simple."

"Red Taddish wouldn't recognize a plan if he was choking on it."

"And you can't take a crap without one."

This time Bike turned away. The shaving cream was drying on his face and he added more and then rubbed it in, taking his time. It could have been a signal that he wanted to end the discussion. But that wasn't what Karen wanted. "What is it with you? Why don't you want to go out with the rest of us tonight?" she said.

"Oh, come on, Karen," and the exasperation was a weight in his voice, dragging at it. "Do you really want to fight that bad?" He was back to looking directly at her, and Karen said, "Oh, for Christ's sake," and moved abruptly away from the sink and sat down. That's the way they left it. She got up later and washed and peeled the potatoes, and Bike finished shaving and took a shower.

81

In the Pace Arrow, Dorothy took hamburger out of the freezer and then discovered that her dishes had gotten dusty sitting in the cupboards and that the table was somewhat grimy. On top of that she couldn't find the extra table leaf. Red was sitting on the sofa wearing just his shorts and drinking a beer. "You ought to pull the shades," Dorothy told him, and he answered that if they hadn't seen it before they wouldn't know what it was anyway. He finished his can of Coors and got up and went to the refrigerator and opened another. Dorothy was cleaning the table and she said, "Will you fix me a Slops while you're there?"

Red emptied a vodka miniature into a glass and poured the last of a soda bottle on top of that and then squeezed in two ice cubes from a tray and handed her the glass. She took a long swallow and went back to the sink and rinsed her cleaning rag in the soapy water. Through the window she saw the single floodlight that guarded the playground at the opposite end of the campground. The playground was empty. "I don't think we've ever been to Hanksville. It seems so far away from everything." She said it in that frail exhausted voice she occasionally used, sometimes honestly, sometimes not.

"I can't hear you."

She didn't repeat it. She knew from experience that her best bet was to start over with something else. She pulled the plug in the sink and watched the water drain out and then she turned her head. "Bike really got on the peck in the clubroom, didn't he?"

"Bike's an asshole."

"It's her fault."

"What's that?" The radio had blared suddenly and he was tuning it.

"It's Karen's fault. She doesn't side with Bike. Whatever position Bike takes she takes the opposite. More and more lately she does that." She paused. "A couple should stick together."

"I don't think Bike's doing his homework." Red's voice was competing with Willie Nelson's now that he had found a new station. *Blue eyes crying in the rain* . . . "Karen's not all that bad. Bike should be plowing that regular."

"Karen's cute."

The music swelled again. "What's that?"

"I say, Karen's not all that bad."

"Right. Great ass on her."

Dorothy took a can of Crisco from the cupboard and began to melt some of it in the two big frying pans. After a few minutes Red came into the kitchen to get another beer and he said to her, "You been awful quiet tonight. You all right?"

"I haven't been quiet. You just haven't been listening." She didn't look at him, didn't turn. "Like usual."

He grabbed her hips from behind and gave her a quick hunch. "I know what you need," he said. "You need a red meat treatment. One of Doctor Red's high-falutin', rootin'-tootin' two-ball solutions."

"How about right now?" and she put the cleaning rag down. "We've got time. This hamburger—"

"Tonight," he said, letting go of her hips. "When we get back from our wingy dingy tonight I'm gonna see you get taken care of. The real palooka."

Her shoulders dropped. "Is there a real palooka, Red?"

Red opened his can of Coors and went back to the sofa and tuned to another station. Loretta Lynn was singing a ballad about a lost graduation ring. Perhaps it was a lost graduation picture, it was hard to make out the lyric. Or maybe it was Tammy Wynette singing. Dorothy sipped her drink. Beyond the window and across the lot the floodlight still stood guard on the empty playground. "Everytime we're in a campground like this on a hunting trip," she said, "I feel like it's a drive-in theater and we came too early and the movie hasn't started yet. In fact, it's like it's never going to start."

Red didn't hear her. She knew he hadn't heard because he

83

didn't ask for a repeat. Tammy Wynette or possibly Loretta Lynn, or whoever it was, went on singing about something that had been lost.

In the El Dorado, Von was sitting at the little fold-out table across from Sandy. He had his shirt off and Sandy was in her panties and bra with a towel draped over her shoulders. She had made coffee while Von shaved in the tiny bathroom. "You know," she said, stirring her cup absently, "it's been a long time since I've seen Bike Kimball carry on like he did in the clubroom."

"He did get a little steamy, didn't he?"

"He was right about the food plan. But he got uptight so fast it stunned me. I couldn't come to his defense. And I wasn't the only one." She stirred her coffee. "But it wasn't just that. It's like we didn't want to help him. Like we couldn't wait to pick a side to fight on."

"There wasn't any fight."

"But there almost was. It nearly came to that. Again." She stopped stirring and studied Von. "Why do we do that? Why do the six of us always start out one way and end up another? We do it more and more. We start out great and the next thing you know we're headed for a crash and burn."

"Hey, it came out all right."

"But just barely. Someone cracks a joke or Karen leads us in a cheer and we're all right again. We get it leveled off." She went back to her coffee but she didn't stir it. "It's like this dream I have," she said. "A dream about a pond."

"A pond?"

"The six of us are all skimming around on the surface of this pond like waterbugs. Happy waterbugs. It's sunny and bright and we're having a wonderful time."

"So?"

"Then the water starts to get foul and we sink down into it. It's a whole different world. It gets murky and we can't see

84

anything. And we're not having fun anymore. It's like we've become a . . . a threat to each other."

Von watched her for a moment and then he said, "I know where there's some water. It's not a pond but it's warm and fresh and you can't sink in it." He got up from the table and pulled the towel from Sandy's shoulders and bent down and whispered to her, "It's called a shower. All you have to do to get in is take your clothes off. Like this," and he stepped back and removed his trousers and his shorts.

Sandy watched him. "What's this hanging down between your legs?" she said, reaching out and touching him there.

"Those are the family jewels."

"Are they on display often?"

"Private showings only."

She stood up and removed her panties and her bra. "Show me this shower thing you're talking about," she said. He took her by the hand and led her to the shower stall and turned on the water and adjusted the temperature. Then they both got in. It was terribly cramped. "Can I soap your jewels?" she asked.

"Yes, but they're very fragile. You can't handle them roughly or they'll break. And you have to pay for what you break."

"I'll pay! I'll pay!" She lathered her hands and reached down and soaped his penis and it got instantly hard. "I like your jewels," she said. "Especially this central pendant here, the long one. Does it always grow big like that?"

"Depends on the soap you use."

She stroked him hard with both hands. After a while he stopped her and soaped his own hands and rubbed them on her nipples. "You got some of this in the front seat today," he breathed. "Would you like to go for the daily double?"

"I think I would," she said, and her voice was throaty. He turned her sideways and stroked her between the legs. She set her jaw to the pleasure and after a few moments she reached out and squeezed his penis and moved her hand up and down

85

its full length. "I like your shower idea," she whispered. They stood in the soft spray and stroked each other and then she grabbed his hand and made him stop. "It's time," she breathed. "But how? It's so cramped in here I can't even turn around. Did you bring an instruction booklet?"

"A good Mormon improvises," he said. He eased himself around in back of her and took hold of her hips. "Spread your legs," he whispered, "and bend forward from the waist."

"I can't. The top half of me will be sticking outside the shower."

"We won't need that half right now."

She bent forward, her head and upper body outside the curtain. "Lower," he whispered, and she bent lower. "Now back into me." She did that too and he guided her and then he was inside her body. He pumped her gently at first, bending forward along her back and reaching underneath to cup her big wet breasts in both hands, rubbing the stiffening nipples with the flat of his palms and then milking the whole breast with his fingers. He quickened his pace. Her hips responded to the new rhythm and accelerated and then he heard her cry from beyond the shower curtain, "Oh, don't stop, Von. Don't stop!" He squeezed her hips tightly and felt her body quiver and then lock convulsively against his. It was a mutual paralysis. His bag pulsed and he shot a jet of his maleness deep inside her.

After a moment she disengaged and turned around in the shower stall and held him. "One thing I didn't like," she whispered in his neck.

"What's that?"

"The only thing I had to hold on to was that stupid shower curtain!"

They stepped out of the stall and dried off and then sat at the tiny table and drank fresh coffee. "Nice shower," she said.

"Beats the hell out of your pond."

Her eyes were soft and unfocused. "If we keep this up when we get home we'll be the cleanest couple on our block."

They all dressed to go out and then assembled at the Pace Arrow. They finished off ten Coors and two Slops in the half hour it took the hamburgers and the french fries to cook and the tiny kitchen to fill up with the smell of hot grease. They didn't leave any of the food uneaten, it was that good. They washed the dishes and left the frying pans to soak and then stood together by the door in a last check, and in that moment they were suddenly a western tableau, a still-frame of that wondrous disparity of contour and size that is modern western garb—the burgeoning hat and the pinched waist, the beige purity of wool vests set against the meanness of denim. They were buttoned and zipped and their boot toes protruded from their pants legs like diamond-headed snakes. It could have been a classic portrait; it would have been except that Bike Kimball wasn't wearing his western hat, but rather his orange cap. The image was irretrievably flawed when they broke apart and began to dig in the impenetrable pockets of their jeans for a flipping coin to see whether they would walk into town or ride. The coin came up ride but Red flatly refused to participate in a second coin toss to determine whose vehicle they would take. It would be his Blazer or nothing, and so they poured outside to help him unhitch it from the Pace. When they had finished with that, Karen dashed back in and brought out the last three cans of beer and in a barrage of cheers egged the guys into a chug-a-lug. Red won handily, Von was second, Bike third. With a burst of noisy instruction, Karen lined everyone up in a rough arc before her and did a couple of fake pom-pom twirls and then led the entire group in the old special cheer. "We're going *where?*"

"OUT AMONG THEM!"

"We're going to have *what?*"

"ONE SWELL TIME!"

"We're coming home *when?*"

"LONG AFTER WE SHOULD HAVE!"

"All right!" Karen shrieked. "Now give me a G!" They gave it to her. "Give me an R!" They gave her the R with equal fervor. They gave her all the letters she demanded of them and then shot the word GRANGER! back at her with a roar that pounded clear across the campground.

Red started the Blazer and raced the motor and when the others had jumped in he popped the exhaust four or five times barreling out of the campground. "Do it, big guy!" Karen cried. "Make this baby fart!" They turned onto the main street and raced toward the cluster of lights that was nighttime Hanksville. Red was wearing his Stetson in a Montana peak and had it squared off just above his eyes, making him look amazingly like Hoss Blocker. The hat blew off his head and nearly flew out the window they were going so fast. Sandy caught it. "Onward and upward!" she cried, slapping the hat on Red's head. "Curfew must not ring tonight!"

"And I used to tell people you were clinging and sedate," Von chided her.

They stopped at the first tavern they came to, which revealed no name on its half-lighted beer neon. They loved taverns with no visible names and Von called for the customary list of possibles, and they ended up calling it Stagger Lee's. It sounded like it would be fun, but it wasn't. The place was ill-lit and barnlike and there was an odor about it that was either undumped ashtrays or toilet bowl deodorizer, they couldn't tell which. They quit trying after two quick rounds and after Red practically went to knuckles with the bartender for refusing to turn the jukebox up. They slammed through the door and stomped out into the parking lot, still carrying their drinks. "It just came back to me," Von exclaimed, "the real truth about Stagger Lee's."

"What is it? What's the real truth?"

"It's a dump!"

They piled into the Blazer and roared out onto the street. "Pop her, Red!" they commanded him, and Red obeyed, repeatedly. He had customized the Blazer shortly after buying it, chromed tubular bumpers front and back, searchlights mounted in trio, twin fogs, grab irons and side irons each side, front axle truss, bed bars, off-road Desert Dog tires—the whole package. He'd replaced the original engine with a 454 block with four hundred horses and four-inch header dump tubes with a glass pack that put him just this side of the legal eight decibels. But the streetlights were beginning to cluster up ahead in a kind of conspiracy and Red reduced the Blazer's speed in time to take the first of the three traffic lights at a prudent creep. The second he had to stop for. There was something obscene in the way the cluttered chrome-splashed Blazer sat there at the light and jiggled itself. It was like a masturbation. "One thing sure," Karen muttered wistfully, staring down the empty main street, "this ain't South State Street in Salt Lake City. Nothing will ever be more fun than dragging South State."

"Those days are gone," Bike said solemnly.

But even as he spoke, a long low lusterless vehicle slithered up alongside them at the light, growling with unrequited power. It was packed with an indeterminate number of local youths who immediately flung an oath-studded challenge from their windows bearing on the courage of the Blazer's driver and the adequacy of his vehicle, if not on his very right to exist on these same streets. "Did you hear those idiots?" Karen shrieked.

Red swept his window down and stuck his head out. "Why, you fuzzy punks," he roared, "I could take that Tonka of yours while I was changing my tire!"

"Give it to them, Red!" Karen screamed.

"You'd be picking my tread out of your teeth for a week!" Red boomed, and the occupants of the slandered chariot beside them threw up a whole phalanx of middle fingers in response.

"Did you see those assholes?" Karen demanded.

Red rammed his head further out the window. "You can get away with racing that shit-colored little tinker toy down these streets," he screamed at them, "because the sheriff is sticking your old lady!" The challenger threw up more fingers, and revved, and Red revved back. "But he ain't sticking mine!" Red shouted. "Which means I can't race this town. So I gotta let you go, Junior. I gotta read your peel marks from the back side and I'd rather eat a shit casserole than do that. But I catch you on my turf just one time," he screamed, his fist in the window now, "and I'll grind up that little antique of yours and use it for *Gum Out!*" The traffic light changed prophetically at that moment and the local vehicle leaped forward with a scream of rubber, leaving only a grinning rear-window death's-head to mock the law-abiding Blazer.

It hurt Red. He swore bitterly and pounded the steering wheel. "I got orientation tomorrow," he moaned. "I got an animal to shoot the following day. I can't spend hunt time looking out a bail bondsman's window. I can't take the chance. I can't!"

They eventually got him quieted down. What did it as much as anything was the towering neon sign that hung in the darkness ahead of them a half block away and on their right. In a throbbing red-yellow pulse the sign proclaimed DANCE, and as they drove toward it they saw that same word multiplied endlessly in the dozen or so car roofs parked beneath it. "Curfew must not ring tonight!" Sandy cried, and Red wheeled the Blazer into the driveway and squealed to a rocking stop in a parking space that appeared as unaccountably in front of him as a spirit sighting. He cut the motor and the lights and they jumped out and ran into the brash gaudy building that had beckoned them from a hostile darkness.

The New Place, for that was its name, did not disappoint. It delivered its promise of crowds and noise and excitement faithfully, as well as the suggestion of clandestine revelry that busy roadhouses always convey. It was the Green Door and Hernando's Hideaway and the After Hours Dive all concentrated into one single throbbing assault on the senses. People were everywhere; there were walkers and dancers and laughers and screamers, and among them like dedicated nurses moved a host of uniformed figures carrying trays of drinks. An elegantly lettered sign at a far end of the principal room announced the appearance at 9:30 that very evening of Carl Custer and his Country Cowboys, and a jukebox buried somewhere in the crowd killed both silence and time until his arrival. "All right!" Bike exclaimed in a momentary ebbing of the din. "This must be the place!"

"Even if it ain't," Karen cried, "I just don't care!"

"I don't care," Sandy shouted.

"I'm sure we'll find the answer here," Von exclaimed.

"Answer to what?"

"Who put the Ram in the Ram-A-Lam-A-Ding-Dong."

"God, I hope so!"

A passageway opened miraculously before them, closed smokily, opened again. They poured into the breach and at the very end of it they threw themselves at an empty table that materialized in the smoke. It seemed a marvelous table, situated far enough from the dance floor to allow for some noise abatement and yet not isolated from it, and surrounded by jolly intimate groups of fellow revelers. In an addendum to the miracle of the empty table, a waitress appeared mysteriously before them. Bike ordered five Coors and a Slops and the bill when the waitress returned was six-seventy-five. Bike gave her seven dollars and demanded she keep the change and they all settled back in their chairs and drank from their drinks and surveyed their new kingdom and tried to adjust their hearing to the new level of sound: It was not harsh intrusive sound, it was more the thick rich choke of gluttony. "Holy Toledo!" they cried. "This *is* the place!"

They finished those first drinks quickly and reordered immediately, for the waitress walked an astoundingly swift sentry of their camp, and it was just after the second round arrived and Dorothy was dumping her Smirnoff mini into a glass of soda that Karen excused herself from the table. Sandy followed her. They didn't actually join up until they reached the hallway where the cloakroom was located, and the restrooms, and the phones. "Someday," Karen said, "Dorothy is going to realize that when you and I leave the table together it's not a piss call. It's so we can find the phones and call the kids." They made their calls and kept them short; it was the custom. "It's possible," Sandy remarked when they had finished, "that Dorothy already knows. She may realize that we're trying to protect her. I can't really tell. But I'm sure of one thing. The hurt's still there. Did you see her tonight?"

"No."

"It happened again. We'd just gotten to KOA and she was sitting in the Pace Arrow staring into the sunset when all of a sudden she jumped out and started to run. I caught her before she went two steps. Poor baby, she always says the same thing, *I shouldn't have left, I should have stayed*. And her eyes, Karen! Her eyes get so desperate. I can't stand the way her eyes look when that happens."

They started back to the table, and they found it. There were new drinks waiting and Bike immediately threw a scare into them by wanting to know what took them so long. "I was about to send the dogs after you," he said, but Karen stopped him with a quick shush when she sat down and Sandy said, "The johns are as busy as the bartenders." That seemed to satisfy Bike, what little satisfaction he had wanted, and he turned away from them and studied the dancers on the floor. He had his cap pushed back and his forehead, which there was a lot of, was beginning to shine a little from the heat and the alcohol. The receding hairline didn't detract from his looks; there wasn't much that could. He had good features all around; black bushy eyebrows and blue eyes. He affected caps and dark turtleneck sweaters and there was a craggy aspect to him. What he looked like mostly was a U-boat captain waiting to go back to sea. He drank the last of his beer and ordered another round from the waitress. Sandy was singing along with the music and Red was into one of his violent belching spells. Dorothy kept feeding quarters to the jukebox and when she came back to the table she would isolate herself in the music, moving dreamily from side to side, humming along with the lyrics but not actually singing them, and all intently, all separately, trying to ride that single track of music alone through the noise. At one point, Linda Ronstadt was singing something and Dorothy sat in her grim swaying seclusion and whispered, "Sing it, Linda. Sing it good."

Only Von heard Dorothy's remark. Something crossed his face and he set his can of beer down and looked at Dorothy and said, "Did you play the Ronstadt just now? 'I Fall to Pieces.' Is that what you played?"

"Yes," Dorothy answered, only half hearing him.

"How about 'Stand by Your Man' earlier?"

"Yes, I played that. Good, huh?"

"And the Charley Pride?"

"That too," she said, but she wasn't swaying now, surprise was beginning to show in her face. Von lifted his can of beer and took a drink and then set it down again. "When?" he said sharply. "When did we change?"

"What?" It was everyone's question, almost in a delayed chorus, and then it was Sandy's singly: "What did you say, hon?"

"When did we start to become Country Western nuts? In high school we wouldn't be caught dead listening to this kind of music. It would have been unthinkable. The shame of the century. We'd have lost every friend we had. It was pure doo-doo then and now it's the only music we like. The only music we buy. Why? When did we change?"

"What are you talking about?"

"What happened in the last fourteen years? Did Country Western get that much better? Or was it better all the time and we didn't know how to tell? What happened to the Beach Boys? Herb Alpert and the Brass? Little Anthony? Are they still cutting records? Do we even know who's cutting records these days beside Tom T. Hall and Conway Twitty and Tanya Tucker?"

There was a difficult moment, a little core of silence cut out of the center of the clamor that surrounded them. Red muttered, "So big deal. Music is music," and that broke the stillness. But only the stillness. The surprise, the awkwardness, remained. "It's important," Von said. "I think we have to understand why we change."

Karen stared at him. "Oh, for Christ's sake," she muttered, and Sandy reached out and touched Von's arm. "Hey, big happy time on the town, remember?" but Von kept right on. "Is it time that does it?" he said. "A change in taste that's programmed in us somewhere? Or is it because our intelligence changes? What?" He glanced at them individually. "Maybe we just go along, maybe that's it. Maybe we ride whatever horse is popular at the moment. Never mind making a judgment, just go along. Do it because that's what everybody else is doing. Is that what happens to us?"

"Oh, for Christ's sake," Karen said.

"I just came in to drink and dance a little," Bike said, trying a smile at anyone who would look at him. No one would. "Just once," Von said, "wouldn't it make sense just once to ask ourselves why we do certain things?"

Dorothy stared at her drink and Red looked like he wanted to say something but his belching wouldn't let him. It remained for Sandy to do it. "Hey," she said to Von, and it wasn't cheerful. "Hey, come on," and she kept that up until he looked at her. "I'm getting the pond image again, mister," she said to him. "And this time it's you who's fouling the water."

"I was just asking a question," he said. "Just wondering. Haven't you ever done that?"

"*We'll* do that," Sandy said. "You and me together. Alone. Right now I want you back up here on the surface with the rest of us." And he came back. He did it with a kind of shrug of his shoulders and a little boy grin on his face.

"All right!" Bike toasted, holding his beer up. "Here's to the rest of us, whoever that is."

94

"I'll drink to that," Dorothy chirped.

"Hear! Hear!"

Dorothy got up to play the music box again but Red stopped her. "I think," he belched, "that Carl Custer finally got here," and everyone looked at the stage.

It was true. But it took the Country Cowboys a full twenty minutes to set up. The bulk of the stage stood in shadow and the individual members of the band were merely milling figures in floppy western hats, positioning this instrument here and rigging that instrument there, hitting a riffle of chords on a banjo and twanging a violin and tuning some sort of electric instrument from alto to unbearable chalk-on-the-blackboard tenor and back to alto again. Carl Custer himself was a short thin-faced man under a monstrous hat who walked the brightly lit front part of the stage with tentative toed-in steps as if his boots hurt him. When he was introduced by the club manager, Carl kept his head down and mumbled unintelligible words into a microphone, but when he sang his "first selection of the evening," which was a ballad, he lifted that tiny hat-oppressed face and fixed his eyes on a spot a couple of feet above the head level of his audience and never abandoned that stance. It was as though his lyrics were printed on some smoke-shrouded wall across the room and he didn't dare take his eyes from them. Whatever the reason, it worked—his voice didn't blur, his enunciation was clear and strong. The man could sing.

Carl's second number was different. He didn't sing this time, he played. The selection was a low-down gutbucket violin rag and he bounced and jerked across the stage like a snapped string from his own guitar. The entire Granger bunch jumped up from their table and poured out onto the floor. They were good dancers, all of them. Since the beginning there had been a kind of unspoken competition among them on the dance floor. In the early years they had switched dancing partners often among the six of them; now they never did. Karen was perhaps the best dancer among the girls, more acrobatic, less inhibited.

95

She loved to fast dance; she loved to have people watch her and to watch in turn their admiration. Bike was the other best dancer, but the surprise was Red. For all his size Red Taddish was amazingly quick on his feet. They all knew it wasn't inborn, that he'd had to learn and that it had been difficult for him, how to sense his own weight and control it in a tiny space on a tiny dancing area. "You are *not* blocking out the entire center of an opposing defensive line," Dorothy had scolded early in the lessons. "Good dancing is not power. It is not size. It is *balance!*" He had done it, he had learned. Scarlet-faced and grin-locked and sweaty, Red Taddish basked at each dance now in that special approbation people reserve for big men who move with grace. And he had been at it long enough to adopt certain mannerisms. One was that he always danced with his hat on, which gave him the appearance of even greater bulk, and the other was that he never looked at Dorothy while they danced. He would look to the side a lot, and sometimes at his feet, but mostly he looked at the other dancers. Here at the New Place in Hanksville, Carl Custer's violin rag was a raw pounding thing and the sweat began to gather in Red's sideburns. Karen and Bike stomped past him, Karen's hips and shoulders rocking in a wild dissonance. Red's hand shot out and slid over her gyrating rump. "Must be jelly!" he shouted, " 'cause jam don't shake like *that!*"

Karen didn't react. The music was loud, her eyes were glazed and her jaw hung loose; she was locked in a mindless addiction to the beat. But perhaps not totally mindless, for when the piece had finally ended and they were weaving their way off the dance floor, she whispered in Sandy's ear, "Watch out! The beer's getting to Taddish."

"I think it's getting to all of us."

"I mean Red's into his touch-ass moves. He just got mine. Yours is next."

Back at the table they ordered another round and drank it quickly, quenching the fires left over from the rag. They were watching the dancers and awaiting a chance to go back out when two couples approached the table and spoke. "We saw your orange cap," the shorter man said, addressing Bike. "We figured you were hunters. Are you coming back in or going out?"

"Going out."

"Then you've got buffalo permits."

"Hey, we do!" Bike exclaimed happily. "That's exactly what we've got."

"So do we," the shorter man answered, grinning warmly. "We'll be shooting at the same thing you are."

"That's great!" Bike beamed. "Tell you the truth we were getting a little lonely. I knew there had to be somebody else in town holding permits."

"You're the first buffalo hunters we've met," the taller man explained, and then he took the arm of the woman beside him and said, "We're the Garlands, Ted and Jeannie. With us is Bill Hall and his wife, Martie," and he indicated the shorter couple.

"Red Taddish here," Red boomed over a burst of music from the bandstand, not extending his hand, not getting up. The rest of the Granger group introduced themselves individually and then Red said, "Where you from?"

"Bountiful."

"Know some people there."

"Great town, Bountiful," Von put in.

The taller of the two women picked Dorothy out and asked her where they were from, and Dorothy answered that they were all from Granger. "Do you always go along with your husbands?" the woman asked Dorothy.

"Yes."

"Do you like it?"

"What do you do in Bountiful?" Red asked.

Neither of the men answered and Red repeated his question and the shorter man, Hall, answered finally that he was a dentist. "Garland here is in veterinary medicine," he added.

"That's great!" Bike exclaimed. "Now I'll know where to go when my dog and I get a toothache." He said it perfectly, it was opportune, they all laughed. "Where are you folks staying?" asked the shorter woman, whom they believed now to be Mrs. Hall.

"We're at the KOA," Von replied. "We've all got motor homes. How about you?"

"Motel," Garland answered, and he turned to his wife and they could see his lips ask the name of the motel but she didn't answer him, she shook it off as unimportant and said, again addressing herself to Dorothy, "Do all of you hunt? Do you all have permits or is it just the men?"

"Just the men," Dorothy answered.

"Do you like hunting? Do you go out with the men and help? Do you actually go into the woods with them?"

"I do," Karen said with a shrill laugh. "Or the bedroom. Or the haymow. Or the backseat—"

"Are you going to that school tomorrow, Doctor?" Bike asked Garland, and the veterinarian answered that it was mandatory. It was not an option. "We all have to go."

"Tags, you think?"

"Tags, certainly. Hunt area rundown. Herd information. That type of thing."

"Long time since I've been to school," Von said, and one of the words slurred a little. Listening, one would have guessed the word was "school," but it could have been "since."

"It's an orientation actually," Hall said, "rather than a school. You can bet they'll get into permits. That's how they control this thing. There's only a couple dozen of us, I understand," but he looked at Bike.

"Twenty-four on the money," Bike answered. "Twenty-two resident and two non. That's been the ratio in previous years too."

"That's right, it's every year, isn't it?"

"Since 1960."

Red blurted abruptly, "Will you have a drink with us?" and Bike added that it sounded like an excellent idea to him.

"Yes," Hall said, "but only if we can buy."

"That's not my deal," Red came back, and his head snapped up too quickly when he said it so that he had to search for the Bountiful people for a moment, sort of focus them in, and everyone saw it. But when he called for the waitress she appeared instantly and he began with an order. Mrs. Hall stopped him, or perhaps it was Mrs. Garland. "We've got a seating problem here," she said graciously. "Your table's too small for the four of us to join you," and everyone looked at the table accusingly. "Actually," the woman went on, "we had just ordered a round of drinks at our own table when my husband spotted the orange cap. We just wanted to say hello. We should be getting back to our drinks."

"The waitress will think we've left without paying," the other woman said. "But we'll see each other again, I'm sure. After all, we're in the area for the same thing, aren't we?"

"Right!" they agreed, and the Bountiful people went back to their table, wherever it was.

Carl Custer filled the void immediately with "Orange Blossom Special" and Von gulped his drink and grabbed Sandy and headed for the dance floor. The others followed. At some point, her hands clutching Von's at the far dizzying periphery of a twirl, Sandy felt a hand slide down over her buttocks. A voice followed it, thick, slurred, building no real emphasis anywhere on the long string of the words: "Must be jelly 'cause jam don't shake like that."

"Karen was right," she said to Von when the piece was finished and they were working their way back to the table.

"Right about what?"

"Red. He's doing his annual grabbies."

"I'm not surprised. He looks like he's feeling his drinks."

"How about you? How are you doing?"

"Feeling my drinks."

"You silly nump," she said. They had no sooner reached the table than Carl Custer started up again with a ballad, "Ribbon of Darkness", and Sandy turned Von completely around and steered him back to the dance floor. "Oh, I love this song," she crooned. "And that little cowboy hasn't got the worst voice in the world. You just don't dare look at him when he sings. It ruins it." When they regained the floor Sandy's arm circled Von's neck and she pressed into him. "It's so danceable. See how nicely it moves."

"I can feel something move," Von said, "but I don't believe it's the music."

"Silly," she said, and then she said, "Von?"

"Yes?"

"I love you, Von."

"That's nice to hear," he said, "but I know your kind. You're one of those wild denim dollies that prowl the road-houses in this part of Utah. You say you like to dance to slow music but all you really want is my body."

"And want it and want it and want it," she laughed. "Get it a lot too."

> "Clouds are gathering over my head,
>   They chill the day and hide the sun,
>   They shroud the night when day is done,
>   Ribbon of Darkness over me."

Von cleared his throat and Sandy said, "You're not going to sing along with Carl, are you?"

"Not unless I'm asked."

"Good, you won't be singing then." Later she said to him, "Those Bountiful people were nice, weren't they?"

"Yes, they were. I was impressed. I'd like to talk to them some more. In fact, I was thinking of going over to their table if I can find it."

"Von?"

"Yes?"

"Will you take Red with you?"

"Right."

> "Ribbon of Darkness over me,
>   Where once the world was young as spring,
>   Where flowers did bloom and birds would sing,
>   Ribbon of Darkness over me."

"Take Bike too, Von. Karen's been wanting me to dance with her and this will give us the chance. I think Bike's pretty well danced out anyway."

"Right." He squeezed her gently. "Sandy?"

"Yes?"

"I love you, Sandy."

> "Rain is falling on the meadow
>   Where once my love and I did lie,
>   Now she is gone from the meadow,
>   My love . . . good-by . . ."

Von located the Bountiful people in a big booth against the wall. Their greeting was pleasant, if not exactly exuberant, and they scooted in toward the middle of the booth to make room. Bike and Red sat together at one end and Von seated himself at the other. "Our gals told us to get lost," Von began with a self-effacing smile. "Said they weren't interested in guys who were danced out. So we thought we'd look you up."

"Glad you did," said the taller man, whom Von was sure was the veterinarian, Garland.

"Just don't ask us to dance," Von said, and one of the women laughed. "We won't," she said. "That's a promise."

"Tell you folks the truth," Bike put in with an exaggerated grimace, "I really *am* danced out." He followed that statement with a quick smile. "But I'm not talked out. Not yet. And I've still got a little beer room left. I guess we all have. That's why we brought ours with us." He glanced around the table. "How about you folks? Can we get you something?"

"Our treat," Garland said, and ordered three Coors from the waitress. Bike removed his cap and placed it next to his bottle of beer. His high elegant forehead glistened with sweat and his eyes were bright. "Do you gents hunt much?" he asked, pouring beer into his glass. "What I mean is, have you always hunted?"

"Not with the success we usually expected," Garland smiled, "but yes, we've given the whole business a consistent effort."

"I think what that means," Hall said, "is that we haven't missed many fall campaigns in the last twenty-five years."

"Know what you mean, buddy," Red muttered, but Hall didn't acknowledge him. "You name it, I've shot it," the dentist went on. "In fact, I'm even a dove shooter now. Doc here," and he nodded at Garland, "introduced me to dove just this year."

Von asked him if he liked dove shooting.

"I do. I like all bird shooting. I wonder sometimes if I don't actually prefer it." He was speaking to both Bike and Von now. "I've done so much of the big game," and he said it with a trace of weariness. "It's really much more fun to drop a big fat ringneck that your best dog has flushed out of cover, and then have him bring it to you and drop it into your hand as gentle as a kiss," and he made a little smacking sound.

"Oh my," Red minced, "isn't that sweet?"

"Bird shooting is okay," Bike put in quickly. "I've blasted some shot at a bird or two in my day. But I think with me it's that I like the bigger target."

"I keep wanting to ask you," one of the women broke in, "how you enjoy hunting buffalo. But of course you can't answer that because you haven't hunted buffalo before, at least not in this state." She laughed warmly. "Not if you're honest."

"Oh, I'm honest," Bike laughed back at her. He was never more sure of himself than at a moment like this, smiling back with the teeth and the eyebrows and the keen blue eyes at an older woman. "There's no way I would cheat on any aspect of this business. You can count on it."

"Man, can you count on it!" Red put in thickly.

"We waited a long time for those permits," Bike continued. "Speaking personally, I don't think I've ever been more excited about a hunt."

"These guys are excited too," Mrs. Garland said, nodding at the two men. "But you know," she went on, turning the glass in her hand, staring into it as though she were looking for something there, "I have trouble associating buffalo with a hunting season. They're not like the other game animals, not like deer or elk or antelope. They seem exempt somehow. They belong to game farms and zoos." She looked at Bike cautiously. "Maybe even museums."

"Go on," he said.

"When you think of buffalo you think of . . . well . . . of Lewis and Clark . . . the Oregon Trail, things like that. You get a picture of wagon trains crossing the prairie and the pioneers building sod houses. You think of Crazy Horse and the Plains tribes and Bill Cody. You're even reminded of Teddy Roosevelt and his foreign prince shooting the buffalo from the platform of a private railroad car. And when you think of the slaughter that took place over those years, the terrible odds the buffalo faced . . . it seems to me there's something wrong with killing those that are left." She stopped. "Am I making sense?"

"Perfectly," Bike replied. "I know exactly what you're saying. Back a hundred years that's all there was out here, the prairie, the space, the animals. But then *we* came, didn't we? And we needed the land. We needed it for plowing and grazing, for railroad tracks. There couldn't be just animals running free out here after that. We couldn't leave the great open spaces to the buffalo any more than we could let the Indian keep it." He paused and eyed her. "And we did stop the slaughter, didn't we?"

"But so late," and she frowned when she said it. "What was it the buffalo were down to finally? A single herd of a few hundred out of an original fifty *million*?"

"It was close, yes, but we can't go back to the fifty million days. We simply can't restore the old buffalo herds to their original size. That's not our goal. There's too many fences now, too many deeds of title and rights-of-way. What we need to do is control their numbers relative to habitat."

"That sounds so cold, so scientific."

"That's Kimball," Red blurted, pouring his new beer into a glass and spilling much of it. "Mr. Game Management."

"Of course you're right," Hall said, directing his remark to Bike. "There's only so much space available on this earth, isn't there?"

"And you want to remember," Bike went on, "that it's man himself who's protecting the buffalo, who's keeping him from becoming extinct."

Dr. Garland's wife gave a tiny bark of a laugh. "That's like the guy who stops beating the puppy because his arm is tired, and then gets credit for being kind to animals."

"You need to explain something to me," Mrs. Hall broke in. "How does killing a certain number of buffalo every year protect them?"

"Easy," Bike answered. "The hunt is only eighteen days in duration. Eighteen days out of three hundred and sixty-five."

"But you've got twenty-four hunters out there. Where's the protection in that?"

"Ah," Bike exclaimed, holding up one finger, "but only one animal is allowed per hunter. That means that even with one hundred percent harvest you still reduce the herd by only twenty-four head. That's not excessive at all. And it's only allowed once a year. That's herd management at its very best. That's what the Utah Division of Wildlife Resources is all about."

"Are you with Wildlife?"

"No, I'm with Highways. But I know the Wildlife Division in

this state and I know its programs. I happen to be a member of the Citizens' Advisory Board, plus I tithe a certain percentage of my yearly salary to the Big Game Habitat Development Fund. So I know what they're doing over there at Wildlife. I assure you that it's only through control of these herds that we can help them. And we've got to continue that policy. We've got to manage herd size, herd harvest, the whole area of general welfare—"

"You use the word harvest as if you were a farmer."

Bike laughed graciously. "I can relate to that. My father's a farmer. He's got a place out in Heber Valley but he doesn't farm it so much as he *manages* it. For example, he'll allocate a certain percentage of his total acreage to crops and so much to pasture and so much to orchards and woodland. He'll let a particular piece of ground lie fallow one year and then seed it the next. Or he'll let it go to pasture. In short, he rotates his resources in order to achieve a desired yield."

"What has growing things got to do with killing them?"

Bike smiled at the question. "That wasn't the exact comparison I was trying to make." He leaned forward and slid his glass of beer aside. "Management is the key word here. My father *manages* what he produces, what he can expect to harvest. The state *manages* its animal herds, its wildlife. And that's a resource no less than land is."

The woman smiled wanly. "You make it sound so benevolent. You're going to help the animals but only by reducing their family size every year. Wouldn't natural processes achieve the same end? Survival of the fittest, that sort of thing? You see documentaries on TV where predators take down a moose or some such animal that's been injured or is sick and can't keep up with the herd. Isn't that a case of nature controlling its own numbers?"

"That's a good example, no argument there. That *is* nature's way. But it's not enough, you see. For one thing it's too slow. It's like never cutting our fingernails because we know they'll eventually get so long they'll break off anyway. How much better it is when we accelerate the process, when we cut our nails before they get so long we scratch each other when we touch. Or before we're no longer able to pick up some tool we need." He waited and then went on. "A herd of wild animals can be managed today just as easily as a herd of milk cows. And that same kind of management philosophy can be used to benefit the human population as well. Recreation, for example. Have you ever been on Lake Powell?"

The woman answered that they had, many times.

"Not only is it beautiful down there but thousands of people are able to enjoy it now simply because it's managed. We controlled the flow of a muddy little river that was cutting through here on its way to Mexico and doing no good whatsoever for anybody."

"Sitting here talking like this," the woman said, "it all seems so high-minded, so . . . noble."

"With our wild herds," Bike continued, "it's a matter of utilization programs. We're always looking for that spot on the graph where the lines of area and population cross. Optimum utilization, we call it. In business and industry it's known as the point of diminishing returns. Management really starts when that point is known."

Mrs. Garland remained quiet, studying the contents of her glass, and then she looked up. "I should think a herd of animals in the wild would have gained enough intelligence to recognize its own best size. Wouldn't it have the common sense to search for new grazing grounds when the old gave out? Why does man feel *he* has the responsibility? After all, the herds were here before man was."

"Yes, they were," said Bike, his look one of forbearance. "But there was a lot of distress, a lot of suffering. Nature isn't merciful. There are droughts and floods and blizzards." He studied both women closely. "Have you ever seen a wild animal starve to death?"

"No," answered Mrs. Garland, "but—"

"Have you seen what happens to a herd when there's too many of them packed into an area that's been overgrazed?" He didn't wait. "After all, we're talking about herbivores, aren't we? They're not meat eaters like the coyote or the cougar, they can't track down and kill their food. They exist on vegetation and when there isn't enough to go around they begin to suffer. Their coat gets dull and ragged and big chunks of hair start to come out. Their bellies swell and their wind gets rotten, so rotten you can't bear to get down wind from them. Their eyes start to sink into their head. They stand motionless for long periods and just stare and their bones begin to stick out like the poles in a collapsed tent. Then one morning the animal sinks to his knees and his head drops down like he's begging. Pretty soon he falls and he can't get up. It's brutal, those last few days. You can literally hear the animal's agony. Compared to that kind of suffering the bullet from a .270 Winchester is an absolute mercy."

Mrs. Garland shook her head uncomfortably, saying nothing, looking at no one.

"How horrible that must be," said Mrs. Hall quietly.

"Actually," Red blurted, "a .375 Magnum would be better than a .270 Winchester."

There was a dead moment and then Dr. Hall said to Bike, "You were talking earlier about depleting the buffalo herd by a certain number each year. I should think that eventually—"

"There is no depletion," Bike said. "Not in the net numbers. What we see each year is a net *increase* to the herd, however small. We know that by actual head count, taken by aircraft."

"I'll be damned," Hall said, and his surprise was genuine. "That would seem to advance your management theory."

"Exactly. The Henry Mountain herd today will number well over three hundred."

"What was the original seed number?"

"Eighteen. They trucked eighteen animals down from Yellowstone in 1941 and turned them loose on the banks of the Dirty Devil River just east of here. Three bulls and fifteen cows."

"Hey," Red blurted, spitting a little, "that's five cows for every bull. My kind of duty." He had finished his beer earlier and failed to lick his lips because some of the foam had dried on his mouth. His eyes were rheumy and beginning to bulge. "Listen," Bike said, putting his cap on and placing his hands palm down on the table, "we've got to be going. Our ladies are waiting for us. That is, if they haven't skipped out with someone else by this time." The Bountiful couples laughed, which seemed to be what Bike had been waiting for, and he pushed against the table and stood up. "I've enjoyed this," he said, "but we've got to go," and he aimed the last words at Red.

"Go," Red mumbled wetly, "gotta go. Gotta get to bed early. Can't go to school tomorrow with a hangover." He stopped midway in his effort to push his body up and dropped back down in his seat. "Fourteen years since I went to school with a hangover," he grunted, directing his stare at Dr. Hall. "Fourteen big ones."

"You won't have a hangover," the dentist assured him. "You're in good shape."

"You ever go to school hung over?" Red persisted. "I did. High school. Played football. All-State '65 and '66. We used to go out at night. Whole team. Get drunk. Big hangover next morning."

"You'll be fine," Hall said.

"Puked all over the boys' dean in his own office," Red went on, his face locked in a lewd soundless laugh.

"We'll see you at the Armory tomorrow," the dentist said to Bike.

Bike tugged at Red's arm and got him to his feet and guided him away from the table. The two doctors watched them go and one of the women started to say something and then she spotted Von. They all did. Von was still at the table, in the end seat, and they looked at him as if he were a package the other two had inadvertently left there. But Von himself didn't seem surprised; they could see in his face that he hadn't forgotten to get up and leave. He studied the woman farthest from him and then the man this side of her and then the woman next to him, and then the man, and he said, "Did you ever see foxes run on a cold morning?"

"What?"

"They like to run on cold mornings. Their breath is silver and their coats are cinnamon. You can't reproduce that shade of cinnamon. The finest chemists working in the finest laboratories in the world can't duplicate that color."

The two couples stared at him.

"And they mate for life, did you know that? For life. They've got enough intelligence to do that, enough capacity to feel, but otherwise they're inadequate. Poor buggers, they have no speed. They can't outrun a bullet, you know."

One of the men pushed his glass aside and leaned forward. "We've really got to be going. Tomorrow's hell-bent on showing up early. But it's been nice talking to you."

"No more to romp the headland and the hill," Von said quietly. "That sort of thing . . ."

"What?" one of the women said.

"We've really got to be going," the other man said.

Von said, ". . . *on his light there falls a shadow, and his native slope where he was wont to leap and climb floats from his stricken eyes, and something in the darkness draws his forehead earthward . . . and he dies. . . .*"

"It's really getting late."

"I think it's Kelley or Sheats," Von sputtered, and then he stopped and shook his head gingerly. "I mean . . . Shelley or Keats. . . ."

The two couples were on their feet gathering up loose change and purses and cigarettes, shuffling out from behind the table, not looking at Von anymore but merely repeating like a chorus of bowmen marching toward a closing curtain, "Good-by . . . thanks . . . good-by. . . ."

When Von got back to his table, Karen and Sandy were gone. "Dancing," Dorothy explained blearily, and Von plopped down into the nearest chair. He shook his head and searched for Red and discovered him sitting at the opposite end of the table with a column of nickels stacked in front of him. "Show you how to drop a buffalo," Red was muttering, and he picked up a nickel from the stack and flipped it into the air and made a gun with his hand and sighted down the index finger and then triggered a shot by snapping his thumb forward. "*Pow!*" he said in his mouth, spewing beer. "*Pow!*"

Karen and Sandy returned to the table and looked at everyone and decided it was time to leave. Dorothy got up from her chair and Von, and Bike too, but Red wouldn't stir until he had shot the last of his stacked nickels. Then he lurched after the others bellowing, "Piss call!" and when he reached the lobby he disappeared into the Men's, with Von and Bike along to steady him. Karen stopped in the Ladies', and Sandy was left in the lobby with Dorothy. "One of those Bountiful women," Dorothy mumbled, mouthing the words badly, "one of those Bountiful women asked us if we liked to hunt." She stopped and tried to focus her eyes. They looked lost and homeless. "Do we, Sandy?" she managed finally. "Do we like to hunt?"

But the words didn't do anything. They didn't go anywhere. They hung in the air like something isolated by the stream of the crowd, helpless and unreachable, at risk of being swept away.

The air was cool driving back to the campground, but not cold, not what it might have been this late in the year, the night before Halloween. Bike drove by virtue of simply waiting long enough for Red to remove the Blazer keys from his pocket and then grabbing them out of his hand. At one point on the return

110

trip Sandy struggled to rise from her place in the front seat and cried, "Curfew must not ring tonight!" but Karen pulled her down quickly. "It's already rung, Sandy. At least for those in the backseat."

There was no sound from the backseat except from Red. He kept muttering ". . . show you how drop a buffalo," and whenever they approached a streetlight he would extend one arm and sight along it and squeeze off an imaginary bullet. "*Bam!*" and then the next street the same, "*Pow!*" and the next, "*Crack!*" and thus, one by one, he slew all the buffalo.

When they unloaded at the campground there was practically no conversation. Some mumbled good nights, that's all. Bike cut the motor and walked around and dropped the Blazer keys into Red's jacket pocket.

Inside the Pace Arrow it smelled like cold grease and onions and Red and Dorothy undressed without speaking. Red flopped down on top of the bed wearing just his shorts and Dorothy peeled back the blankets on her side and got under them. But almost immediately she raised up and looked out the window. She could see the floodlight beyond the campground standing stark and alone beside the deserted playground. She put her hand on Red's shoulder. "You won't let them kill any of the baby buffalo, will you?" She waited but he did not respond. She bent her head and looked at his face. "Will you, Red?"

Red didn't answer. He was asleep. Slanting in through the window the light touched his mouth, fallen open now, an arc of dried foam still visible on his upper lip.

CHAPTER 6

Dawn came and the Great Light edged up over the rim of the land, pushing a red sky before it that turned slowly pink and then lost all its color like the belly of the fish they sometimes caught in the narrow places where the shallow waters ran. But here by the black stunted trees there was no water, and no fish to eat. Nothing to eat.

They left the rock where they had spent the night and trotted into the trees. There was a strong urine smell and some beast droppings, but the grove was empty. Good Runner climbed into the lower branches of some of the larger trees looking for carcasses the huge cats might have hidden there the night before, but there were none.

They ran from the trees into a shallow valley where thin puffs of fog still hung and where the eye of drying marshes peered bleakly up at the sky. There were no animals there, no hare and no birds. They found a few shriveled seed pods and at the fringe of the marshes they found bush berries and ate them too, although they were little more than pebbles and too hard to break with the teeth. Good Runner had strong teeth; he could crack open a whole pile of small animal bones to get at the marrow. But here there were no bones. There was nothing here and the three of them ran up out of the little valley and back through the deserted trees and across the heat-stained grasses where the rock stood that had held them in the night, and past that and still farther, leaving it all behind.

At some time in the morning the scarred hunter moved up beside Good Runner and pointed with his spear at a low mounding of hills to the side of them, and they veered off in that direction. Where the ground broke at the foot of the hills a small patch of green lay against the earth. When the hunters reached the spot they saw that the green was a straggle of plants clustered around a place where water had trickled out from between the toes of the hills, and now was dried up. They dug at the wilted plants with their short spears and pried a few roots to the surface and ate them. They were juiceless and stringy and had a strange metal taste.

They left the bunched hills and ran on and after several miles Good Runner's stomach began to cramp. He kept running and suddenly the roots he had eaten shot up out of his stomach with a bitterness that burned his throat and made his eyes water. But he did not stop running. A while later his stomach erupted again and he bent down as he ran and grabbed a handful of grass and stuffed it into his mouth in hopes it would absorb the taste.

His feet were becoming sore and he gradually slowed his pace. But he would not stop. The hills disappeared behind them and the Great Light rose steadily in front, and still he ran. The sky seemed huge now, so vast and empty and overreaching that he sensed as they ran beneath it how tiny the three of them must seem to the Great Light, how lost they could become in those endless stretches of grass, how finished and forgotten they would be if they could not get food enough to keep their legs running, if they could not find the beasts.

The Hanksville Armory was a squat brick building that sat on the back side of a vacant lot full of dead grass. Looking at the building you knew that the brick had been fiercely red once but time and the southern Utah sun had faded it into a watery pink that resembled bad salmon. Red parked the Blazer in a parking lot that had hoped originally to be in front of the building but had wound up on the side, and together they approached the Armory.

There was something basically disappointing about the Armory. To begin with it should have been military but it wasn't. It didn't deter or frighten, it didn't throw up stern towers or bristle with *chevaux de frise*. Ticonderoga, Verdun, the fort of Beau Geste, it was none of these. What the Armory actually did was deaden. It deadened by lethargy and inconsequence and when the three of them opened the massive front door and stepped inside the building, that impression was confirmed. A cloak of stale air enveloped them instantly and there was an immediate lack of good light. A glass-enclosed bulletin board hanging on the opposite wall offered an initial promise, but as they approached it they saw that although there was no dust or fingerprints on the glass, still it had an untouched look; there hovered about it the suspicion that the announcements posted there referred to events from a decade ago. The lobby was so leadenly silent they caught themselves listening for the ticking of a clock to prove that time really did move forward there. A hallway led off into shadow on the right, there was another to the left, there were doors there only dimly seen, opening into rooms from which musty unused sunlight would escape with a rush if those doors were ever opened.

In any event, they had arrived on time. It was a few minutes before nine o'clock when they entered the lobby. They had agreed to let the girls sleep in and had awakened them to tell them so—Bike with a slap of Karen's roundness under the blanket and a long buried kiss on the neck that had almost pulled him back into bed again, Red with a swift mount that he

114

finished wetly before Dorothy ever opened her eyes, although she had opened her arms to hold him in that half-sleep before he entered her; Von over a cup of coffee at the table with Sandy, who kept stirring her coffee mechanically and blinking her eyes and repeating, "Would you believe I've got a hangover? Would you believe that?"

When the three men had left the campground that morning they were wearing full orange. "Hunters will be required to attend a hunter orientation course in the Hanksville Armory October 31," Bike recited as they drove downtown, quoting the notice they had received in the mail two months earlier. They'd eaten breakfast at the Shell Casing Cafe on Main Street: omelets, hash browns, bacon, a plate of silver dollar cakes in lieu of toast, and Red had ordered a side of biscuits and gravy. They pronounced themselves fit and healthy immediately afterward, with no serious hangover, although Red broke a lot of foul wind driving over to the Armory and they got on him pretty good about that. Then they were inside the Armory, and after the dismay of the lobby they walked down an ill-lighted corridor to the right that smelled of sweeping compound and whose brick walls bore small sticky-backed arrows pointing them toward an inconspicuous door that read merely ENTER. It was extremely quiet and they wondered if the arrows really were meant for them, but when they opened the ENTER door it was all revealed, abruptly, astonishingly, like a genie uncorking a magic bottle. There was noise, there was a smell of cigarettes and hot coffee, the bustle of a few hunters and the huddled talky waiting of others, the stare and then the wave from the doctors Garland and Hall, the rows of folding chairs and the raised stage, the huge green blackboard with a white projection screen perched in front of it, the long head table with two Department men sitting at one end wearing regulation orange vests and regulation orange caps waiting for nine o'clock to show precisely on the big round black-and-white wall clock so they could stand up and call out, "All right, gentlemen, let's get this thing under way, shall we?" and pass out the first paperset of regulations/instructions: State of Utah; Division of Wildlife Resources: Big Game Department; Controlled Hunt 600; Henry Mountain area; Buffalo.

Karen got out of bed when she first woke up. She showered and washed her hair and ate two powdered donuts and washed them down with a can of Snap-E-Tom. She had felt a slight heaviness at her temples earlier but it went away with the food. She threw on her housecoat and wrapped a towel around her head and stepped across to the El Dorado to wake Sandy.

Sandy was awake. She had showered and was sitting at the little dinette table alternately stirring and drinking a cup of coffee. Her greeting to Karen was a question: "Are we still going downtown?"

"You bet your right and left buns we're going downtown. Hell, we might even buy it!" The excitement shining in her face had bubbled its way into her voice. She had a question of her own for Sandy: "You get a dawn-buster this morning?"

Sandy didn't understand the remark at first, and when she did she answered simply, "No."

"You like it in the morning?"

"Yes."

"I love it in the morning. Sometimes I get off real quick and then get off again before Bike does. It's like my trigger is set real fine when I first wake up." She stopped and took a breath. "That's *some* mornings. What I got *this* morning was what the little bird left on the fence."

Sandy studied her across the top of her coffee cup. "Do you know if Dorothy is up?"

Karen guessed she was but just to be sure she would run over to the Pace and check.

Dorothy was awake but not out of bed. She was lying on her back under the covers looking at the pattern of the wallpaper on the ceiling, the familiar way the circles merged magically

116

into the ovals, the ovals into the rectangles and the rectangles into the squares, most of it somewhat blurry now. What she was trying not to think of was the mess that had seeped out from between her legs since Red had left, sticking part of her nightgown to part of her thigh. She wondered if more of it would seep out if she threw the covers back and stood up. When you were trying extra hard to get pregnant it was recommended that you lie perfectly still on your back with your husband's semen pooling itself at your cervix, trying to get in, wanting to swim up inside and join hands with the little girl eggs who were swimming down searching for that one tiny tadpole who was the strong one, the good swimmer, the survivor in that incredible passage to life. . . . But she wasn't trying for pregnancy now. After Red's vasectomy what did semen do except make a mess that stuck your nightgown to your leg?

Dorothy's eyes flared and her body jerked when Karen pushed open the door and called her name. For her own part, Karen saw the reaction and she said to Dorothy, more to divert an apology than anything, "You're a little quick this morning, aren't you?"

Dorothy had settled back onto the bed. "A little quick," she said, fading badly on the last word.

"You must have got your ashes hauled or something?"

"There were some ashes hauled," Dorothy mumbled, pressing her head into the pillow and closing her eyes. "But they weren't mine. They almost never are." And again the last words trailed off.

Karen closed the door behind her and got an immediate reinforcement of the sense of having intruded, and of being obligated to explain it. "Well," she began uncertainly, "the guys have been in school for over an hour."

"It's not a school," Dorothy said, with just a hint of exasperation.

It struck Karen wrong. "Who gives a shit what they call it?" she snapped. "They're in it, aren't they?" But her pique dissolved as quickly as it had formed. "The lucky thing is, *we're* not in it," she added, "and that gives us our chance to go shopping."

"Oh, Karen . . ."

"Come on, don't be a deadhead. We'll put on our stack-heel boots and our shrink jeans and make a pass through this town. We'll give the local types their all-time biggest thrill. They'll talk about it for years. You want to be part of history, don't you?"

"Oh, Karen, I'm not . . . you've been . . . you've washed your hair and had your coffee—"

"And you're talking like you want to mouse out."

"Can I? I mean, can I join you and Sandy later? Can you guys go ahead and let me come downtown after I get showered and dressed?"

It was easier for Karen to agree than to argue with that fuzzy, up-on-one-elbow, slightly defensive figure in the bed, and she did, she agreed, and then she went back to the El Dorado. Dorothy would join them downtown, she reported to Sandy; she hadn't gotten up yet, she was still in bed. "I had to wake her up. I thought she acted a little funny."

"You don't act funny when you've just been woke up? You've never been lying there hung over and had somebody bust in and start throwing plans at you in a loud voice?"

"Oh, don't be so damned fair!" and she threw the wet towel at Sandy and started to back out the door. "Thirty minutes at my place. Be there!"

Sandy was there in twenty, and it was good timing; Karen couldn't get her jeans on. Sandy found her flat on her back on the floor with her feet jammed up against a wall and her hips arched, trying to pull the jeans over the top of her thighs and onto her hips. "These goddamned pants!" Karen exploded, and Sandy knelt on one side of her and helped pull and then knelt on the other, with as little success, and finally she straddled Karen's head and reached down and together, with a motion like that of rocking a snow-stuck car, they tugged the jeans into position. "I hope you've already gone to the potty," Sandy panted, "because we're not going through this again."

They locked up both motor homes and unhitched the Bronco and drove downtown. The day was an exact copy of the previous one, warm and windless and with an odd onionskin quality to the sky. Karen parked at the far end of the main street and they got out and started the three- or four-block walk to the opposite end.

No one could walk on heels like Karen; no one could fill the hip cup of new jeans quite like she could. It was almost suspenseful. Her buttocks swayed like ripe casks balanced on twin stilts, threatening with every step to topple onto the sidewalk and spill their rich naked splendor out before the hungry eyes that followed her parade. And there were plenty of eyes. Karen knew they were there. She saw the heads turn and the cars slow down and the faces suddenly appear in the store windows as she passed, but she gave no sign. She had long ago mastered the art of indifference and Sandy never ceased to marvel at it. When they reached the end of the street they crossed over and came back down the other side. "I'll say one thing for you," Sandy told her. "You sure round out a pair of jeans."

Karen had been expecting a remark; her head turned to Sandy in response to it. "Sexy?"

"Sexy."

Karen's laugh was ebullient and frothy and she sidled into a wicked exaggeration of her walk. "Bike says when I walk in front of him down the street my rear end looks like two watermelons trying to gang-bang a crease in the tablecloth."

The two Department men stepped down to opposite ends of the first and second rows of chairs and passed out the papersets and then returned to the table. "You're in the number two auditorium of the Hanksville Armory for buffalo hunt orientation," one of them announced. "If the permit you are carrying on your person reads Snowshoe Hare or Alber's Squirrel, please leave immediately, you're in the wrong place. You may even be in the wrong *state*." He waited for the laugh but it didn't come. He wasn't overly disappointed, he would keep trying; one hunter had laughed at that remark one year and it could happen again. "A map of the hunt area has been included in the packet of materials you just received, and if you will take that map and follow along we will outline the boundaries of the area for you." There was a flurry of paper shuffling and when it subsided the second instructor, in an amazingly similar voice, proclaimed as follows: "Hunt area 600, those portions of Wayne and Garfield counties lying within the following described boundaries—Hanksville thence southerly along the Dirty Devil River and Lake Powell to Bullfrog—is there anyone here who can't find Bullfrog on his map?—thence northerly along the Notom road to highway 24 and then east to Hanksville, point of beginning. Any questions?"

There were none.

"That's an area roughly fifty miles long on a north-south axis and forty miles wide on an east-west axis, giving us how many square miles, gentlemen?" One of the maxims of the Department was that asking questions in orientation sessions helped maintain interest and also fostered audience participation. Actually, this particular question was an attempt by this particular pair of instructors to catch the group sleeping. It had happened one year and it could happen again. It didn't work this time. At least one of the hunters was awake and listening because he blurted out immediately, "Two thousand square miles!"

The Department man could have said "Right!" and gone on, but he didn't. He didn't because the program the two of them had developed over the years allowed for several options at this point, options available only to themselves. A reprimand of "Come, gentlemen, let's pay attention," was called for if no one in the audience had answered the square miles question. If there had been an answer but it proved unintelligible, then the instructor's option became "Let's speak up so everyone can hear!" Finally, there was the *last word* option, which went "The area isn't that big, actually," and was used when one of the audience came up with the correct answer but delivered it with too positive a response, as now. Positive responses could not be tolerated this early in the session. They could threaten authority. They could establish a bad precedent.

"Actually, the area isn't that big," the instructor announced, "not when you consider the irregular boundary that Lake Powell imposes in the south. Do you see that?" From deep in the audience came the respondee's voice, "Right. I see that."

The instructor frowned forbiddingly as if to discourage any further dialogue bearing on area, and then continued. "We've got a lot of ground to cover, gentlemen, so let's keep moving. These sessions are for *your* benefit. *Your* protection." He moved without further interruption into a listing of hunter checkpoints that were scattered throughout the hunt area. It was important, he intoned, if not absolutely necessary, to co-operate with official checking-station personnel and to obey the rules relating to the proper registration and identification of kill so that the harvest could be properly tallied and the whole program passed on to future once-in-a-lifetime permit holders without jeopardy or taint. As responsible big game hunters, did they see that? "Let me quote the regulation to you. *It is unlawful for any person to fail to stop at checking stations or road blockages where a stop sign or red or blue light is displayed.* Then there's the exhibition regulation and I will read that as well. *All persons while engaged in hunting or while transporting wildlife shall be required upon demand of any conservation officer to exhibit the required license, permit or tag, or any device or apparatus in his possession used for hunting, or any wildlife in his possession.*" He stopped and asked if there were any questions.

"Not a question but a point," Bike called out loudly. "You

121

omitted part of the regulation. The words *or any other peace officer* should have been included right after *conservation officer*. You obviously overlooked that. Any peace officer can make an exhibition demand."

"All these Big Game regulations," the instructor went on, never once looking at Bike, "must be known and understood. Ignorance of the law is no excuse. Let me begin by restating the license requirements of the state of Utah. *No person shall engage in the harvest of protected wildlife without first having procured the necessary licenses, permits and tags as provided and having at the same time such licenses, permits and tags on his person. Nor shall any person lend, transfer, sell, give or assign his license or any permits or tags belonging thereto or the rights granted by such licenses, permits or tags. It shall be unlawful for any person to use or have in his possession while hunting any license or permit not issued to him.*" The instructor paused and surveyed the group. "If there is any person in this room under the age of twenty-one years please raise your hand."

There were no hands.

"Remember that when you sign for your tags this afternoon we have the right to demand proof of age. And from those found to be under twenty-one we must see a certificate of competency in hunter safety issued by the Division of Wildlife Resources under the hunter education program." Again he paused, ominously this time, confident that after this additional warning there would be a show of one or two tardy hands. Red wanted to raise his hand for a prank but Von stopped him. "Don't try to be funny," he whispered, "when your intelligence is being insulted."

"Was there a question?" the other instructor demanded, hearing the whispering, but then he took over and went on without further delay. "There are some general regs here we should look at. Hunting hours, for example. *It is unlawful to take big game except during daylight hours. Daylight hours are defined as that period between one-half hour before official sunrise to one-half hour after official sunset.* Any questions?"

"Sounds like the question on headlights in the Drivers License exam," Red mumbled, and a man to his left snickered and the instructor boomed, "Was there a question there in the second row?"

"No question," Red boomed right back. "We pretty much know the difference between daylight and dark."

There was an eruption of nervous laughter and the instructor drawled, "Trespass, another general regulation. *Any person entering upon privately owned land of any other person, firm or corporation which is properly posted, without permission from the owner or person in charge, is guilty of a class B misdemeanor.*"

"How are you treating Capitol Reef?" asked a man with an accent in the front row at the end.

"National parks, monuments and Indian lands are closed areas," came the reply. It was weary and automatic. "On hunt area 600 there is no conflict except for a small stretch along Hall's Creek in the vicinity of the Burr Trail cutoff. But the herd won't be there anyway."

"Where will it be?"

"You're the hunters," answered the instructor sweetly, coming back to life. "You figure it out."

The other instructor immediately took over with a regulation he thought was important and should be brought to their attention. It covered tagging of big game. That was followed by a regulation having to do with waste. "*It is unlawful to waste or permit to be wasted or spoiled any big game.*" The recital swung back again to the alternate instructor who, in an absolutely identical voice, warned them of yet another practice the state of Utah deemed unlawful. "*It is unlawful to purchase, sell, offer for sale, barter or otherwise dispose of or obtain for sale, purchase or barter any big game or parts thereof except heads, hides, antlers and horns as provided.*"

123

Listening attentively, Bike gave a confirming nod. "These guys really know their regs," he whispered to Von.

Von swallowed hard. "It's the very soul of hunting, isn't it, Bike? The laws and the unlaws. What to keep and what to throw away. How to tell a rabbit from a deer."

"*It is unlawful for any person to take any form of wildlife from an aircraft, either fixed-wing or helicopter, or any other airborne vehicle or device or any motorized, terrestrial or aquatic vehicle, including snowmobiles and other recreational vehicles.*" There weren't any questions and the instructor went on with a great number of additional maxims laid down by the sovereign state of Utah. Interminably. But he stopped eventually, which seemed startling when it happened, and the twenty-four orange caps in the audience lifted to become twenty-four white faces. It was a unison thing, like a rise of ducks from a morning pond. "What do you say we break here and stretch our legs and grab some coffee," the instructor announced, and his voice had changed, as if monotone was itself a regulation and he had just repealed it. "Smoking lamp is lit. Latrines are down the hall to your left. Let's be back in our seats in twenty minutes."

Sandy and Karen entered practically every store on both sides of the street, or at least studied their window displays. In the Trading Post Gift Shop, Karen picked out two porcelain mugs that carried a decal of Snoopy lying on his back with his foot cocked up on one knee and his hands locked under his head and a cigar in his mouth looking up at the sky and saying, in a little dialogue balloon just above his head, "Screw It!" Sandy bought some underwear and a tablecloth in the Zion Department Store and as they came out onto the sidewalk a semi rig passed in the street. The two women looked up at the noise and caught a glimpse in the cab of gloved hands riding a flat steering wheel and a face pinned in place by sunglasses and then the driver's head shot out of the window in a swift double take, having caught a glimpse of Karen and the lush overripe totter of her walk, and his voice cracked out, "*Hey . . . meat!*"

For the first and only time that morning Karen Kimball glanced back at an admirer. It was a quick glance, furtive almost, but in that instant was revealed a face flaming with satisfaction, gorged by it, to be exact. The truck passed on and so did the moment, and a terrible smugness flooded into Karen's voice. "Let's go get a cup of coffee."

They found a coffee shop and took a booth toward the rear. "I guess you could say that semi driver liked what he saw," Karen began, not forgetting, coming right back to it, and Sandy said, "It's pushing noon. Maybe we should be on the lookout for Dorothy and plan on eating some lunch." But no sooner was the statement made than each of them shot a glance of horror at the other. "Oh no!" Karen cried. "Dorothy's got no way to get downtown. Red's got their Blazer!"

"I completely spaced it out," Sandy confessed, incredulous, but then they decided to go ahead with their coffee and pick Dorothy up afterward and bring her back downtown for lunch. The waitress came and they ordered the coffee and when she was gone Karen said, "What do you think the guy in the semi looked like? Tall? Handsome? Broad shoulders?"

"One hundred and ten pounds at full sweat," Sandy said. "Five feet tall if he wears his cheater heels. Bad teeth. And on a date he'd show up wearing a hundred-dollar hat that was bigger than he was."

"You're no fun."

"You'd think those guys would really be something, sitting up there in those cabs wheeling those big rigs around. But I've never seen a truck driver yet who fits the image. When they open that door and step down onto the pavement they're a real turnoff."

"Not for me. They're a turn on. A big one."

"The rig or the driver?"

"Listen," Karen whispered, leaning forward, "I keep having

this dream. Maybe it's a fantasy. Fantasy seems to be the in thing now, male and female both. You read a lot of books about it. Actually, I think they're dirty books masquerading as scientific studies."

"We'll call it a fantasy. What is it? Is it bad?"

"Hell no, it's not bad. It's great." She took a sip of coffee. "I'm hitchhiking on a highway somewhere and this semi stops and picks me up. We drive a few miles and then the driver pulls off onto a side road and stops and drags me back into the sleeping compartment, that place back of the seat where the relief driver usually sleeps."

"I know."

"It smells real sweaty and sour in there, and the blankets are all messed up. There's a little red light up in one corner. The driver takes all my clothes off and then takes off his. He's got a great huge thing with a big head on it and it's hard and he rubs it against my belly and in my armpits and all around my nipples. The red light makes my nipples look like pieces of red licorice and he keeps sucking on them. Then he puts his thing into me and I can feel it way up under my ribs. It hurts but he starts balling me and I have one climax after another. He gets me in all kinds of positions, you wouldn't believe some of them. I just keep coming and coming and coming. I get so weak I can't move and I just lay there and this guy keeps pumping me. After a while I fall out onto the front seat. Then the dream stops, right at that point. It's like I wake up, except that sometimes I haven't even been sleeping."

"Sounds more like hot pants than a fantasy."

"But isn't that normal? Isn't that what they're saying now, that it's normal to think about sex with someone else, someone new?"

"Who is *they*? Besides, I think it depends on the individual. The one having the fantasy."

"Don't you have them?"

"No, I don't, Karen."

"Not even little ones? Quick happy ones when you see a neat guy somewhere?"

"No."

"Maybe it's you that's not normal." She drank from her coffee. "According to what I read—"

"I think if your love life is satisfactory you don't think about anyone else. Truck drivers or cute guys or anybody."

"But that's just it. My sex life *is* satisfactory. Bike takes good care of me. He's always ready and he knows what to do with what he's got. I know a half dozen girls in the bowling league who'd just love to get into his shorts." She stopped and winked lewdly. "So do I. It's fun in there."

"Then you don't need your truck drivers."

"But I *think* about them, Sandy. I guess it's because they're new. After all, I've never seen another man naked. I've never seen what their bellies and their chests look like. If their cans are any good. What they look like hard. Don't you ever wonder about strange guys? After fourteen years with the same one, don't you wonder?"

"I was right," Sandy said quietly. "You've got hot pants."

"But I wouldn't do anything, Sandy. Honest. I wouldn't do that to the Bishop. It sounds corny, but I really wouldn't betray him. We argue a lot anymore and I get so damned pissed at him sometimes I could knock him in the head. But I wouldn't be untrue. I mean it." She waited. "But I still think about new guys."

"The way you wear your jeans you shouldn't have much trouble attracting somebody new."

"Maybe some big horny driver will throw me down and just take it."

"You mean rape?"

"Why not? At least I'd get some strange stuff that way."

"Oh, Karen!" and Sandy laughed in spite of herself. "In the first place, rape isn't really a sexual act. And secondly, wanting to get raped would be the same thing as stepping out."

"Why would it?"

Sandy answered right away, but the words didn't come as easily as she'd hoped they would. "Because it would give you a chance not to be responsible. You could hide behind it. We have to be responsible. It's a matter of being honest, really, and I think that's important."

They finished their coffee and left the shop and turned down the street toward where they had parked the Bronco. A pickup truck drove alongside and then stopped in an explosion of brake lights. The window on the right side rolled down and a young man popped his head out and made a loud exaggerated panting sound. As Karen moved moved away down the sidewalk, pretending to ignore him, the young man stuck an arm out the window and began to pound on the car door. "Horny town," Karen sniffed when the pickup had finally gunned away down the street.

"That was pretty young stuff."

"Who cares?" Karen said as they got into the Bronco. "I hear they can go night and day. Just like my dream driver."

"It shall be unlawful to possess or use weapons in the taking of any big game while under the influence of alcohol or illegal drugs. It shall be unlawful for any person at any time to take big game with the aid of a dog or dogs. It shall be unlawful for any person to aid or assist any other person to violate any rule or regulation."

"It shall be unlawful," Von muttered, "for any state in the union to have this many unlawfuls."

"Every person," recited the instructor in his wooden monotone, *"while hunting big game animals shall wear a minimum of four hundred square inches of hunter orange fluorescent material on his head, chest and back."*

"Did he get it right, Bike?" Red whispered.

"Basically, yes. But he left out *Other red and yellow colors do not comply with this regulation.* That's actually part of the

128

regulation. Lots of guys try to cheat on the color but it's got to be orange. Hunter's orange."

"God forbid," Von muttered, "that any of us would try to cheat on color—"

"Let's move right along," the instructor exclaimed. "*No person, other than peace officers or other officially designated persons, shall carry in or on any vehicle, including any two-wheeled conveyance, any firearms which have live ammunition in the firing chamber.* In other words, gentlemen, don't carry a loaded gun in the car. I'm sure you've all heard that one before. It's the one your father pounded into your head when he got you your first rifle." He stopped and surveyed the group paternally and then swung into an additional warning that primitive weapons, as defined, were not allowed on hunt area 600. "Also, handguns aren't legal for the taking of buff. I'm sure you all knew that. *It shall be unlawful to employ any firearm using rimfire cartridges, or any type shotgun, crossbow or a non-expanding type bullet when taking buffalo.*" He stopped and took a breath. "Any questions on this last set? Any discussion?" When there was only silence from the floor the Department twins, as Von now thought of them, continued their recital. When they got to the regulation prohibiting the discharge of firearms across any public highway, "*except as provided for in the Wildlife Resources Code of Utah Section 23-20-13,*" there was a collective catch of breath from the audience. "My God," Von groaned, "they're not going to read that entire section, are they?"

They did.

But it ended eventually. One of the twins abruptly laid aside his papers and looked up and took a deep breath and let it out slowly. "All right, gentlemen, our morning session has come to a close," and he smiled benevolently. "You've been so nice we've got a surprise for you. The Department is going to pick up lunch." He waited for the cheers and they came, exultantly. "There's a restaurant directly across the street with a banquet room that's been reserved for us," the instructor announced, and he maneuvered his wrist so he could read his watch, "and we're going to leave for that banquet room . . . right . . . about . . . *now!*" His dropping his hand, as if it held a starter's flag, had the desired effect. The group exploded from its chairs and jammed into the narrow exit door before the instructor could step off the platform and join his double. The two eventually worked their way to the front, however, and together they led their orange-splashed charges down the antiseptic corridor and through the morbid lobby and into the autumn sunlight.

The banquet room was furnished with six or seven large round tables and Bike managed to isolate Dr. Hall and Dr. Garland and convince them to share a table. Everyone introduced himself again—it was odd to see the faces this clearly—and Garland, whom they knew for certain now was the veterinarian, taller and a bit younger than the dentist Hall, who ran to portliness and wore glasses, told the three Grangerites they appeared to be full of the requisite piss and vinegar. "I saw you come into the auditorium this morning," the vet said cheerfully. "The three of you combined couldn't have made one decent hangover."

"I drank a little more last night than I usually do," Von told him. "In fact, I don't remember the last part of the evening." Red added that he himself hadn't drunk so much, but it hit him harder than usual for some reason.

"It will do that sometimes," Hall said.

Lunch was a small fruit cup, sliced roast beef under brown gravy, mashed potatoes, peas, one roll with butter, coffee or iced tea and possibly a small dessert later, the waitress couldn't be sure. "I sent this meat out for analysis," Bike remarked when the plates were served and the waitress gone. "The results have just come back."

"And?"

"It *is* roast beef."

They all laughed politely. "I don't think they brought mine back from the lab," Garland said, poking in the gravy with his fork, and they all laughed again, more warmly now. Addressing Red, Garland said, "I forget the exact conversation but I recall you saying last night at our table that you thought the .375 Magnum a better cartridge than the .270."

"Oh hell, yes," Red answered, but it was obvious he was trying to remember the remark.

"A better cartridge, or more powerful?" Hall asked.

Red stared at him, and then Bike stepped in. "I don't believe," he grinned, "that Mr. Taddish makes that particular distinction."

"What's your rifle then?" the dentist asked Red, and Red answered that it was a Colt-Sauer bolt, .375 H & H Magnum.

"That follows," the dentist smiled, and then he said, "I've got a good friend who lives up in Logan. He was trying out a Ruger No. 1 that he was considering buying, which is also chambered for .375 Magnum, as you know. Well, this one day he picked me up and drove me out to the rifle range and asked me to shoot the Ruger. I did." He paused dramatically. "That's what is defined as a powerful rifle, gentlemen. The recoil damned near knocked me down."

"A .375 will kick on you," Red agreed, involved now. "But that's what I like. Man, I got a belly full of sweet little guns that won't kill. My first rifle was a .22 short that I used on squirrel. It would bust up a lot of shoulders and ribs but it wouldn't put them away. I had to swing the damned things up against a tree to get it over with. I don't want that shit anymore. When I pull trigger now I want to feel some jolt. I want to hear some blast. Only a Magnum's got that kind of power."

"Too much," Von put in quietly. "Too much blast. Too much power. You don't need it to be a hunter."

"Bullshit," Red huffed. "When I throw a barrel up to my shoulder I want to knock something down."

Von said, "Like the rabbits? Tell them about the rabbits."

But Red had his mouth full of food at that moment so Bike told the story. "The day Red got his Colt-Sauer he wanted to try it out so we drove over after work to Dugway, over in Skull Valley. But it was dark by the time we got there and all we could do was shine jacks."

"I got the top of my cab rigged with lights," Red broke in. "It's a Power-Pak triple mount." It was in his face that it was important Hall and Garland knew that.

"But just killing the jacks wasn't enough," Bike went on. "Red wanted to put some hair in it, like the pool sharks do. The bet he put up was who'd be the first to blow a jack's head off with each of us shooting our big rifles." He grinned. "You can guess who won."

"Shit!" Red snorted. "I had me a head by the second shot. It went flying off into the sagebrush somewhere."

"Some shooting," Dr. Hall declared.

"Not really," Von said.

Bike chuckled. "Meet Sergeant York," he said, nodding at Von. "He's our rifleman. Our sharpshooter."

"Is that so?" It was Hall again.

"Red was firing a 300-grain bullet," Von explained, sounding obligated. "You hit a rabbit at fifty yards with a bullet that big and naturally you're going to blow its head off. It's too much power. You don't need it. Besides, where's the sport in blowing away a hypnotized rabbit? In those lights you could have walked up and wrung its neck."

"And it's illegal," Bike broke in. "You shine a jack in this state and you are flat breaking the law."

"Bike is our Prophet, Seer and Revelator," Von explained. "He was originally with the church and now he's with the state. He interprets all the regulations for us. He tells us how close we come to going to jail. And how far we are from heaven," he added.

But Dr. Hall wanted to get back to something. "So you're the shooter in the bunch?" he said to Von.

132

"A purist is what he is," Bike put in, grateful for the change in subject. "He even hand loads."

Hall kept going. "Factory loads today are perfectly adequate. Why hand load?"

"For a lot of reasons," Von answered. "Economy. Performance. But mostly I like to tailor my loads for the specific type of hunting I'm going to do."

"How about tomorrow? What will you take out tomorrow for the buff?"

"My .270 Winchester."

Hall was eating from his fruit cup and he stopped. "Isn't that a little light for buffalo?"

"It's a pussy gun," Red broke in. "Girl Scout model. It shoots peas through a hollow tube like I used to shoot at the girls in grade school. If he pulls down with that thing tomorrow the buff won't even know he's been hit."

"I don't want him to know," Von said quietly. "I want it over with that quick," and he snapped his fingers. "What I *don't* want to do is blow his legs off and let him bleed to death in a draw somewhere. I don't like to track cripples."

"It's dangerous," Garland said.

Von said, "It's unnecessary."

"Tomorrow?" Hall repeated at Von. "In the field, what kind of bullet?"

Von took a sip of coffee and sat his cup down. "I'll shoot tomorrow what I put together last week in my basement. A Nosler Partition 180-grain Protected Point. It'll hold together in bone and it'll give me the expansion I want. But I won't take the shot unless it's a brain shot. That way, a hit's a sure kill and a miss hasn't got any pain in it."

"Sounds good when *you* say it," the dentist exclaimed. "Me, I'm not a good enough shot. I'm taking the same weapon out tomorrow that I took to Africa a couple times—once for water buffalo and the other time for elephant. It's a .45-70 Government. Big Flat Nose, is what I call it. That bullet is going so

133

slow a hundred yards out from the muzzle I swear you can actually see it." He waited while the waitress refilled his coffee cup and then he sought Von out again and winked at him conspiratorially. "Wouldn't you just love to get your hands on one of those old-time .55 Sharps that had a barrel as long as a tree branch and would kill your animal at a thousand yards?"

Von answered that it would be a real challenge. He remembered that in the movies Burt Lancaster and Jimmy Stewart always made that shot. "For myself, I won't lift for anything beyond three hundred yards. Almost all your big game is killed this side of three hundred. If I'm not good enough to get closer then I'm no hunter. Anything over three hundred and there's too much chance of merely wounding the animal. There's no real accuracy at the longer ranges. Firing a .270-caliber 150-grain Spitzer boattail sighted in at one hundred yards, that bullet will fall ten inches below the target when the target is three hundred yards away. At four hundred yards, the bullet will fall twenty-four inches low. Just think of it, that's two feet lower than what you aimed for! Hell, at that distance you're not aiming anymore, you're praying with your eyes open."

Hall agreed that Von could be right, but his words were an amenity only. He had already turned to Bike, whose growing restlessness he must have seen out of the corner of his eye. "And you, sir? What's your weapon?"

"I'm an ought-sixer," Bike answered gratefully. "As far as I'm concerned, the .30-06 is the best cartridge ever invented."

"Hard to argue with that."

"It puts me right straddle of this power business," Bike went on, glancing both at Von and at Red. "I can go either way from the middle if I want to. From antelope up to buffalo. Or back down."

"Safe," Hall said, sipping his coffee. "You've got to admit it's safe."

"And you, Dr. Garland," Bike said, as if having regained control of the conversation, some responsibility had passed to him. There was a lot of the master-of-ceremonies in Bike Kimball and it never revealed itself more than at moments like these. "You've let the rest of us do all the bragging. Certainly you've got a favorite rifle you'll throw onto your shoulder tomorrow morning."

"Yes, I have," Garland answered. "My Palmer Cap-shur."

Bike was lifting his coffee cup and he set it back down. "Your what?"

"My Cap-shur," the veterinarian repeated solemnly. And then, having gotten the reception he obviously sought, his face broke open and he let the enjoyment show. "That's what I'd *like* to shoot."

"What the hell is it?" Red demanded.

"It's the rifle that shoots an immobilizing drug into an animal's hide. Veterinarians and zoo officials use it. I'm sure you've heard of the practice. It enables the animal to be anesthetized so it can be tagged or examined or transported or treated, whatever. I'm sure you've seen it done on TV. Certainly in *National Geographic*."

Red was incredulous. "You paid a two-hundred-dollar permit fee just to stick a buffalo with a dart?"

Some of the mischievousness went out of the tall veterinarian's voice when he spoke. And he didn't look at Red. "As I said, that's what I'd *like* to shoot. In fact, I spent a whole month trying to get permission to do it. But I got turned down." He gave a laugh that was somewhat condescending. "You wouldn't believe the looks I got when I told those clerks in the Department that I didn't want to kill the buffalo, I just wanted to immobilize him for a few minutes so I could study him. Do some tests, that sort of thing. I'm sure they thought I was crazy. They couldn't really come up with a good reason why I couldn't do it so they just kept saying that it was too dangerous. That an accident could happen. That a buffalo was unpredictable and what I wanted to do at this time presented too much of a risk. *At this time*, they kept saying, as if another time would be perfectly all right, except they didn't ever say when that would be. Typical bureaucratic runaround."

135

"But why?" Bike asked, and he was nicer with it than Red had been. "I don't understand exactly. Couldn't tests like that be done in a zoo? In a more controlled atmosphere?"

"I'm sure they could," was Garland's answer. "But I don't own a zoo. Besides," he added, "there's the challenge to it. The sense of the dare."

"The truth is," Hall broke in, "the good doctor is tired of bullets. He wants to try darts."

"That's crazy," exclaimed Red. "What were you going to do, comb the buff's hair and count his chin whiskers and then slap him on the ass and tell him to get lost?"

"Something like that," Garland shrugged.

"Shit, man," Red argued, "this is a once-only hunt. Once in a lifetime. Why waste it? You want a nice buffalo head for your den, don't you?"

"Actually, I haven't got room," the veterinarian drawled. "The only spot that's even a little bit possible is right next to the boar I took in Sonora. Of course, I could take the Guaymas sailfish down . . . donate it to the club. . . ."

Red laid down his knife and fork. "Tell you what I'll do," he said. "You go ahead and kill your buffalo. Check him out and run all the tests you want to run. Then give him to me. How's that? That will solve your space problem."

Bike said, "You cannot sell, offer to sell, barter or otherwise dispose of big game."

Garland shrugged his shoulders at no one in particular. "Looks like I'll have to go out tomorrow and bag my bull like everybody else. But I would like to use the Cap-shur. Just once, that's all I ask. I'd like to try it just one time."

Von stirred in his chair. "What's the rifle like?" he asked Garland. "Can you tell me something about it?"

Garland pushed his plate back and lit a cigar. "The rifle is made by Palmer. Cap-shur is the model. I think Palmer makes only two or three models."

"Does it have any power?"

"Well . . . yes. But power is relative, like you were saying earlier. All I ask it to do is carry at least fifty yards. Fifty and under is the effective range. The shaft of the cartridge, if you want to know about that, is made of aluminum, maybe two inches long. The needle is attached to that, of course. It's approximately the same length."

Bike's interest was up now. "Is it like a harpoon?"

"No, the needle isn't barbed. There's a slight collar on it but that's all. The drug is released on impact. There's a little powder charge that drives the syringe plug down the barrel and forces the liquid through the needle into the animal's flesh."

"Is there a best place on the animal?" Bike asked.

"Any large muscle mass is good. The haunch or the thigh. The dart will work itself out when the animal gets up and moves around again."

Von got back in with another question. "Is there any danger to the animal while it's unconscious?"

"It's never unconscious," Garland replied. "The drug is a muscle paralyzant only. The animal remains fully awake and alert. It just can't move for fifteen or twenty minutes, that's all. The drug itself is somewhat dose sensitive. You have to be careful. You're talking approximately two milligrams of drug per kilo of body weight, so you've got to stay within those parameters as much as possible."

Von asked if the drug had a shelf life.

"I'm not sure exactly. It's succinylcholine chloride, that's its generic name, and I buy it in a bottle and prepare my own charge in advance. I can load the rifle as much as twenty-four hours prior to use. Beyond that I don't know. In my practice I've never had the chance to use it on a *big* animal. That's why I wanted to use it on the buff. Hell, a big bull is liable to go fifteen hundred pounds." He glanced around the table and then he smiled and the impishness was back. "You know what I'm going to do? I'm going to load up that Palmer fresh every night and when I see the right buffalo and get my chance I'm going to go ahead with the dart anyway."

"I wouldn't do that," Bike cautioned. "You'll be breaking

the law. You could wind up paying a healthy fine and losing your Utah hunting privileges."

"Who's to see me?" Garland said, and it was pleasant enough. "The dart can be pulled out and destroyed easily, and there goes the evidence."

"Something else, too," Von put in, "if you lose your license you won't be able to kill any more animals. You don't want that, do you?"

"Hell, no," Garland winked. "What would become of the taxidermists in the Salt Lake area? How would they survive without me?"

"Speaking of taxidermy," Hall interjected, touching his mouth with a napkin, "you could say that being big in the animal world incurs a penalty. You don't see many of the little animals, squirrels and prairie dogs, mounted on plaques. But there are a hell of a lot of kodiak and moose and polar bear looking down from den walls in this country."

"True enough," said Von. "There isn't a lot of drama in busting a prairie dog."

"Give me the big animal every time," Hall said.

"They fall so hard," Von said quietly, after a little silence. "That's what bothers me. It seems like it takes them forever to hit the ground."

"So?"

"If they'd just fall quietly, maybe it would be easier. But they don't. They make that sound that isn't like any other sound in hunting. It has no echo. It's so heavy, so ... . final. I guess if I had my way I'd make a regulation that would erase the sound of their falling."

Hall tried a soft laugh. "Maybe you should change your standards and start shooting at long range so you wouldn't have to listen to it."

Von drank coffee and put his cup down. "You're right about the bigness penalty, Dr. Hall. These big animals pay it. They're proud and they're arrogant and they strut around showing off their size and all of a sudden a bullet hits them. They don't even see it and it humiliates the hell out of them. There's no way they can fight back. Nothing to fight. A lot of the time the bullet doesn't kill them right away and that's even worse. Then the pain comes. And the rage." He sipped at his glass of water but he didn't look at anyone. "My dad doesn't hunt much anymore," he went on, "but when I was a boy he'd take me and my brother Orin hunting with him. This one year he took us on a pack-in for elk up in the Warm River Basin in Idaho. We were after winter meat. Something for the table. That's rugged country up there and in those days a bear tag was automatically a part of your elk license. I remember my dad's brother was with us this time. He was carrying a .257 Roberts, which is fine for a small white-tailed buck but not a twelve-hundred-pound grizzly, which is what he flushed up during a drive he was making. He got off three shots. We heard them and all of a sudden here comes my uncle busting through this brush. 'Bear! Bear!' he was shouting. 'Big grizzly! I think I hit him but he ran off into a draw!' Well, we headed off in that direction but we couldn't hear anything. Then this noise started up. Scared the hell out of me. I can still feel my hair standing up on the back of my neck. It was a horrible noise, growling and thrashing and breaking. I haven't heard anything like it since. It kept up for maybe ten minutes and then it stopped and that draw got real still. My dad said we had to go in and find the bear because he was too dangerous to just leave be. But we should wait a bit, he said, and we did. We waited at least an hour. My dad said the bear needed that amount of time to lay down and stiffen up, if he was ever going to. Finally we went in. The draw was a jumble of brush and deadfall and for about a hundred yards all we had to track was these splotches of blood. And we were creeping, I can tell you, rifles out in front and the safeties off. Suddenly we broke out of the cover into this little clearing and I've never seen such a mess in my life. It was total destruction. The earth was all torn up. Trees four inches thick had been busted and bent over and big rocks had been thrown around everywhere. A dead tree laying on the ground had been ripped to pieces and scattered over the clearing. We spotted the bear piled up against the base of a lodgepole pine. He was dead. One of the bullets had smashed his hind leg just below the knee. Another had plowed into his rump. The shot in the lungs was the one that eventually killed him, but not soon enough. He was hurt bad and he didn't know why and he couldn't stop the pain. So he went into a rage. This great huge powerful animal was fighting back in the only way he knew." Von picked up his coffee cup but he didn't drink from it. "I can still hear that anger, I can still see it. I've never forgotten."

There was no dessert, the waitress announced, and they finished their coffee and left the restaurant. "That was a damned good story," Red remarked to Von as they crossed the street to the Armory. "You should have finished it."

"What do you mean?"

"Well, shit, you didn't say whether you ever got that big grizzly down off the mountain."

Karen parked the Bronco in front of the Pace Arrow and she and Sandy got out and ran in to get Dorothy. Sandy knocked once, more as a joke than a consideration, and they pushed open the door.

Dorothy sat slumped at the end of the sofa with her eyes closed and her head leaning against a bookcase that abutted the sofa. She was still in her nightgown. In her lap and on the cushions and on the floor at her feet lay perhaps a dozen empty Smirnoff minis. Karen took in a startled breath and dropped into a chair that stood by the door. "Oh, for Christ's sake," she said. And Sandy, still standing in the open door, said flatly, "She's drunk."

"Blotto," Karen said. "Bombed. Stinko. Loaded."

Sandy closed the door and crossed to the sofa. There were some flakes of dried saliva at the corner of Dorothy's mouth and her face revealed the blotches of freckle that the cake makeup ordinarily hid. Sandy reached out and laid a single finger on Dorothy's shoulder. "Dorothy?" It was tentative, as if she didn't actually know the person slumped there and was approaching with some apprehension.

"Stoned. Zonkered. Smashed," Karen chanted, her voice rising indignantly with each word. "In the bag. In her cups. Out cold." She stopped finally. "For Christ's sake, what do we do with her?"

"We sober her up," Sandy said matter-of-factly. "It isn't the first time, is it?"

Karen groaned and shook her head. "Man, you've got to be real hung over to get drunk again by noon the next day."

"Either that or real unhappy," Sandy said, and she reached down and pulled Dorothy's head away from the bookcase. "Okay, here we go," she said to Karen, and together they lifted Dorothy to her feet. Her lips moved and she spoke a harsh mumble of Sandy's name, and what they thought was Karen's, and then her face twisted into a grimace as though she'd been struck by an intense pain. But she never once opened her eyes. "I think she wants to sleep," Karen said.

"She can't sleep. She's got over a pint of vodka in her stomach and it's got to come up. Now."

Karen protested. "I'm not getting puke all over these new jeans."

With the toe of one boot, Sandy reached out and snared the leg of the chair that stood by the door and pushed it next to the kitchen sink, and sat Dorothy down in it. "Hold her there," Sandy said. "I'll see what's in the fridge." She found a carton of milk, and in the freezer section a quart of ice cream and a small tin of strawberries. "Oh, for Christ's sake," Karen said, "I know what we're going to do and we don't need the strawberries!" Sandy returned the strawberries to the freezer and located the blender and plugged it in and filled it with the ice cream and milk. The whir of the blender got absolutely no response from Dorothy. "A bucket," Sandy said. "I need a bucket." She found a plastic bucket beneath the sink and placed it on the floor between Dorothy's feet. She poured part of the milkshake into a glass and held it up to Dorothy and said, "Drink this!"

Dorothy must have recognized the voices for her head came up and her mouth opened momentarily, and Sandy poured half the contents of the glass into it. When the cold milkshake hit Dorothy's throat her eyes popped open and she began to swallow rapidly and her cheeks ballooned and there was a desperate *whuh whuh* sound in her throat, and then her head snapped forward and a thick clotted mass shot out of her mouth into the bucket. It smelled fiercely of liniment, and of milk that has gone sour. After a few seconds Dorothy's mouth blew open again and another white rope of ejecta arced into the bucket. Karen grabbed Dorothy's hair and pulled her head up. Her eyes streamed water and she gulped air in frantic bites. Sandy jammed the glass against her mouth and forced the remaining liquid into it. Dorothy's eyes rolled and she began a series of hiccups that started in her diaphragm and moved progressively upward and then her mouth exploded with a new gush of vodka-stained milkshake. Again the odor of liniment rushed at them. "God," Karen winced, "it smells like the athlete's foot solution we used to have to stand in at Granger High just before we took a shower."

Dorothy began to moan pitifully and her head sagged in Karen's grasp. Sandy emptied the contents of the blender into the glass and motioned for Karen to get ready and they repeated the entire procedure. Dorothy drank and vomited, and vomited again when they drained the last of the shake into her mouth. Following this, they pushed the bucket aside and stood Dorothy on her feet and forced her to accept her full body weight. Sandy then made her drink a glass of milk without the ice cream. Dorothy promptly threw it up and crumpled into the chair.

They got her to her feet and made her look down at her toes

and then up at the ceiling, down at her toes, up at the ceiling, toes, ceiling, toes, ceiling, faster and faster, and Sandy got the bucket up in front of Dorothy just in time to catch the last wrenching spasm of vomit that was ever going to come out of her.

Sandy rinsed the bucket in the toilet while Karen dumped a tray of ice cubes into a pan of water and soaked a washcloth and applied it to Dorothy's forehead. Dorothy peered pathetically at her through rheumy eyes and Karen didn't give up the washcloth treatment until her fingers got numb from the ice cubes. At that point, Sandy ordered Dorothy to take a quick shower in cold water. When she had finished, the two of them toweled her dry with a vigor that brought from Dorothy the first successful attempt at speech. Sandy said, "We need to get something in her stomach," and Dorothy said, "Seems fair to me, you got any vodka?"

"Oh, for Christ's sake," Karen sputtered. "She's still drunk."

The something for Dorothy's stomach turned out to be a can of Snap-E-Tom and a half dozen saltine crackers. Miraculously, despite several near disastrous hiccups, Dorothy managed to keep the food down. They got her into a pair of slacks and a jacket and after a second Snap-E-Tom they all three went outside and walked. They walked at least thirty minutes at a brisk pace, and then questions began to pour from Dorothy in a thick gummy voice: *What time was it? What time did they find her? Had she said anything foolish? Had she fought with them? Had Red been home? What time was he coming home?*

"Quit talking, damn it!" Karen ordered. "Walk hard and breathe fast!"

In a few minutes Dorothy began to cry. The tears soaked her face and a stringy loop of spittle hung from her mouth but they would not free her hands so she could wipe it away.

At two thirty they went back inside and while Dorothy drank another can of juice, Karen and Sandy combed and brushed her hair until the sheen came back into it.

At three o'clock, without support this time, Dorothy walked

with them across the parking grounds and back. At one point they encountered a knot of schoolchildren carrying papers covered with orange pumpkins and brown witches, and Karen made a mental note to remind Sandy that they should call home that night and trick-or-treat the kids by long distance. They could probably call from the KOA clubroom. When they got back to the Pace Arrow they made fresh coffee. Apart from her voice sounding scratchy and her eyes being puffed, Dorothy was much improved. The color was struggling back into her face and she had decided to put on some makeup. She started to thank the two of them again for what they had done and Karen lifted her hands in a gesture of protest and said, "None of that shit, huh? A little hangover on your part wouldn't be entirely out of line so don't get too well. You put a lot of booze away last night. We all did. But this business today, this bullshit never happened, okay? The three of us drove downtown and window-shopped and drank coffee and then came home. You got that?"

"When will the guys be home?" Dorothy asked.

"Soon."

They got home shortly after four o'clock. They came shuffling into the Pace Arrow carrying two cold six-packs and they made a stab at being bright and talky but it was obvious the day had dulled them. They had a tendency to stare at what they looked at and they repeated everything that was said to them as if they were sizing the words up, measuring like carpenters to see if they would fit into their understanding. "How to have your intelligence insulted in the name of sport," Von grumbled.

"They kept telling me it wasn't a school," Red yawned, "but you couldn't prove it by me. I had a civics class in high school that wasn't this boring."

"We had a film this afternoon," Bike announced woodenly.

"What was it about?" Karen asked and she waited while Bike fixed on Von and Von glared back and they both started a couple of times to answer the question, but before they could accomplish it Dorothy said to Red, "Well, what was the film?" and Red answered, "Shit, don't ask me, I was asleep."

But the first six-pack of Coors twelve-ounce cans began gradually to work its magic and the men were into the second before they realized that neither Karen nor Sandy had joined them, and that Dorothy hadn't asked for a Slops. If they noticed her eyes being swollen they didn't mention it.

"What's the plan for tonight?" Red wanted to know.

"I don't think there is one." It was Dorothy. Her voice had settled into a coarse flutter.

"Bike won't like not having a plan," Von said.

Bike said, "Be nice. Let's have fun."

"Whatever we're going to have we should have it early," Karen put in. Sandy wanted to know if anyone was hungry and the response was mixed. Red was, Dorothy wasn't, and the others couldn't decide. Karen suggested that each couple fix whatever they wanted in their own rig and then they could all get together again afterward, maybe in the clubroom where there was shuffleboard and a couple of pool tables.

That got agreement, and leaving the Pace Arrow Karen took Sandy's arm and said, "There are some phones in the clubroom. We'd better call the kids now. If we wait till later Dorothy will be there and she'll hear."

They made the calls and then went back to the Wallaces' El Dorado. Von broke out a six-pack and Sandy played a Tammy Wynette tape and long before it was finished Von opened a second six-pack. It was completely dark outside now. Sandy put in a Linda Ronstadt tape and just when the vocal of "Love Has No Pride" started, a knock sounded at the door. Sandy went to answer it because it was her motor home and Karen got up too because she was closer, and they were both standing together when Sandy opened the door.

What was there was a skull.

It was an animal skull hanging in the top half of the doorway, a white night-eyed apparition of bone leering in at them, terrible in its disembodiment and fearsome in the demented mocking grin that was its greeting.

Both women screamed and fell back from the door at the same time that Von and Bike caught a glimpse of the specter and shot to their feet.

The skull spoke. Muffled. Sepulchral. "Trick or treat!" After an interminable moment, two arms reached out from the draped conical mass below the skull and lifted it up to reveal the leering face of Red Taddish.

"Oh, for Christ's sake!" Karen hissed, and Sandy gasped something unintelligible, and Red boomed, "Had you going there, didn't I?"

"Hey," Bike sputtered, "you did, you had us, you certainly did," and only then did he and the others laugh, but nervously, for a skull that speaks from the darkness is the very heart of terror, the nightmare child of shadow and unreality. Von, feeling the adrenaline drain from his stomach, said, "I think I'll go for the treat. I don't want a trick from a thing like that. What the hell is it?" and his words were an exhalation of relief as much as anything. "Where'd you get that outfit?"

Red was standing inside now, fully revealed and exuding some of that sheepishness that accompanies the act of unmasking, and he answered that he'd seen the skull in the clubroom last night. "I spotted it on the top of a filing case in this little office they got. I went over tonight and asked the guy if I could borrow it for a while." He eyed them. "Great skull, huh?"

"Great. I don't think I've ever seen a buffalo skull."

"And this other," Red said, holding up the robe, "this is my moose hide. I keep it in a footlocker in the Pace. It's the one my old man gave me a long time ago."

"Right," everyone said, for they vaguely remembered the robe, but their eyes were still full of the skull.

"Hell, it's Halloween!" Red trumpeted, as if they had forgotten. "And I still don't know what I got at this address, trick or treat?"

"Treat, for God's sake!" Bike cried. "Treat!" and he thrust two cans of Coors into Red's hands. "What did Dot think of your costume? I'll bet she got a kick out of it."

"I didn't show it to her. She was taking a nap." He stood stiffly, clutching the skull of the buffalo and the two Coors, the gag dying now. "Listen, about tonight," he said, overly loud, "we're going out, aren't we? Could be a wildass time. Let me know when," and he turned and left the camper, looking strangely ancient and ceremonial as he disappeared into the darkness.

Bike and Karen couldn't decide right away what they wanted to do. Maybe if they went back to the Huntsman and grabbed a snack, something would come to them. "But we're game for anything," they insisted, and left the El Dorado.

While Sandy showered, Von stepped outside and stood in the darkness and studied the lamppost that guarded the deserted playground next to the parking lot. Peering into the darkness beyond the light, he said, aloud to himself, unbidden, "My God, it starts tomorrow." He stood several minutes longer and then went back inside. He sat down on the sofa and began to rub his stomach. Sandy had finished her shower and was standing by the sink brushing her hair. "What's the matter?" she said, eyeing him.

"Stomach feels funny." He rubbed harder and made a face. "Got the cramps," he said. "Better forget tonight. Maybe tomorrow too."

Sandy placed the hairbrush on the counter and moved out from the sink and sat down on the edge of a chair. She looked squarely at Von. "Is this going to happen all over again?"

Von stopped rubbing his stomach. "What do you mean?"

"Last year you got sick to your stomach just before elk season and we almost stayed home. The year before that you missed the first two days of mule deer with cramps."

Von shrugged. "So?"

"What is it, Von?" she asked quietly. "What's the matter?"

"What do you mean, what's the matter? A guy can only get sick at certain times, is that it?"

"I think that's what you're doing, yes."

"Hey, come on. It's probably just the excitement." He looked away from her. "A case of nerves."

"You don't get nerves. Ever. I've seen you take home too many trophies."

"Glass of milk. Good night's sleep. I'll be all right." He got up from the sofa and opened the refrigerator and poured himself a glass of milk and drank it.

Sandy stood up from the chair. "I'll go tell Bike and Karen we're going to stay in tonight," she said with a certain resignation. "They can tell the Taddishes."

When they got back to their own rig, Bike stopped Karen at the door and asked her if she was going to fix a snack.

"Yes."

"You go in then. I'll be with you in a minute," and when Karen had disappeared inside he walked back a few feet and studied the sky to the south. The moon had come up, a cream-white ball hanging low in the sky. He had seen a ball of cream-white opal lying in black velvet once at a rock and gem show in Provo. He had studied the display a long time, he remembered, and circled the floor and then gone back to study it again, it was that singular, that unique. The moon was like that now, an opal imbedded in velvet. He continued to watch it and then he turned and went inside. Karen was sitting on the couch eating from a plate in her lap listening to a Waylon Jennings tape, and even before Bike got the door closed he said to her, "Just think of it, babe. I'm going to kill an American buffalo tomorrow."

"Just like a thousand other hunters before you," Karen said, not looking up from her plate.

"But that was their hunt, and this is mine. And I get to do it only once. Once in an entire lifetime."

148

In the Pace Arrow, Dorothy was nursing a Slops and reading *Parents* magazine. Red returned his dress jacket to the closet and took off his Levi's and got into his old clothes. "Bunch of gutless wonders!" he snorted. "If they ain't tired they're sick. Truth is they can't take it. They're too light for this heavy work." He picked up the buffalo skull like he would a bowling ball, with his fingers in the eyes, and made a mock roll at a set of imaginary pins. He repeated it several times and then said to Dorothy, "I'm gonna take this thing back to the clubroom," and he was out the door before she could acknowledge him.

The night was starless and the moon was up. Red thanked the manager at the clubroom for the loan of the skull and didn't stay to talk, although the man seemed to want to. Walking back, Red noticed there weren't many rigs parked on the grounds. He wondered where the two dozen hunters were staying. In motels in town? At Bullfrog Marina down on Lake Powell? He wondered where the buffalo were. He stopped and looked into the sky above the lamppost that stood on the far side of the campground, and then he raised his fist at the sky and shook it. "Get ready, you hump-backed bastards! Taddish is coming!"

CHAPTER 7

Good Runner saw the beasts from a long way off, a discolored island in the straw gulf of the grass. An inexperienced hunter might have mistaken them for a grove of trees, so dense and unmoving were they, but Good Runner knew they were not. They were beasts of some kind and he knew that distance caused them to be clumped, that as he neared them they would gradually grow larger and more distinct, that they would splinter off from their clustering like branches of a winter tree when the Great Light got behind it. And they would be big beasts, he knew, not the small swift animals. Even to be seen from this distance proved they would be big. He slowed to allow the two trailing hunters to draw abreast and then he pointed at the beasts with his spear. The hunters nodded and pumped their spears over their heads and stayed abreast of Good Runner for a few minutes, but then dropped back into the plodding hypnotic ranking that custom and fatigue had locked them in.

When Good Runner finally stopped and shielded his eyes from the Great Light he could see that the beasts numbered as many as the fingers of both his hands. They were the shaggy beasts with the huge hump and the fierce outward-curving horns, and he was pleased. The floor of his cave was covered with the fur-clotted hides of these beasts, his foot wraps and his head coverings were the gift of these creatures, as were the skins softened by chewing that he wore at the ceremonies when the good hunts were celebrated by making a cairn of skulls within a ring of fire and dancing around it. He had clubs fashioned from the heavy shoulder bones of these beasts, scrapers and fleshers made from the smaller bones of their legs, rattles made out of their horns and filled with the stained nuggets of their teeth. And they were good eating, these beasts. Their flesh was firm and blood-warmed and sweet to the taste.

He began to run forward again and as he did he studied the terrain. The ground to one side of the beasts' feeding area appeared to be broken but he was still too far away to be certain. It would have to be scouted to see if there was a ravine hidden there that they could use in their attack, a cliff with a sheer edge. He glanced at the sky. Was there time for one of the hunters to reconnoiter that ground and establish an ambush at the base of the cliff? Could the remaining two hunters drive all those beasts straight enough and far enough toward that cliff to make the plan succeed? And most important of all, what was the path of the wind?

As he circled in the grass, Good Runner could see that the beasts had not detected the hunters' approach; the shaggy club-like heads did not lift and sniff the air and search for them. They had slept and they had wallowed in their strange dirt ovals and now they were hungry and would feed.

Good Runner waited for his two companions and in the dirt of an abandoned wallow he drew with the tip of his spear a sketch of the terrain and then announced his plan. He pointed at the Great Light and expressed his concern with the time that was left to them, and then he ordered the scar-faced hunter to begin his scout of the mispatterned ground to the left of the area where the beasts grazed.

The hunter departed immediately, circling far out to the side to avoid detection, running in a crouch with his spears held low *to the ground, not looking back, shrinking gradually as distance and the tall yellow grass reached out and pulled him in.*

———————

The day began in a drifting grayness that would not pull back as the morning advanced but insisted on stalking them as they drove south out of Hanksville on state 95. They had not started especially early but they were in two vehicles as usual, the men leading in Red's Blazer and the women trailing in the Bronco with Karen at the wheel. "We won't find buffalo to the left of this highway," Red declared for the second or third time since leaving Hanksville. "There won't be nothing between here and the Dirty Devil River. The herd will be to the west. My bet is that we'll find the animals after we turn off onto 276 and start toward the Henry Mountains. That first ten miles on 276, that's where we'll see buffalo."

"Maybe," Von said, although he figured Red was right about east of the highway. It was painted desert country on that side, treeless and flat with a lot of sagebrush and snakeweed that had faded into each other this late in the year. Ordinarily a cloudy morning would bring the earth colors out more, the reds mostly, although never exactly the same shade in any two places. But not here. It was as if the land couldn't decide what color it wanted to be and maybe didn't care either; it had been abandoned, no doubt about that. It put up a brave front in certain areas but if you looked at it long enough you could see that it was pretty forlorn. Red was right; to the west of the road, on the mountain side, was where the buffalo would be. There was sage there too but it climbed into juniper and hogbacks and some spruce breaks instead of staying in the flats. There were escarpments back in a ways that you could see parts of, and canyons you could only guess at, and beyond that, higher up, beginning on what you might call the flank of the mountains, there were meadows. Now on the first day of November the meadows had been robbed of color too but they weren't scrubby, not sand-patched like the flats. There was a genuine carpet of grass up there, even if it was going dead, and Von supposed that animals could figure certain things as well as man could, where food was to be found, where there was cover and some safety. He almost spoke these thoughts to the two men in the front seat but at the last second he held back. All he said was, "Maybe," and settled into his seat. Talk had become sporadic anyway, decreasing proportionately as they increased the distance from their starting point, squeezed out by noises that had no real purpose such as the roar of the Desert Dogs on the blacktop and the wind at the open windows. What conversation there was had lost its spontaneity; it tended to drop its head and fix on near simple things like a tiring long-distance runner. Bike turned from the front seat and said to Von in a shout that didn't develop because of the wind and the tire roar: "I like our chances better toward the mountains, don't you?"

"Definitely. Definitely the mountains," but Bike had already turned back to watching the road and the speedometer by the time Von got his answer out, and he returned to looking out his window. The sun was completely hidden, although the air was as warm as it had been the day before. Von knew that November weather could change rapidly. He thought of November days as a rear guard of defeated soldiers trudging toward the end of the year who could turn suddenly at unexpected places and lash out in a savage attack. The earth on both sides of the road was level and unlifting and the shadowless pressing of the sky would lend it no depth at all. Occasionally a little lake of grass struggled to become a separate part of the land and at one point they passed a group of animals obviously headed toward it. Von didn't see them right away. The Blazer was traveling at high speed and he was beginning to be a little hypnotized by the blur when suddenly there was a blotch of white on the red earth just back from the highway. The Blazer was past before Von realized that what he had seen was terribly out of context, and he had to sit up in the seat and look back and locate the white blotch again to verify that it was after all, there in the spaces, a flock of sheep. "Sheep," he called out, but the wind from the open window snuffed the word and the men in the front seat didn't turn around, for they had not heard. And they hadn't seen the sheep.

For Red Taddish it was no loss. Not only had he never been a sightseer but he was now totally preoccupied. Expectant, to put it more accurately. It showed in the way he sat behind the steering wheel, not slouched against the seat in the manner of a carefree surveyor but tilted forward instead, hunched in the shoulders and yet still trying to stay loose as though he were engaged in a playful sparring match with a large dog and he needed that position for his best counterblows. And then he spoke. "A couple miles and we hit 276." His words were peppy. "Then the buffalo, guys. The old *bison bison*!" and in an exuberant motion he popped the steering wheel with a fist and a thick white index finger shot out and he sighted along it and fired expertly through the windshield. "*Ka-whoom! Ka-whoom!*"

The road dropped into the open tube of a canyon and there abruptly was highway 276 angling off at a sharp right, climbing back out of the narrow canyon by means of a drywash bridge and a hill made of flaming red dirt and dead sage that had been waiting a long time for the road to climb it. Red hit the brakes and made the right turn onto the bridge and stopped. But Karen, following in the Bronco, couldn't get braked in time and screamed past the turn in an agony of locked rubber, not getting stopped for another forty yards. It grew totally still then in the vacuous way that only a high desert canyon can, and Red stepped out of the Blazer and called to Karen in that shrill too-high voice, "How long have you been driving professionally?"

Karen gave him the finger and said something they couldn't

hear. "I'm glad I didn't hear that," Bike said, but everyone gathered eventually at the edge of the bridge and the whole business turned to giggles and some grabby kisses, except for Dorothy. "Why did we stop?" she wanted to know.

"Because we're all going down under the bridge and get laid," Karen said.

"This is our turnoff," Bike explained. "We're headed for those mountains over there. The Henrys. That's where Red figures the buffalo are."

"There aren't any buffalo," Dorothy said.

"See if you can stay a little closer to me this time," Red called to Karen as he got back into the Blazer, and as soon as Bike and Von were in he took off. But he acted nervous; he kept looking in the rearview mirror, trying to locate the Bronco and fix it in view. Karen turned onto the bridge at the bottom of the hill just as Red gained the top of it. "Hot shit!" he blurted, and shot the Blazer over the crest and down the other side into the rolling terrain that waited for them.

Bike wanted to know what the hell he thought he was doing. "Watch," Red answered. "Just settle your ass in place and watch," and he hit the foot feed. The Blazer careened out of a curve and into a straightaway and into another curve, and even when it had gained the far end of a long straight stretch between two drumlike hills the Bronco was still nowhere in sight. "It worked!" Red cried. "We've lost them!" At the top of a small hill the speedometer read sixty and below them the highway stretched empty and straight for over a mile. "Hang on!" Red cried, and he tromped it. The speedometer hit seventy almost immediately and the roar from the Desert Dogs was shattering.

"Hey!" Bike screamed over the wind. "The speed limit is fifty-five here the same as every place else."

"Fuck that!"

Ahead of them lay a long supine grade and behind them there was nothing.

Seventy-five.

"You're breaking the hell out of the law, Taddish!"

"You see them yet?" Red screamed, and his words were like tiny scraps of paper that the wind had torn apart and blown out the window.

Eighty-five.

"Man, they will . . . throw . . . the . . . book . . . at . . . you!"

Ninety.

"Anything yet?" Red screeched. "Are they back there?"

The highway lay stained and discarded behind them like a shed snakeskin. Suddenly, with the Blazer popping and straining as it slowed to make a curve, Von spotted something. Tiny, remote, fixed in the extruded distance like a flaw in cement, an object broke into view. But far. Incredibly far. "It's them! It's the Bronco!" and this time Von made the shout heard.

In the Bronco, cresting the knoll and surveying the basin ahead and the grade that led down into it, Karen cried, "There's that asshole!" just as a tiny blue-and-orange dot disappeared off the opposite end of the highway. She sat bolt upright and gripped the steering wheel. "Hang on, gals! We're about to play a game of catch-'em!" and she jammed the accelerator straight at the firewall.

Karen eventually overtook the Blazer but there was no victory in it for her. Roaring down that particular hill and up the next ridge and down into a farther basin, and another, and yet another, she finally caught sight of the Blazer again. But it was stopped, sitting on the right shoulder of the road with that disconsolate air that parked vehicles take on. Karen slowed the nearer she came to it and was just barely creeping when she pulled the Bronco off the road and edged in behind.

With its grotesquely outsized tires the Blazer seemed an alien thing, as if the tires were the vehicle and the body merely an optional accessory that had been added later. Its three occupants stood in a knot at the rear and did not wave as Karen drove up. They did not perform comical antics or surge toward the Bronco in greeting. The Rear Mount Swing Away Tire and Can Carrier, another Blazer accessory Red had installed, had been swung away and a gas can stood by itself on the ground. Karen came to a full stop and cut the motor. "Guess what?" she said to Dorothy and Sandy, and it was fiendish. Quiet, but fiendish. "Off-road Man just ran out of gas."

It was true. Red didn't confess it—he never opened his mouth or left his position against the left rear corner of his vehicle—but Bike did, rather sheepishly now that the women were out of their own vehicle and the moment had come. "There wasn't even any gas in the spare can," he finished limply.

The stillness of the open land with no car engines running was awesome. Their voices boomed when they spoke. "Nice of you to wait," Karen snapped at Red with a flip of her head, and Red stirred finally and stepped away from the Blazer. "First one who laughs gets shot," he grumbled, and Sandy said, "No, I don't think so. I think what's in order now is for you to personally ask Mrs. Kimball if she has any gasoline you can borrow."

Red didn't speak. He didn't look at anyone.

"I'm Mrs. Kimball," Karen said. "And I'm waiting."

Red looked at the ground and then at Bike and said, "You got a can of gas in the Bronco?"

Bike didn't have. The Bronco had a gas can flanking its spare wheel but it was empty. Bike started to apologize for not filling the can that morning but Sandy stopped him. "Don't apologize. At least you filled your tank," and then she turned back to Red and said, "Do you still do that gasoline dance you did in high school?"

"I remember that dance," Karen said. "I thought it was cute."

"I thought it was stupid," Sandy said. "But I could be wrong. It's been a long time. If I could see the dance performed again . . . maybe . . ."

Red looked at the empty gas can and at the Bronco and then

at Bike. "All I've got is what's in the Bronco," Bike said, anticipating him. "But you're welcome to siphon what you need. The problem is I don't have any tubing."

Von broke in to remind them that Red must have forgotten he had some quarter-inch tubing rigged up to an extra water can in the back of the Blazer. Gravity feed, spring-pinch cut-off valve, the whole palooka. "That ought to work."

"I was saving that tubing," Red protested. "I was going to use it to wash up after I dressed out my buffalo."

"Suit yourself," Bike said, and he leaned back against the Bronco and folded his arms.

It was early afternoon by the time Red finished his siphoning and restarted the Blazer. He used a whole can of Coors to rinse his mouth and wash his hands, and then he shut the Blazer down and they all gathered at the tailgate of the Bronco to eat lunch. They agreed they would continue down this road for maybe five miles, but it was risky to travel much beyond that. "Our supply of gasoline sorta sets the limits," Bike summed up, and there was no rebuttal. "It's a tossup how many miles we could go with the gas that's left. It's best not to take any chances. Not in this country. Not with only four hours of daylight left."

"Probably less," one of them said, and they all glanced at the sky. It was a poor clock; the pressing grayness still shut out the sun.

When they resumed their trip they split up as before, the men leading in the Blazer and the women following in the Bronco, except that Bike removed his binoculars from the Bronco and scanned the left side of the highway while Von, using Red's 8×30 armored Bushnells, searched the right. The land began to take on a little more rise and fall as it neared the Henry Mountains, but it remained treeless. And empty. "There's no buffalo out there," Von reported matter-of-factly, lowering the glasses. "Your prophecy was a dud, Taddish. You need new tea leaves."

Red muttered under his breath.

"Don't sweat it," Von came back. "This is only the first day. We've got plenty of time. But I think we ought to turn around now and go back, like we agreed."

Red slowed dutifully and turned the Blazer around and headed in the direction of state 95 and Hanksville. As they picked up speed the road sounds took over again, the fierce vacuuming of the wind, the thrum of the huge bloated tires. When they passed the spot where the Blazer had run out of gas and they had stood beside the vehicle, Von remembered the eerie stillness that had descended upon them. Once the protection of being inside a vehicle was removed you felt vulnerable, exposed to an open treeless country that had mysteriously quadrupled its size. The earth no longer seemed to be the ally it had always been, no more the safe haven. The sky was so vast it was threatening. Against wind or lightning or deluge you had no chance at all. You were helpless. And you sensed that the wind that was blowing had a mind of its own, that it blew not because there was nothing to stop it or because it was coming from a beginning and moving toward an end and had simply touched you somewhere in the middle of its passage, but because like light and air it was an ancient thing and belonged there. The land stretched away on all sides without familiarity and there was the feeling that if you left the highway and penetrated deep enough into the distance and the stillness and the space, you would reach the beginnings of time, that the horizon would prove to be what you had feared in childhood it was, the very edge of the world.

CHAPTER 8

The grass was waist high in the place where Good Runner waited. He dropped his head onto his knees and closed his eyes and let his thoughts run with the short scar-marked hunter who had gone to scout the broken ground beyond where the beasts fed. The man had been a hunter among the People for a long time, as long as Good Runner himself. They had been small together in the days when they had lived in the snowlands that lay beyond the smoking mountains to the north. They had played the Boy games together. They had stayed behind with the Women and helped them with their work while the Men hunted. They had waited in impatience to grow big enough to perform the hunter tests of manhood and when the time finally came they had taken the tests together, and had endured, and come home to the People. Good Runner's father, the leader of the tribe, had built the fire of welcome in the central cave and danced alone for the two of them in front of the People and had given Good Runner for his reward the white ceremonial beast robe with the head and the horns still attached. For his achievement the scarred hunter had received one of the sacred bone carvings that were highly prized among the People. They stayed friends, the two of them, and years later when the scarred hunter's Woman and her Children had been killed in their cave by a marauding cat, Good Runner had accompanied his friend on the pursuit. Bleeding from a deep claw cut in his face and chest, the hunter had finally cornered and crippled the cat and Good Runner had held the animal down upon the ground while his friend shattered its fangs with a rock and then cut into the cat's body and tore out its heart, as the ritual required. The years passed. The scarred hunter had been one of the few to side with Good Runner when the People broke into two groups over their fear of the continuing ash storms and their belief that better hunting grounds lay to the south. Good Runner's group had left shortly afterward, taking with them their personal weapons and their tools and the ritual skulls and the sacred white robe of ceremony that would belong to Good Runner forever.

Lying in the high grass now with the blood drying in painful patches on his feet and his stomach swelling with the gas of its emptiness, Good Runner tried to swallow the dryness out of his throat but he couldn't. He rose to his knees and shook his head in an effort to ease the pain of his effort, and finally it went away. He stood up and peered out across the flats and saw that the beasts were still feeding. At almost the same time he spotted the solitary figure of the scarred hunter returning from his scout. He was approaching cautiously, showing no weapon, making no sound. The beasts did not see him and suddenly he was standing before Good Runner, his blood-threaded eyes telling partially of his discovery before he dropped to his knees and reported it.

There was a ravine in the broken ground. It was deep and well hidden with a cliff above where the grass grew right up to the edge. There were boulders at the bottom of the cliff and there were rocks that could be held in the hand and used to slay an injured beast. And there was more good news. The wind. The wind was blowing from the far side of the ravine. It would blow across the beasts before it reached the hunters. They *would be able to approach directly into it when they made their attack.*

The third hunter, the tall one, was sitting on the ground rubbing his legs and listening to the report, and when the scout had finished he got to his feet and offered him his stabbing spear. It was refused. Good Runner then made an offer of his own spear, and it too was declined. This ritual concluded, the scarred hunter turned back into the grass and moved away toward the ravine to set up his ambush.

Good Runner and the remaining hunter slipped into the grass and as quietly as possible tore up the tallest plants and tied them to the ends of the two long spears they carried. Finishing this they peered out along the top of the grass and studied the beasts where they grazed. The herd remained oblivious to them, feeding into the wind as usual, their massive heads down and their tiny tails switching contentedly across their rumps. Good Runner informed the tall hunter that he should make his approach on the right flank of the herd while he himself would take the left. They must stay close to the beasts once they had leaped from cover. They must drive them hard and not allow them to veer off to either side. This was of the greatest importance; they must keep the leaders on a straight line for the edge of the cliff or the attack would surely fail.

Then they began.

They crawled for a ways and then stopped, crawled and stopped, taking deep gulps of air and holding them in an attempt to make their need to breathe a noiseless thing, taking delay in all their actions, easing their bodies through the grass slowly, never looking ahead, never rising up until the smell of the beasts was heavy in their nostrils and the sound of their feeding the only sound upon the wind and then . . . Aaaaahhh! . . . they leaped from the grass with their arms thrust skyward shaking the spears and making the strands of grass a sudden rustling terror to push at the frantic, head-jerking, wild-eyed beasts. Aaaaahhh! . . . and the screams ripped from the hunt-

ers' swollen throats with a terrible agony. Their stomachs pumped strange fluttery liquids and their legs trembled and their eyes burned with fear. But they leaped straight at the huge beasts, who swung instantly into flight, bellowing and blowing, their massive heads skimming the ground and their humps rolling and their tiny tails waving like the toy wands the Children sometimes made out of seed husks and reeds.

The beasts did not veer from their course. Peering over the low black mass of pounding bodies Good Runner saw that they would reach the unseen cliff before their panic deserted them, that there was only a short stretch of grass remaining before the leader and one or two of his nearest companions would plunge, still running, still blinded by that senseless terror, into the waiting pit of rocks and death.

But it was not to be.

Out of that last few yards of grass whose density and color seemed as something fallen from the Great Light itself, two forms leaped up, terrified by the trembling of an earth they had briefly hidden in.

It was a pair of the small swift animals.

They bounded from the grass and into the haven of air at the last possible moment, their tails bushy as winter pods and their faces as tiny and as daintily hewn as those of their young. The long furred arc of their leap was an explosion of crimson against the yellow grass.

The front beast veered instantly to avoid colliding with the leaping pair, his head jerking back and his jaws blaring in a new terror at the eruption in front of him. And he was so close to the ravine that slabs of sheared sod and stubble broken loose by his braking hooves clattered down into the chasm and onto the naked back of the hunter waiting there.

But no beasts fell. They had wheeled to safety and were trotting away now across the flats, their panic broken, their heads up searching for the Man threat that was even then being forgotten, stopping to paw arrogantly at the ground and to

163

*break fetid blasts of wind from beneath the foolish mast of
their tails.*

*Good Runner collapsed into the grass and rolled onto his
back. Pain squeezed his chest and he gulped desperately for air
amid the clouds of chaff and dust that settled to earth about
him.*

———————

They came out to the Blazer in the morning, the three men,
and before they reached the vehicle they began sniffing at the
sky. "You smell it?" one of them said.

It was snow. It wasn't visible but it was in the air, a wet raw
heavy essence that begged to be detected. The men didn't get in
the Blazer right away. The smell was so overriding that they
were sure some snow had already fallen and they simply hadn't
seen it. Perhaps it was on the roofs of the vehicles, or on the
hookup stanchions in the deserted parking grounds, or maybe
in the tops of the dwarf maples that made a windbreak near the
clubroom.

But there was no snow. It hadn't fallen yet. It was somewhere just beyond, beyond this street and the next, beyond the
farthest limit of the town, waiting out there somewhere for a
kind of trigger, waiting for more warmth or more cold perhaps,
perhaps for time. "You smell it?"

It was in the clouds certainly. They were thick and sullen
and they had slipped in during the night to cut off the tops of
things that were tall and towering like the peaks of the Henry
Mountains off to the southwest. "I can smell it, by God. It's
snow."

"I'm not surprised. It's overdue."

"I wouldn't mind a little snow. It would help us track."

When the wives were ready the party drove downtown in two

vehicles and ate breakfast at the Shell Casing on Main Street: omelets, hash browns, bacon, juice, a plate of silver dollar cakes in lieu of toast, and Red ordered a side of biscuits and gravy. The waitress was young and chunky and believed that insolence was a form of maturity. "You folks was in here yesterday morning," she said, addressing no one. "You must like the food."

"You bet," Red grunted, and they didn't speak to her again until they had finished eating and she brought the check, and then Red asked her in what he thought was his chummiest voice, "You talked to any guys who've bagged their buffalo?"

"Buffalo?"

"You talked to anybody who's seen the herd?"

"A herd of buffalo? No."

Red took his wallet out of his pocket and laid it on the table. "Are you from Hanksville?" he asked the girl.

She was.

"Have you worked here long? Here in the cafe?"

She had. "Two years. Since high school."

"I'll bet you've waited on a lot of buffalo hunters in that time."

"I'll bet I have."

"I'll bet they've talked a lot about where they found their buffalo."

"I'll bet they did." But for the first time she actually looked at the person who was talking.

Red picked up his wallet and opened it slyly as if there was a surprise inside and took out a five-dollar bill and laid it in a visible space next to his coffee cup. "This could be bonus time if you felt like helping a bunch of guys out," he said to the waitress.

The waitress looked at the bill. "Man, I like fives," she said. Her voice was throaty. "Fives are good feedstock. But I don't know where no buffalo are. I know guys hit this town every fall and come in here to eat when the bars close, but I don't pay much attention to what they're hunting for. Besides the obvious, that is."

Red picked up the bill and rubbed it seductively between his fingers. "A real nice tip, look at it that way."

The waitress looked suddenly put upon. "What's with you, man? You want me to give you the name of some phony place so I can earn the five? Is that what you want? Man, if that's what turns you on I can do it," and she made a grab for the money.

Sitting next to Red on the inside, Dorothy snatched the bill out of his hand and said to the waitress, but not angrily, considering the swiftness of her move, "Never mind, honey. Mr. Sportsman here got a little anxious, that's all."

"And a little confused," Sandy said. "There's only one fee for this hunt and we've already paid it."

Outside on the street the six of them stood at the hood of the Blazer and began to discuss possible routes into the hunt area. Two were mentioned, a backtrack on highway 95 to 276, or a new approach on an unimproved surface that led straight south out of town toward Bull Mountain, the first peak in the Henrys. But Red wouldn't listen to either plan. He wanted 95 all the way south to the Colorado River, with no turnoff on 276, and as if it were already decided he got into the Blazer and revved it up with such insistence that people began to stare out the restaurant window. Getting into the Bronco parked behind, Karen remarked that she thought Red was right: "I think the herd's more apt to be by a river than by mountains. I know I've heard Bike say that stocked animals will often return to where they were first let out."

"Wrong river," Sandy said. "They weren't let out on the Colorado. It was the Dirty Devil. And besides, that was thirty-five years ago. The original buffalo are gone by now."

"They're all gone," Dorothy said quietly. "There aren't any buffalo."

"Funny, funny," Karen said, and pulled out into the street behind the Blazer.

There was a full tank of gas in each vehicle, plus a full can on the rear rack of the Blazer. Red was quite smug about that particular precaution, but it was the only emotion he showed. He sat stiffly behind the wheel and stared straight ahead as the highway wound itself up on the empty spool of the tires. The windows were closed against the grayness that looked like it was freezing cold, but wasn't. Bike sat in the front and Von in the back again, looking out. It was all a repeat, tableland left, tableland right leading to the cloud-flattened mountains where even now it might be snowing. Bike was glassing the area on both sides of the highway and after a while he put the binoculars down and removed the strap from around his neck, which meant that he wanted to talk. "That's a lot of boondocks out there," he said, nodding toward the south. "If our quarry has found itself a little oasis on some back corner somewhere, with grass and water and some wallow dirt, they're going to be hard to get to. This hunt area 600 is the biggest one in the state. Biggest one in the country probably. You could fit two Rhode Islands in it and still have room for a committee meeting."

Red belched some of his breakfast. "So?"

"But it's got the fewest roads. We could have trouble getting to our game even if we spot them. I almost hope they're not out here in this section at all. I don't think they are. My gut tells me they're below the Henrys, up above Bullfrog."

"Fuck that," Red said. "They're in this southeast corner, down by the bridge."

"Suit yourself," Bike shrugged, but he wasn't quite ready to submit and he turned to the backseat and asked Von where he thought the buffalo were.

It surprised Von; he'd been watching out the window and only half listening. "I'm not sure," he said, recovering, clearing his throat. "I don't do forecasts. I've been wrong too many times. I know I've seen a few Herefords moving through the brush. Can't see a rib on them, which means the land supports cattle. Which means that it can support buffalo too. God knows why they'd choose it. If I were a buffalo standing out here year after year with the wind in my ears I'd sooner or later spot one of those high meadows in the Henrys and figure out a way to get up there. That's most likely where they are. But I'm not going to swear to it. All I'll sign my name to is that the buffalo is a herd animal and they'll be together when we find them."

"Maybe," Bike said, and it was as subdued as he could make it; it was obvious he didn't want to sound like he was advancing an argument. "Karen and Sandy went to the library right after our permits came and took out a book on buffalo. Maybe she told you," he added, glancing at each of them. "Anyway, this book said that a buffalo cow will leave the herd in the spring and go off by herself to drop her calf. And she stays with that calf for at least six months. They're real loyal mothers I guess. What I'm getting at is that there's got to be a period when the herd is split up. Maybe it's now."

"I don't give a shit what a book says," Red snapped. "Von's right. They'll be together. From a distance they're going to look like cattle or a bunch of juniper, but they'll be together."

The talk fell off after that, the way it had the day before, and in the back with his legs stretched out in the seat, Von concentrated on the world outside his window. He noticed that the same sky that had threatened snow all morning had eased up and let in a little more light. It was like a curtain parting just enough to show that the *real* day, the day intended all along, was the one that was out there now.

After a few miles they burrowed into the shallow canyon that yesterday had tried to hide the intersection but today could not, and as they roared past the little bridge it looked abandoned and faintly wistful. But where Von expected the canyon to lift again, it did not, it deepened; it took on walls and a rim at the top. Color too, a red-brown varnish as though it had been an artery once and blood had pounded through it. Gone now, of course, except for the stain. There were juniper and pinyon pine lining the rim and from the canyon floor the trees resembled a line of mounted Indians standing motionless, watching the vehicles pass below. At certain places on the rim they seemed to turn away from the edge and disappear, as though they were going to creep down to the canyon floor and make an ambush in the willow thickets along the highway.

Later, the road lifted and the canyon walls folded back, like the lips of a deep wound that hadn't healed and was never going to. The flatness reclaimed everything, the emptiness, the waste. It was waste breeding waste, wallowing in it, abandoned to it. It was as though that same insane earth artist of Capitol Reef had prepared a pot of thick red paint and stirred it and thinned it and strained it and boiled it unmercifully until it became merely a pink watery slurry. Then, not knowing what to do with it and unable to restore the original color, he had poured it out upon the earth. While it was solidifying he had squeezed it into weird knobs and columns and spires like a degenerate schoolboy playing in a purloined sandbox. When he had finished and the land was fully hardened he called it southeastern Utah. Stark and tortured and shattered and desolate, and utterly magnificent.

But it held no buffalo. The empty miles swept past the prow of the Blazer like an ocean might have, and suddenly they came upon the bridge over the Dirty Devil River where it joined the Colorado. The river had backed up there, making gooseneck canyons into which that same perverted schoolboy had emptied ink bottles, royal blue in some and in others kelly green. The bridge itself was a spun silver magic, a tall thin stiltlike span that men had built to connect the leftside emptiness to the right, believing with the simple purity of engineering that the two halves were meant to be a whole. To cross that span was to pass beyond the boundaries of hunt area 600, so they stopped and ate a wordless lunch atop the winded heights, and then turned back toward Hanksville.

They saw no buffalo on the return either. Red Taddish slapped the steering wheel repeatedly and Bike Kimball muttered about the possible mismanagement of the Big Game Habitat Development Fund, and Von Wallace sat in the back-seat of the Blazer and stared out at the emptiness and listened to the scream of the red-gray wind.

CHAPTER 9

He lay on his back in the grass until the air came into his chest without pain, and then he closed his eyes. There was no sound anywhere except the noise the wind made blowing across the grass. It was like the hum of an insect cloud when it hovered over fresh meat. Good Runner thought of fresh meat and the way the blood ran wetly from it when it was warm, how the blood lay upon it like a dew when the meat was cool. He remembered how the tongue of every beast he had ever slain tasted good in his mouth regardless of whether it was eaten raw or roasted. He thought of how the organs in beasts' bodies were nearly always in the same place so that when you opened a body with the knife you knew where to cut and what to push aside, and that the organ you finally took out would be firm and somewhat rubbery like a young Woman's gourds, and sweet to the tongue, and still warm when you stuck the ball of it on the point of your knife. He remembered how the blood would spurt a little when he sawed the little pieces off. His stomach cramped with the remembrance and he had to draw his knees up against his body and think of something else before the pain would go away.

When he opened his eyes again the scar-faced hunter was slumped beside him in the grass with his face hidden between his knees. He sat that way until his chest stopped heaving and then he lifted his head and looked at Good Runner and at the tall hunter, who had also stirred and was squatted on his haunches shaking his head and rubbing his throat. They should make another attack, the short hunter suggested, while the Great Light was able to give them help. The wind was still right, it had not changed direction. The beasts had not fled too far, in fact they had gathered in a bunch and were feeding again. The three of them together, he argued, could make a new approach and attempt to down at least one of the beasts. They had to try. Otherwise . . .

Good Runner got to his feet and gave his consent, and the three of them readied their weapons and prepared for a second attack. The scarred hunter trotted off to his ambush in the ravine and Good Runner and the tall hunter started once again through the grass, locked in the old pantomime of caution, edging stealthily toward the tiny herd in the last tawny slantings of light, scarcely breathing, creeping steadily forward, seeming to be themselves the very substance of grass. . . .

Then the sudden leap upward, the shouts, the thrusting grass-bound spears catching light like strange wands. But their shouts were bleating and feeble and although the beasts reared up in a frantic renewal of their fear and fled headlong into the grass, the pursuers quickly fell behind. Their bodies failed them. Like ragged scarecrows set upon an alien field, they could not consummate the chase. They stood waist deep in the grass and watched helplessly as the beasts first slowed their flight and then stopped, milling about and staring back at the hunters with a glowering contempt.

The Great Light dropped quickly below the edge of the earth and the moon rose from the opposite side and crept over the land, looking like the mysterious single-eyed obsidian fetish that his father's shaman had sometimes carried. The stars emerged from their faraway caves and floated overhead like tiny silver leaves on a pond of black water.

Good Runner watched the stars for a long time and then got to his feet. He walked back to where the beasts had first fed upon the grass and with his foot he kicked at several piles of droppings he managed to locate in the darkness. Miraculously, he was able to separate out from one of the piles a few seeds and berries. He pushed them into his mouth but his throat was swollen shut and he could not swallow. He removed the hide pouch from around his waist and dumped out the tools. Holding the pouch in front of him he drained his body water into it, and then drank. He put the berries and the seeds into his mouth and swallowed a few times, and drank again, and at last they went down.

Hunt area 600 lay upon the land in the shape of a horse collar. The Henry Mountains ran in a rough north-south line down its middle with the peaks rising over eleven thousand feet toward the northern end of the range but scaling down considerably as they neared the impounded waters of the Colorado River in the south. The river had wandered for centuries across that corner of Utah, not doing much of anything except living on past glories and a colorful history, and then down by the Arizona state line near a sleepy little place called Glen Canyon the government had thrown a huge cement dam across the river and backed it up. The river water had been a cinnamon paste most of its life but the dam forced it to stand around in the canyon mouths and it rewarded everyone by settling out and turning blue. And green. And blue-green. And emerald and beryl and aquamarine. They gave the resulting body of water the name Lake Powell after the one-armed explorer who had ridden the river in its angry days a hundred years before, and some entrepreneurs came up from Phoenix and built some

173

ramps out into the lake and constructed a few marinas—a name they had borrowed from southern California—and called the big one on the north shore Bullfrog. That's where the Granger group established their new base at noon on Monday, the third day. "Circling the wagons" is how Bike Kimball referred to it, remembering the Mormon pioneers, but Red Taddish called it "getting our ass where the buffalo are." At least that had been his definition the night before in Hanksville when he had pretty much demanded a move to a new location. Von had questioned the move and Bike had turned the logic inward and wrapped enough enthusiasm around it during the course of the evening to make it seem like an alternative proposal rather than the grim demand it started out as. "It'll give us a whole new attitude," Bike had expounded, "as if we were just starting out. It'll make us sharper. It'll make us better hunters. After all, this is one hellacious big area we're hunting in."

So they left Hanksville in the morning and now they were at Bullfrog, fifty miles south. They made their hookups in the camping park section of the marina and had a ham-sandwich-and-beer lunch that was mostly talkless except for Bike, who was still selling the relocation as if it had been wholly his idea. "Down, Bishop, down," Karen finally admonished him.

They decided when they finished lunch that there was time enough left in the day to backtrack on 276 to where the Notom road branched off to the northwest, a distance of approximately five miles. They might be able to find a decent road that branched off from that one and paralleled Bullfrog Creek, which came straight south out of the Henrys. There might be buffalo in there. Von suggested they take his Jimmy this time, maybe it would change their luck.

"Bullshit," Red muttered. "We're going off road and I want the Blazer." Von wanted to know what the difference was: "We take the Blazer whether we go off road or not."

Red didn't answer. When the women were ready he told them he didn't care what vehicle they followed in, as long as it wasn't his. "Why can't we all go together?" Dorothy asked, and it was so unexpected and plaintive that they all stared at her. "We go out dancing and drinking with six people in one vehicle," she went on, "why can't we do it hunting?"

"You'll have to ask your old man," Bike said to her.

"Why is that?" Sandy asked in the awkwardness that settled in." Is it Red who decides on vehicles and groups now? Who gave him that responsibility? Do you do all the planning for us now, Red?" and her voice sought him out where he stood sullenly beside the Blazer.

"There's three couples and three vehicles," Dorothy kept on. "What's wrong with each couple going in their own vehicle for a change?"

"We seem to have better luck," Bike put in, "if we follow our normal plan. One vehicle for the guys and one—"

"That's the way we left home, isn't it?" Dorothy persisted. "Each couple together? If it's good enough driving out from Granger why isn't it good enough at Bullfrog?"

"The language can get pretty rough sometimes," Bike argued.

"Worse than *fuck*?" Dorothy said. The word hung there in front of them like a splatter of mud on a clean windshield. "I've only heard that word forty million times." Her voice was beginning to get ragged. "Why do we always have to separate? Why do the women have to tag along behind the men like we don't belong to the same club or something? Like we can't be trusted?"

"Oh, for Christ's sake, Dorothy," Karen snapped. "Can it!"

Red was standing with his hand on one of the Blazer's grab irons and he let go and walked out to Dorothy and bent down to her. "That's right," he blurted, "can this shit! We got game to track. You women get together and decide whether you're going to follow in the Bronco or the Jimmy, but get with it. The day's wasting," and he wheeled around and marched back to the Blazer. "Whoever's with me, get in!" he barked. "Otherwise it's the pussy wagon."

"There are worse fates," Bike laughed, and he made a dancy little show out of joining the women, but then he stopped and scooted back to the Blazer and climbed in with Von and Red.

Dorothy got into the back of the Bronco, sprawling out in a way that would ensure her getting the seat alone. Before leaving Hanksville that morning she had refilled eight miniatures with a mixture of vodka and orange juice and stuffed half of them into her purse and the other half in the right-side pocket of her jacket, and she groped for one now and found it. She checked the rearview mirror to make sure she couldn't see Karen's eyes and then she unscrewed the cap and cupped the miniature in both hands in such a way that when she brought it to her mouth it looked as though she were blowing on her thumbs, or pretending to whistle through them in the way you could teach a child to whistle. She emptied the bottle in three separate tips and then recapped it between her knees while she was still leaning forward, pretending to study something through the windshield, and then she dropped the bottle into her empty left-side pocket and leaned back in the seat.

The country climbed perceptibly going north out of Bullfrog. Now at midday it was a dull pink color, still treeless and with some scarp faces and perhaps a few canyons back off in the distance, but they were petty and shadowless and would not hold the eye. The sky looked like something that had been hung on a rack and bled. There was the threat of snow in it still, or maybe it was rain. Whatever it was it just hovered there above them, making no move.

Watching the Blazer ahead of them on the highway Dorothy saw the brake lights go on and then it turned left onto a gravel road. Karen slowed the Bronco and followed. Against the colorless gravel the Blazer resembled a saucy blue-and-orange lunch box dropped on the road by some departed picnickers. Maybe it was rock hounds. Geologists? Who would come out here? Only crazy people, Dorothy concluded, and slipped another bottle out of her purse, pretending to be rummaging for a cigarette. It was noisier now on the gravel, and rougher. Karen was talking about the string of first day kills her father and her brothers had established over the years, certainly a record. Sandy was watching the road and listening to Karen and it was easier this time for Dorothy to tilt the bottle back and drain it. She slipped the empty into her left pocket and then leaned back against the seat with a kind of sigh as though she had given up waiting to break into Karen's long monologue and was going to concentrate instead on studying what lay beyond the window on her side.

Some ten miles north of the road the Henry Mountains rose up out of the plateau like a castle. A deserted castle, Dorothy thought, and forbidding too if you looked at it long enough. There was no movement about the distant towers, no banners fluttered there. The road leading into it was choked with tumbleweed and there was no moat. There was no entrance to the castle for them, she suspected, no friendly drawbridge to crank itself down and welcome them in. They had fouled the kingdom with their bullets and their rifles; they had dishonored the king. There would be no flourish of trumpets for them, no tables in the cavernous halls laden with feast of food and drink, no silver goblets glowing in the flare of wild rumbling fires.

A mesa loomed suddenly before them in the road, an alkali-stained gray-yellow wart that looked as if it had been picked at enough times to make it stop growing, but not enough to make it disappear. And still big enough to force the road to split around it. The Blazer stopped and Red got out and walked back to the Bronco. He kept his eyes on the ground and wouldn't look up. His orange cap was pulled down and his orange jacket was buttoned tight and he resembled a brightly costumed carnival giant stomping back and forth between tents, upset somehow about the choice of grounds. When he reached Karen's window he spoke only to her. "According to Bike this is Thompson Mesa. The road splits around it for a couple miles and then joins up again. You take the right fork and we'll take the left and we'll meet you at the other end."

"What if we get lost?"

177

"You won't get lost. Just pay attention to where you're going." He continued to look only at Karen. "You seen anything?"

"No."

"You been looking?"

"There's nothing to look for," Dorothy said from the backseat.

Red turned and walked back to the Blazer and gunned off down the left fork. The fork Karen took hugged the base of the mesa for most of its length and then flared out when the mesa began to break up into a field of splatter cones. Everything in the area was a leached-out gray color, even the splotches of sagebrush. It was all badlands, all scoured and tortured and bleak. Karen was appalled. "How could buffalo ever find enough to eat in a godforsaken place like this?" She swore disgustedly. "They couldn't even breed in this crap. I know I couldn't."

Sandy laughed in a kind of relief and Dorothy said, "Yes you could, Karen. You could breed in anything."

Karen's shoulders bunched up under her jacket and she was getting something ready, you could see it, but the Blazer reappeared suddenly on their left and the two branches of road got ready to merge back into one. Karen fell in behind the Blazer and seemed relieved by its presence. Not Dorothy. "Isn't this fun," she muttered, "looking up the ass end of a Blazer?"

Farther on they came to a crossroads where a small weathered sign stood, the sign colored exactly the same as the soil. On the sign was printed SHILAMARING SEEP with a crude arrow pointing to an unreadable number that was probably the miles. Someone had made a t out of the l in SHILAMARING. SHIT-AMARING. "My sentiments exactly," Karen grunted.

"At least some other humans have been out here," Sandy said.

"Humans maybe, but no buffalo. You've noticed that, haven't you? They're too damned smart."

178

"There aren't any buffalo," Dorothy said, sitting forward and dropping another empty into her pocket.

"Why don't you stow that crap?" Karen snapped, but Sandy jumped in with a statement that went back to the road sign. "It proves what I've always believed, that people are basically funny. Humor is innate in people. They see a sign out in the middle of nowhere and right away they've got to change it to make it funny."

"It's because they didn't have a rifle with them," Dorothy said. "They'd rather shoot a hole through a sign than write on it. I've seen more bullet holes than funny words. People would much rather destroy. *That's* what's innate in them."

They quit talking then. It was argue or be silent, and they were silent. The road turned and it wasn't gravel anymore but packed clay that was crumbling in places where the dry streambeds snaked out of the draws. Another Slops made the stealthy circuit from Dorothy's full pocket through the cup of her hands and into the empties pocket on the other side, after which she lit a cigarette and leaned back in the seat and closed her eyes. According to the book she'd gotten from the library, buffalo weren't too bright but they'd have to be downright foolish to try to exist in a wasteland like this, even though the state must have assumed they could survive when they released them here. Were the state's big game people cruel or were they just unfeeling? She felt that man didn't truly understand the animal anyway. He could *see* the animal, he could define him and illustrate him perfectly, like in the book, but he didn't *know* him, couldn't grasp the spirit and the essence of what an animal really was. God knew. God had made the animal to be exactly what he was, a brother to man but a lesser one, and man was to learn the difference and allow for it with an emotion called pity. But he forgot. In gaining knowledge and then taking on arrogance for what he had learned, he lost the pity. Oh, a few retained it, Dorothy supposed. More women than men certainly. And all the children had it.

Dorothy rolled the window down and flipped her cigarette butt out. She saw that the road was climbing an approaching mesa rather than skirting it like before. The snakeweed and sage gave way gradually to an area of bunch grass interspersed with clumps of alder thicket, and it was while she was staring at that incongruous hilltop oasis that she saw the buffalo.

It was a cow, alone, with her calf beside her. She was standing motionless at the back corner of one of the alder thickets, chewing her cud and staring out across the steppes in a kind of heavy-lidded idleness, not seeing anything in particular and not needing to see, not fearing anything. Her calf stood slightly out in front of her, its reddish-brown body all in miniature, its upper lip still too short and its face just beginning to show the peculiar puckering of the buffalo, the eyes perfectly round and impish, depthless in their innocence. Behind, comforting and rocklike, stood its mother, the head a great inverted pyramid, chin-whiskered and gartered and shaggy beyond comprehension. A graceless misbalanced nearly deformed beast, like all her kind. Her hindquarters were so narrow and delicate that that part of her seemed a different animal altogether, one who was merely masquerading as a buffalo. Her tail was much too tiny for her body. A ridiculous tail really, tufted and far too feminine for the rest of her. An outrageous afterthought. How truly ugly the buffalo cow was, Dorothy thought, and yet how determined, separating from the herd to birth and nurse her calf, not wanting the bulls around, not accepting their strutting and their sniffing about, not needing the wanton arrogance of their ways. That small helpless round-eyed baby was all she needed, and the calf needed only her. Dorothy saw the two of them as the very symbol of life, the mother and her child together in kinship; valiant, elusive, hiding from those who wanted only to use and to destroy them.

In the very moment of the cow and calf passing from her sight Dorothy realized that neither the men in the Blazer nor Karen and Sandy had seen the animals. She sat forward in the seat and lit a cigarette and began to question whether *she* had seen them. She turned and looked back and searched for the two animals but they were gone. The mesa top was deserted. She turned back toward the front seat and Sandy's head came up a little from watching the road and she said to Dorothy, "What were you doing?"

"Looking out. At the country."

"You were so quiet I thought you were asleep." And Karen said, just at the point of hearing, but not to Dorothy, "I would have guessed drunk."

Dorothy's response to the remark was to remove the last two minis from her jacket and drink them openly.

The road edged southward as they bounced along it, but deceitfully, as if it were attempting to hide its real intent. After a mile or so it gave up the pretense and turned straight south, and almost immediately the land began to tilt downward before them, sloping away toward the great rift in the earth that marked Lake Powell. Dorothy suspected they had spent more of the daylight hours in the search than planned because with every mile they traveled the sky darkened. The land took on depth as though the sunset were a magnet that pulled all the forms of the earth upward when the daylight died, that drew shadows out of hidden places and stretched and angled them and gave them back a touch of the nobility they had had at dawn. Before Dorothy's eyes the high desert became a magically altered place, a child's fantasy realm of fairy things. It became a rock wonderland full of elves and goblins and long-necked clowns on stilts, and squat bulbous toads poised to leap. Yet even as Dorothy stared out upon the land it changed again. A silence descended upon it. It grew brooding and mysterious. Something had crept across the earth and was hiding in it, otherwise why were all the shadows gathering protectively under the scarp faces, guarding the canyon mouths and peering out suspiciously from behind the shattered colonnades?

When they parked at the marina, Bike walked back to the

Bronco. "Did you guys see anything?" he asked, and Karen answered, "Nothing," and Sandy said, "We didn't see a thing."

"How about you, Dot?" Bike asked, bending, looking in. "You spot any buffalo for us?"

"You'll never see any buffalo. They're gone. They got tired of man tracking them down and destroying them and they went away. You'll never see them again."

CHAPTER 10

Good Runner slept badly with his stomach cramping and his throat burning and his mouth dry as the fluff of weed pods. The Great Light rose with an early heat and when he finally pushed himself up from the ground his legs shook and the flesh of them had no feeling like the flesh of his hands when he had held them too long in icy water. He drank his body water again and tried to chew the roots of a plant that grew at the base of a boulder, but he could not. While the Great Light climbed the wall of the sky he stood with his two companions and shaded his eyes and peered out across the grass.

At the farthest end of what his eyes could reach, Good Runner saw them, looking like a tiny brown island in a lake of yellow water. They were perhaps the same beasts of the day before, feeding now in that dumb forgiveness that characterized the bigger beasts, forgetful of old dangers and fearing only those that could be seen. Good Runner could not determine in which direction the beasts were feeding and he stripped a handful of chaff from the grass and tossed it into the air. The particles drifted lazily away to his left and he knew that the beasts would be facing the opposite direction. The three hunters picked up their pouches and spears from the matted grass and trotted off to the left.

The run did not last long. Their legs would not sustain them and after only a short distance they settled into a walk. Good Runner took a position slightly ahead of the other two and attempted to set a pace, tossing up a handful of seed periodically and adjusting the long arc of their approach according to the way the material sifted down. The air grew hot and his chest began to hurt. His legs still felt partially dead and the blood was beginning to ooze again from the sores that the days of stones and stubble had made on his feet. He kept his eyes fixed on the brown clumping of the beasts in the grass and again he regretted that he had not brought with him from the caves his pouch of sacred objects. He had accumulated the objects from his youth; the shaman had blessed them repeatedly and they would have surely lured the beasts to his spears. If yesterday he could have burned sweet grasses in the carved horn and passed his spears through the beads and sung the chants, then his spear points would glisten now with blood instead of just the light. Without the magic pouch he could call down no promise of help from the Above People. He knew, watching the humped beasts grow slowly larger, that without a kill they could never make it back to the caves. They would fall and not get up. The wind and the Great Light would dry them where they lay in the grass. The Women and the Children would watch for them from the ledges above the caves, but they would not come. The Women would give up waiting and gather the Children and the Old and retreat to the back of the caves. And they would never emerge. The Great Light would never fall upon them again, nor the wind reach out and touch their faces.

The beasts were near, feeding with their heads in the grass and only their giant humps showing, revealing no alarm, smelling only the hot wind, hearing only the brittle juiceless grasses cracking in their own jaws. There was no ravine this time for the hunters. There would be no help from the earth. Good Runner knew they would have to creep directly up to the massive creatures. There could be no retreat. Face to face, they

184

*would have to stand at last under the great shaggy loom of the
beasts and make their attack.*

After breakfast the men gassed up the Blazer and drove north
on state 276 for approximately ten miles and then turned off on
the Maki Tanks road and drove northeast another ten or twelve
miles onto Ticaboo Mesa.

Ticaboo was an immense upland terrace that time had failed
to damage much, although you could see at the edges that it
had tried. Erosion and slides had cut at it. A dirt road climbed
boldly up its west face but turned quite timid by the time it
reached the eastern rim and wound back down. There were no
buffalo there. Red shut down the Blazer and they got out and
walked up to the edge of the mesa and worked the binoculars
across the dead stone gardens that lay below, but there was
nothing. Eventually they gave that up and just stood there
under the gray implacable sky, looking like three contest shoot-
ers who had dressed up in their orange-and-brown suits and
come to this out-of-the-way park looking to enter a champion-
ship shoot. It was the wrong park, of course, and it was
empty.

Red gunned the Blazer pretty good going back to the highway. They bounced viciously crossing the rocky bed of Smith
Creek, a dried-up waterway that had the temerity to show a
sign. "I'll tell you one thing," Von said, and his voice sounded
warped and stale as if it had been sitting out in the sun in a
closed box for several days. "If I had a name like Smith I'd
change it the first chance I got. It's too common."

"Common my ass," Red muttered. "The founder of our
church was named Smith."

"Joseph Smith," Bike exclaimed in his most unctuous pedan-

185

tic tone. "And the name didn't seem to bother God any. He came down and talked to Joseph several times."

"Probably asked him to change it," Von said.

"Remember," Bike admonished them, "that Joseph Smith was the first Latter-day Saint. The first Prophet of the People. Our first Seer and Revelator. He deserves our respect. After all, God made a direct revelation to Joseph. He became God's instrument here on earth."

"He was an instrument all right," Von drawled. "Anybody who claims he had lunch with John the Baptist on the banks of the Ohio River in 1824 is an instrument. You can bet on it."

"I'll tell you what we don't need right now," Red grumbled, "is a lot of silly talk about Joseph Smith."

"You started it," Von came back. "I'd have let it go but I figured you and Joseph were real close."

"Kiss my ass," Red blurted. "If you two bastards would spend more time looking for the herd we might get somewhere. You act like you flat don't give a damn."

Von said tightly, "We give a damn, Taddish. We just don't let our milk turn sour as quick as you do."

"What's that supposed to mean?" Red flared, searching for Von in the rearview. "You pushing to be a smartass or something?"

"Be nice," Bike broke in. "Let's cool this thing. He was turned sideways in the front seat, studying both of them like a solicitous counselor. "Let's be looking for some buffalo to shoot."

"Dorothy says there aren't any buffalo," Von said. "She claims they're gone."

"Dorothy's been sucking too long on vodka bottles," Red muttered.

They boiled dust all the way back to 276 where the women were waiting for them. Once on the blacktop, Red turned north again. There was a succession of gravel roads branching off from the highway, roads that started out decently enough with good culvert drainage and generous shoulders and a solid bed, but after about two or three miles something invariably happened to the roads. They narrowed quickly and the shoulders began to squeeze in as though they were afraid of the emptiness on both sides, and the gravel graded to dirt and the washouts deepened. After that, the road shallowed into tracks and just quit altogether. There was always a certain disgust associated with it; it was like they'd been deliberately duped, and at one dead end Red let it blow. "I shit turds longer than these god-damned roads!" he exploded.

"I told you this country down here wasn't famous for its roads."

"They don't go nowhere! Is that the best your goddamned Highway Planning Department can do?"

"We do a good job. But roads like these are mostly ranch access, or they're left over from when this highway was built. They receive very little state upkeep. In fact, you'll see signs reading END STATE MAINTENANCE. If you'll look for those signs you can generally tell when your road is going—"

"Jesus Christ, I'm looking for buffalo and you're reading road signs."

Bike took a deep breath and let it out slowly. "If you want to know the truth, mister, I've spent most of my time looking back to make sure the girls didn't get left behind."

"My ass," Red spat. "If the girls want to come along they gotta keep up." It was obvious he wanted a confrontation of some kind but the particular road they were on gave out at that moment and Red swore and whipped the Blazer around in a snarl of dust. When he got completely turned, there sat the Bronco directly in front of him. Karen and Sandy popped out of the doors so exactly in unison that it looked like one of Karen's old high school routines they had spent the morning rehearsing. They charged the Blazer in full stride and when Karen spoke her voice was scathing. "Are you turkeys practicing off-road trials or are you really looking for some game to shoot?"

187

Bike chose the role of spokesman, probably because it was Karen and because he wanted to blunt her a little, and he flattened his response out to a sleepy almost second-thought thing. "How you guys doing? Okay?"

"How we *doing*?" Karen shot back. "Considering we missed lunch and our rumps are boned out and our kidneys have ruptured, we're doing great." She wiped at her nose with a big hand and glared in at Red. "What the hell are we doing out here anyway? We haven't flushed up as much as a collared lizard. My old man would have shot himself out of pure shame by this time."

"Then you tell us where the buffalo are," Red answered, and it was gritty, barely contained. He was like a jar with the lid on wrong, ready to spill.

"Well, they're not *here*, are they?" and Karen practically screamed it. "A one-legged blind man from Jersey City could tell that! And it wouldn't take him three days either." She stopped and wiped at her nose again. "Three days hell, it's four! Four days of eating your dust and we've got a belly full of it!"

Sandy said, but much quieter, "What Karen's trying to tell you nimrods is that we're going back to Bullfrog." An unusual sarcasm crimped her mouth. "But don't worry, you'll be all right. I've plotted your position and have determined that you're equidistant from absolutely everywhere. You can't possibly get lost." She swept all three men with a glance. "If you ever get tired of chasing dust devils come back to Bullfrog and look us up," and with that the two of them returned to the Bronco and started it up and backed it around and drove off. Perhaps a half mile down the road they escaped the dirt and got back onto gravel again, and the curls of dust at their tail grew smaller and less angry.

That evening in the Pace Arrow, Red broke into a six-pack of Coors and brought the Colt-Sauer in from the Blazer and

188

removed the Outers kit from the foot locker and started to clean his rifle. Dorothy fixed herself a Slops and put the Merle Haggard record on real low and began to leaf through the pile of *Woman's Day* magazines she always brought along on the trips.

Red unzipped the case and lifted the rifle from its nest in the soft flannel lining, then laid the rifle across his lap and closed the case. He detached the sling from the swivel studs and began to work it real good with the Hard Leather Dressing his brother Dee had given him for Christmas the year before. It did a lot better job than that stupid saddle soap Von used. When he had finished dressing the sling he laid it out to dry on the flannel rags he kept with the kit. Next he removed the scope from the mount and rubbed down the tube and the base and the rings with gun oil. If you bought a good scope you had to take care of it, which is why he'd gone ahead and gotten the scope cover like the salesman suggested. It was good tan leather with a strap connecting the front and back caps and not like that abortion Von used that was nothing more than a strip of old inner tube stretched around the two ends of the scope where the lenses were. Von wasn't very classy when it came to equipment. That Winchester of his was a mess, worn bluing and a beat-up stock and no more shine to it than a dried-up yucca. And Von had been the last one in their crowd to go to a scope. When they'd first met in high school Von was mostly a varmint shooter, using iron sights on a .220 Swift with a barrel heavier than an elephant's balls, insisting that he'd never stoop to looking through a magnifying glass to find his target. He had to hand it to Von, by God, he was a deadeye with those iron sights. He could drop a coyote with a head shot at a hundred yards any time he got serious about it. He claimed it was because he hand loaded, because he knew ballistics and had learned how to press a perfect bullet, one with just the right amount of powder behind just the right shape of lead in a cartridge that was exactly the right one for the game he was planning to shoot. Bullshit! No guy reloading at an old wood bench in his basement under a hanging light bulb was ever going to improve on a factory load. Even that dentist from Bountiful, Hall, had said they were adequate.

Red reassembled the scope and attached it to the mount and when he sighted through it at the bathroom light he remembered the time his old man had rapped him on the head in an argument over a sight. He'd been a kid living in Richfield, eleven, maybe twelve years old, and he had this old rimfire .22 with an open sight that had a gold bead in the front and a U-notch in the leaf at the rear. If he wanted to adjust for elevation he'd slide a tapered rail under the leaf and if he wanted to change for windage he'd tamp the rear sight left or right with a punch and hammer. Nothing to it. That sight had played hell with the fox squirrel population down in the scrub oak flats along the Sevier river east of town. It must have been on his thirteenth birthday that his old man bought him the big rifle, the Winchester 94 Lever with a Redfield peep. Jesus, that was a gun! It was *the* gun of the West, actually, the famous one. Just holding it in your hands made you feel like Palladin and Sugarfoot and Wyatt Earp all at the same time. He'd done so well with the open sights on his .22 rimfire that he thought he'd change sights on the Model 94, replacing the receiver peep with his old reliable rear leaf. He made the switch one Friday night in the garage and the next day his old man took him up on West Taviputs for the October Buck Only, Seven Day. The first hour out on the first morning he missed three straight shots at a six-pointer standing broadside to him no more than a hundred yards away. His old man howled up a storm on the first two misses and on the third he spotted that old .22 leaf on the rear and yanked the rifle out of Red's hands and banged the barrel up against the side of his head so hard his ears rang for three fucking days.

Next, Red got out his Marten's Select Hardwood Treatment that he'd looked all over the city for and began to dress the stock. He'd customized the hell out of that stock. It was made of imported Fajen walnut, not your common walnut finish over white ash, and attached permanently to the butt was Pachmayr's finest recoil pad, a rich honeycombed rubber baffle one inch thick. He tipped the bottle of Marten's and let a few drops run out onto the flannel rag. It had a musky pungent odor, like good pussy, he thought. He rubbed the stock all over, first along the comb and then down onto the swell of the belly and then out to the grip and the fore end with its skip-line checkering, stroking the rich wood with a gentle motion up and down, back and forth. Finishing that, he removed the trigger plate assembly and brushed it with some solvent from the Outers and then blew it dry and reoiled it. To be sure there was no moisture accumulation he ran a rod and patch down the barrel bore and wiped all the action parts and reoiled them too. Next he jerked the bolt and exposed the chamber and cleaned it with his new chamber brush, and when he was finished he ran his finger around the lips of the chamber. The chamber was the heart of the weapon, the place that birthed the power. He loved that power, loved the smooth shiny cartridges and the dull metallic bullets that would lie there in that darkness just waiting to explode when the pin struck them. A .375 H & H Magnum with a 300-grain bullet was what power was all about. Von with his .25-06 and .243 cartridges and his 120-grain bullets and his refusal to fire anything that was Magnum—that kind of hunting was for girl scouts and old ladies. It was pussy stuff. Face it, Von himself was a pussy. So was his old lady. He laughed. A pair of pussies, that's what they were. He wondered what kind Sandy had. Probably one she thought smelled like a lilac bush in April. If you thought your shit didn't stink you probably figured the same for everything else you had. Miss Snooty, Sandy was. Miss Superior. What kind of body did she have, he wondered. Good tits for sure, big ones, tits that bulged even when she was trying to underplay them with a tight brassiere. What kind of hair in the crotch? A blond duster? Brown? Probably not interested in using it except once a month, and then only when she could hear the angels singing. Karen now, that would be something else. Karen would have a big hairy bush that showed black and cushiony under her panties. That's what she would stress, that pussy, not the hard knobby tits she had but the ride she could give you in that hair saddle. The way to fuck Karen would be to set her on top, to get a good hold on the big soft cheeks of her ass and then slide her up and down on your bolt like you would a washer, up and down, up and down until the steam built up and she blew her valve. She'd probably scald you with it. Small-titted broads could really ball you. They seemed to concentrate on it, figuring that way you wouldn't pay much attention to the boobs. Like what's-her-name on the mill floor last year at the smelter. What was her name? Janet, that was it. God almighty, you talk about a wild piece of ass—!

He heard a soft sound like something falling and he glanced at Dorothy and saw the Slops glass lying on the floor beneath her hand and her head fallen back against the sofa and her mouth open. "Jesus, woman," he said, but he didn't get up. He put the Colt-Sauer back in the case and closed the kit and put them both away. Then he went over to Dorothy. "You passing out on just one drink now?" he said, for when he bent down and picked her up to carry her to the bed he didn't see the other minis jammed down in the cushions and behind the stack of *Woman's Day* magazines.

Dorothy didn't wake up when Red dropped her onto the bed, or when he left the next morning in the Blazer. Or rather started to leave, for Bike and Von pulled up behind him in the Bronco. Bike shouted for him to let the Blazer set and climb in with them, said maybe it would change their luck, they had to do *something*, and Red got into the Bronco, in the backseat. He told Bike to go back up to the Mt. Ellsworth side of Tica-boo but where Bike took them was way past there to a road leading in toward Mt. Hillers, which was a couple of thousand feet higher than Ellsworth. Where they eventually wound up was more or less southwest of that mountain, in a place the map called Indian Spring Benches. Actually it was Von's idea to go to the benches. "We've got to go up higher and look," he kept saying, "up where the trees are. Where you've got trees you might get grass that's still fit for browse. And there's more apt to be water up there. A buff won't go to a stock tank down here on the flat like a Hereford will."

Red grunted and Bike said, "Sounds good to me," and when they reached the benches they got right at it, actually making a couple of drives. There was a good growth of Gambel oak and shadbush in the area and they purposely moved around a lot and talked in normal tones, like they would with muleys when they wanted the bucks to get curious and show themselves so they could get a good shot. But they didn't jump anything. Von got out the 20X spotting scope and took a rest across a boulder and put a good scan on the open grassy drainage up above Hillers Creek. He had been right about the vegetation, there was grass there in abundance, but there weren't any buffalo. All he saw was a pair of redtail hawks circling against some rock ledges high in the mountain.

They drove back down to the highway and turned south toward Bullfrog. By the time they reached the marina they had decided that first thing in the morning they would leave and make a new camp. They'd go north along the Waterpocket Fold and into the Tarantula Mesa country, maybe even as far as the Notom Benches if they had to, they would just wait and see what happened. Bike had lunch with Karen and then walked down to the water to look at the houseboats. Von caught Sandy waking from a nap, naked and breast-heavy and sleek with sleep, and they made love. It was a great way to wake up, she told him, and he laughed about how horny he got on these hunting trips when he knew they were alone and the kids weren't going to bust in on them. He seemed relaxed, not nervous at all about the days passing empty-handed. When they got out of bed they dressed and ate a little supper and just at dark a knock came at the door. It was Dorothy. Red had gone to the marina lounge to get some beer and some vodka, she told Von, her breath sour. "That was two hours ago. He hasn't come back. What do you say we join him?"

"I like it," Von said, and he pulled Dorothy into the El Dorado to wait while he and Sandy got into their jackets. They picked up the Kimballs and together the five of them walked down to the lounge. The approaches weren't well lighted and it was full dark, a darkness that was faintly threatening because there was water there, backwater from a river they couldn't see and didn't think would be that quiet.

The lobby of the marina lounge had that ambivalent air of an off-season place: there were lights but they hadn't all been turned on, there was a full staff of employees but you could see only one or two of them, there was full service but you had to wait a long time to get waited on. The bar sat at one end of the dining room, which was partly draped off by loops of thick solemn theater rope. There was a radio playing in a back room somewhere but they couldn't quite make it out, whether it was music or news. A foursome was seated at one of the darkened tables and a single figure sat at the bar. It was Red. He saw them at the same time they saw him. "Just coming get you guys," he called, and it was much too loud for that room, too intrusive. They ordered drinks when a bartender finally appeared and then took a table. Red joined them there, dropping heavily into the end chair. His cap was off and the white empty face was fakey with unnatural color. He took a long drink from a can of beer and then leaned on his elbow and stared at them. His elbow slipped off the edge of the table and he lurched rather badly before he caught himself. "Good see you guys," he sputtered. "Waiting for you."

"I can see that," Dorothy said.

The bartender brought the drinks and when he had collected the money and left the table the stillness closed in behind with a rush. Bike coughed and said, "Golly, this is what, Wednesday?

Would you believe we could go five days into a season and not drop a four-legger of some kind? Can you believe that?"

"Buffalo," Von said. "It's buffalo we're after, Bike. Not quarry or game or four-leggers. Why don't you go ahead and try the word?" and he spelled it out. "Go on, say *buffalo*."

Bike's response was a scowl.

"Animals have names," Von went on, "and you should learn them. If not the Latin at least the English."

Karen said, "Tell the man to be nice, Bishop. That's what you usually say, isn't it? Be nice?"

"Hey, cool it," Bike said, responding to her, trying a smile but unsure of it. "You guys are ganging up on me."

"He's right," Sandy said. "Let's drop the language lesson," and while they were watching Von for his reaction, they missed seeing the foursome across the room leave their table and slip into the chairs at the table next to them. "Anybody seen any buffalo hunters around here?" came a man's voice, and they all turned and looked for the speaker.

"Oh, for Christ's sake," Karen exclaimed, and Sandy laughed expectantly, and Von said, "I'll be damned, it's the Bountiful people!"

"Bountiful people," Red repeated woodenly.

Bike declared his surprise with something of a flourish. "The doctors Garland and Hall, I believe," he announced grandly, "with party," and Sandy immediately asked them how long they had been at Bullfrog.

"We got in late this afternoon," one of the women answered, and went on to explain that they had driven last weekend to Dr. Hall's sister in Moab and had spent the intervening days flying over the Arches and the Canyonlands and the entire length of Lake Powell in the sister's private plane. Bike couldn't wait for her to finish. "Then you haven't filled your tags yet?"

"Filled tags," Red mumbled.

"What Bike means," Von put in, "is have you shot your buffalo?"

"Not yet," the taller man answered. The taller man they remembered now as Garland, the veterinarian; the short man had to be the dentist, Dr. Hall. "We'll probably come onto the herd tomorrow," he added promptly.

"Allow us to save you both time and gasoline," Bike offered graciously. "We've searched the entire south and southeast quadrants of the hunt area. We've covered every inch of that ground, foot and glass. There's no buffalo in there."

"Then where did you take yours?" Hall asked.

"We haven't," Bike told him.

"You haven't?" and he couldn't keep the relief out of his voice. And it was too loud. The two tables were quite close to each other and no one had need to raise his voice. Now, after that final bleat of surprise, no one did. "So where does that put us?" Hall said, making conversation.

"We're in good shape," Von answered him. "There's plenty of time left. Almost two weeks."

"I'm not so sure," Garland put in. "If you haven't seen a single buffalo, not even tracks—"

"There are no buffalo," Dorothy said.

One of the wives coughed and Dr. Hall looked at Dorothy and said, "That's good," and the four of them laughed in the embarrassed mannerly way they would have laughed at a poorly told joke. "But I imagine we'll be able to scout up something in the next few days," and it was a little haughty, sort of a dismissal, the way Hall said it.

It didn't work. Karen made a slight interruption by excusing herself from the table but the taller woman, Dr. Garland's wife, came right back to Dorothy's remark. "Wouldn't that be something?" she said, searching the remaining faces. "The exposé of the century. The state sells all those buffalo permits and takes in all that money knowing full well the herd isn't even in the state."

"Maybe it moved into Colorado," Dr. Hall's wife said. "Maybe there's grass over there." She waited a moment for the complaint part to sink in, and then went on. "We left Moab this morning to drive over here to Bullfrog, and we came through some truly *desolate* country. I mean, it is *desert* out there, especially when you get near the river. It reminded me of the country in North Africa where the land begins to merge with the actual Sahara."

"Well," Bike began somewhat defensively, "the terrain in this part of Utah has always been arid—"

"We even saw *sand dunes*," Mrs. Hall said.

"Sand dunes," muttered Red, who had also left the table and had just come back. After a moment Karen returned, and having everyone present again seemed to activate Bike. "We've had our little laugh over the elusiveness of the herd," he began, coughing for attention. "But if I may get serious for a minute I'd like to remind you good folks of something. Two some-things really," and he smiled officiously. "One is that we're in the middle of a change of season, and the second is that our friend *bison bison* is still a migratory animal. His natural food supply is dwindling this time of year and he's getting a little restless. After all, he's not bright enough to understand why the grass is bad and why his hide is getting shaggy. All he knows is that it's getting a little colder every day and his body seems to be changing. So he's beginning to move around. It's pure reaction with him. No logic. No analysis. Just instinct."

Von broke in dryly. "We will now have a three-hour address by our resident wild game scientist, Dr. Balance of Nature."

"I want someone to hit me in the head if it runs that long," Bike laughed, and the Bountiful party laughed back at him. "I only wanted to remind everyone," he went on easily, "that what we're seeing here is perfectly normal for this time of year and that we shouldn't get discouraged by the fact that the herd hasn't exactly been following us around. I guess my bottom line is *don't . . . give . . . up*. After all, what we're involved in here is a *controlled hunt*. It isn't merely to give us a chance at a new head mount for the den wall, however nice that might be. The

197

plain fact is, these annual hunts have been set up to regulate the size of the Utah buffalo herd. That's been the goal every year since the first one. And we have a responsibility to join together in meeting that goal, don't we? To contribute to the program that the Department has set up."

Von said, "Hell, I thought we were tracking down some rogue bulls that have been terrorizing the local villages. Stomping on the natives and like that."

Bike smiled. "Von's going to have his little joke, but my point is still valid. It would be a tragedy if each and every one of us holding a tag didn't *fill* that tag. The Utah Division of Wildlife Resources has had a one hundred percent kill on this animal for twelve consecutive years. I don't think any of us wants to be the first to break that string." He eyed them accusingly. "I know *I* don't."

It got formal for a moment, but then Dr. Garland's wife, who all this time had been watching Von instead of the speaker, said clearly, "I know someone who wouldn't be too disappointed in not getting a buffalo."

Bike saw she was looking at Von and showed his surprise with a nervous laugh. "Von Wallace? You've got to be kidding. Von's our marksman. Our pure hunter."

"Pure shooter maybe," the woman said. "Not hunter. He doesn't like to hunt. He doesn't like to kill animals."

They all turned and stared at Von. Von was staring at the woman. "You're mistaken," he said to her.

"I don't think so."

"I've hunted all my life."

"I'm sure you have."

"I even had a slingshot once." He smiled and looked around the table. "And a rubber gun my dad made for me out of clothespins and some strips of inner tube. I used to shoot barn swallows with it."

"That doesn't change anything," Mrs. Garland said. "How you start doesn't matter. It's how you end." She fixed Von's

198

eyes with her own. "No more to romp the headland and the hill, that sort of thing."

"What?"

"Did you ever see foxes run on a cold morning? Their breath is silver and their coats are cinnamon."

Von's face drained; it was noticeable even in that impossible light. The woman said, elaborately, distinctly, ". . . *and then from whence he knows not, on his light there falls a shadow and his native slope . . . floats from his sick and filmed eyes, and something in the darkness . . . draws his forehead earthward and he dies. . . .*"

"What are you talking about?" Sandy said to her.

"That's the poem your husband recited that first night in Hanksville. When we were all in that dance hall."

"Oooohh, not me," Von crooned, and for the first time he broke away from the woman's stare. "I didn't recite any poetry."

"You thought it was Kelley or Sheats. And then you corrected yourself. Shelley or Keats, you said."

Von laughed redly. "You've got the wrong guy. We'd all been drinking pretty heavy that night, I remember. You as well as me."

"It's Tennyson," she said. "It's Tennyson's poem, not Shelley's or Keats's. You may want to remember that."

From a back room somewhere came the sound of glass breaking. They all waited for it to come again, as if to prove it really had been glass, but it didn't. Dr. Garland shoved his chair back and announced that they had to be going. "But it was nice seeing everyone again." Dr. Hall and his wife rose too and offered basically the same sentiment. "Where will you look now, Doctor?" Bike put in quickly. "Where will you head tomorrow morning?"

"The Henry Mountains probably," Hall answered, moving from the table. "West side. Or north. But the high meadows in any event."

"Good choice," Bike called, sending the words after them. "We were up near the meadows. But on the south side."

"Right," Hall called back. "Good to see you again," and then they were gone.

Von and Bike pulled Red to his feet and together they walked him out of the lounge, following Dorothy. Karen and Sandy brought up the rear. "Some crazy night," Karen said.

"How do you mean?"

"Do you remember when I left the table?"

"Yes."

"Well, I went out to the phone and while I was bent over talking to the kids, Red came up behind me and started hunching the hell out of me."

"Are you sure?"

"Of course I'm sure."

"It wasn't another one of your fantasies?"

"For Christ's sake, Sandy, I ought to know if someone is hunching me. He came up and grabbed my hips and started pumping away. He said, 'Gotta get my spoon in this jelly,' or something like that. It was hard to make out."

Sandy was silent and then she said, "I don't know, Karen, sometimes I think you ask for it. And I think someday you're going to get it."

"Well, not bent over a public telephone in a lobby, I hope." She started to laugh and then broke it off when Sandy asked her if she had slugged Red.

"No. He was drunk."

"So was that guy in Wendover at the casino. You slugged him. In fact, you broke his teeth. But not Red. Not now. Why is that, Karen?"

"Oh, for Christ's sake," Karen said, but not immediately, there was a delay. "For Christ's sake," she said again, and the slighty swollen face sagged in upon itself just a little. "Maybe Von was right."

"Right?"

"That first night in Hanksville, in that roadhouse when Dorothy kept playing the country music on the jukebox? Von said we had changed. You remember that? He said we had changed but we didn't realize it, that it had sneaked up on us during fourteen years. Maybe he was talking about me, Sandy. Otherwise, why *didn't* I break Red's teeth?"

When they had gotten Red safely into the Pace Arrow and returned to their own rig, Sandy put her hand on Von's arm and stopped him just inside the door. "That Bountiful woman," she said. "That Mrs. Garland. It's funny, isn't it, that she would be the one to tell on you."

"She was wrong."

"Stop it, Von. Please. You said once we had to be honest with ourselves. That it was important." She peered up at him, her face pinched with disappointment.

He turned his face away and would not look at her. "I don't remember quoting the poetry."

"It's not the poetry I'm talking about. It's the other. It's about being a hunter."

CHAPTER 11

Whispering the words that were the commands, Good Runner ordered the two hunters to stay close to him during the advance. They would attack the rearmost beast whatever it was, bull or cow, and by staying together they could concentrate their power and strike the animal with a trio of spears instead of one, killing it before it could stampede the herd to safety. They no longer had the strength to pursue even a badly wounded beast.

It seemed an impossible distance to where the tiny herd grazed. Good Runner could feel his body rebel against the awkward cramping of his crawl. There seemed to be no air within the cover of the grass. The sweat ran into his eyes and where it hung upon his shoulders, his hair was wet with it. His tongue was a rope of fur and his mouth stank like the flesh of a rotting animal. Lifting his head he saw that the herd was much closer and that a cow was in the lead and that a huge bull brought up the rear. On the flanks, a pair of smaller bulls fed; in the center milled three cows and a pair of their young.

Gradually, the hunters neared the rear bull. They began to smell him, the strange musks and the eye-burning sharpness of the body water that stained the tangled hair of his underbody. Close up, he was massive. Thrusting out nearly curveless from the sides of his head, his horns were as long as a stabbing spear and as big around at the base as triple fists. His chin whiskers dragged the ground and his knee garters draped his feet and the fur lay thick and matted upon his back as though he wore a pile of his own hides.

Finally reaching him, the three hunters rose from the brittle sanctuary of the grass and drew back their spears to strike the hairy creature towering above them.

But in the shock of seeing the grass suddenly reveal three threatening shapes, the beast jerked his head abruptly to one side.

The tall hunter was standing on that side. He was standing so close to the bull that he could have reached out and touched him with his hand, and when the giant head swung out and up the tip of one massive horn penetrated the hunter's body just above the hip, impaling him.

It was a mortal breach. In a trumpet of terror the bull lowered his head and then raised it again. The movement flung the impaled hunter free of the horn and for a terrible moment he was airborne, suspended above the beast with his arms and legs rigidly extended.

And when he fell it was not to the ground but onto the beast's back. He lay spread-eagled there, stricken, staring in terror at the sky.

The bull gathered itself and leaped forward into flight, and the wounded hunter was carried with him for a moment, there upon his back.

When the herd had finally galloped off, the two remaining hunters followed them a short distance and retrieved the body of their comrade. He made no sound of words but moaned only, and they sat beside him in the trampled grass for the balance of the day and into the time of starlight and shadow. Sometime then his face became merely the colored reflection of the moon itself, a pale remnant that had broken off and fallen to earth, and the air ceased to move in his chest. They tried to dig a final place in the ground for him but Good Run-

*ner's spear broke in the hard dirt and they were both too weary
to dig with their hands. When the Great Light returned to the
sky the two hunters scraped dirt onto the body of their dead
companion and limped off after the herd.*

Except for that one day on the benches, Bike and Von rode no
more in the Blazer with Red. He was becoming too belligerent,
unable to participate in choosing routes or planning the day,
and unwilling to talk to them on even the simplest matters. He
got into it with Von one morning, demanding to know why they
hadn't run into any hunters. They were in the Muley Creek
headwaters area, two days after they had pulled out of Bullfrog.
Why, Red wanted to know, hadn't they seen a single fucking
one of those two dozen orange jackets from the Armory session
except those two rich bastards from Bountiful who hunted only
because they were bored and were looking for new ways to get
their kicks? Dart guns and that kind of horseshit! Had they ever
put in a decent day's work in their fucking lives?

Von asked Red if he thought he had some kind of corner on
hard work. That immediately set Red off. He slammed on the
brakes and threw open the door and invited Von out. Bike
stopped it before it went any further, but after that Red got so
wild he gunned the Blazer unmercifully. At one point he was
speeding down a crumbly clay road at the base of Tarantula
Mesa when the left front wheel dropped unexpectedly into a
washout and both Bike and Von were catapulted straight up
out of their seats and into the roof.

The two got out of the Blazer rubbing their heads and swivel-
ing their necks, and then proceeded to walk the three miles
back to the sandy patch next to the Notom road where the
motor homes were parked. "That's it," Von explained to

Sandy. "That's the last time I ride with Taddish. Bike can ride with me in the Jimmy and that'll leave you gals the Bronco if you need it. But no more trips with Taddish." Later, when he was soaking his feet in a bucket of ice water and drinking a Coors, Von told Sandy he thought Red was cracking up. "He tromps that Blazer continually. Full blast. He lays on the horn till you think your ears are going to blow off. He pounds the steering wheel. He cusses out the window at the buffalo. Hell, there isn't a buffalo there to even hear him!"

"It's odd," Sandy said, "but just yesterday Karen was saying she wondered if you guys knew how to track anymore. She said that over the years you've gotten so accustomed to road hunting and taking game the first day of the season that she wasn't sure you knew how to be hunters when the going got rough."

Von didn't answer. He sat in the chair and wiggled his feet in the water and looked out through the window of the El Dorado at the sun going down. The day had finally revealed the sun and now it was going to hide it away again behind Capitol Reef, but with a lot of color and show this time, even some drama. The canyons were filling with darkness from the bottom up, like strange rising seas, and what the huge tilted mesas of the Reef looked like more than anything was a fleet of stricken ocean liners sinking into the canyons without a sound. But with color, as if they were burning.

The following afternoon found Von staring again into the west, this time on the slope of a long ridge in the South Notom Bench area, overlooking a defile called Bloody Hands Gap. That morning he and Bike had cut some tracks—fresh spoor mostly, and a few prints they figured could be buffalo—and Red had come onto pretty much the same kind of evidence just over the hill to the east, and after lunch the three of them had taken up stands on three separate sections of the same ridge.

On the ridge opposite his section Von could see clumpings of short grass and thickets of manzanita, patternless vegetation that was caught on the earth like tumbleweed on benchmark posts, but he could detect no movement anywhere. There was a storm forming in the clouds overhead but it wasn't finished yet, it was still drawing into itself all the electricity and darkness and power available to it, all the evil things, like a boil seeking a core. Part of it was thunder. It was strange to Von that there would be thunder this late in the year. He sensed that the rear guard of November days had at last turned and made their stand, lashing out not with any hope of advantage but sullenly, with despair.

It was growing colder. Von pulled his cap down, sensing the perfect brightness of the orange in that flawed light, and he flipped up the collar of his jacket and checked the extra cartridges in the slot bands on the front of his vest.

Then it was, just at that moment, that he saw the bull buffalo.

It sauntered into the corner of his vision from somewhere upslope and then stopped and swung its great head and looked down at him, a gross front-heavy beast as suddenly unnatural in that place as a satyr. The hump on his shoulders seemed a massive thing, a kind of deformity. The front legs were hidden in garters of hair and the head would have been sinister except for the ludicrous goatee. There was a certain scorn in the way the bull stood there. He was like a sentry from some mythical Hall of the Mountain King who had come forward fearlessly to investigate an intruder.

Von had been seated on a boulder and without getting to his feet he pressed the Winchester to his shoulder and settled his cheek against the cold wood and fixed the buffalo in the long tube of the scope. His judgment told him the distance was a hundred yards, that the wind was from the left quarter and stronger by twice at the target. But just at that moment the bull disappeared from the bore of the scope and began to move diagonally across the slope toward him. It was an unhurried approach, almost an amble, and when the bull had descended the ridge perhaps twenty-five yards he stopped.

206

Again Von lifted the rifle and took a focus in the glass. For a moment he considered a shot just behind the shoulder directly into the lungs and he inched the sight across the bull's thick winter-bobbed cape. But he thought better of it and swung back. He wanted the instant kill and he settled the Zeiss cross-hair onto the base of the bull's ear and steadied himself. Just then, just as he was zeroing in, assuring the bullet a precise target, a peal of thunder rolled swiftly downward from the darkness overhead. It was first a great rage of sound and then a sob, a sob such as a wounded animal might make, an animal helpless and maimed and in pain, crying out in a final agony.

Von never took the shot.

He never pulled the trigger. He got to his feet and lowered the Winchester and worked the bolt and methodically ejected all five of the shiny three-inch cartridges from the chamber, their expulsion making a harmless spent sound there on the quiet ridge slope he and the magnificent bull buffalo shared.

CHAPTER 12

It took some time for Good Runner and his remaining companion to catch up with the herd, for their feet were badly swollen and they had to stop several times in the course of their pursuit. It was not a chase. After goring the tall hunter the beasts had not run far, perhaps only as far as their fright, for they were poor-witted and forgot quickly.

They were also poor-sighted and because of this Good Runner stopped a short distance away and explained a new plan of attack to the scar-marked hunter. They pulled grass again and tied the strands together and wrapped them around their neck and waist and draped them over their shoulders and wound them in their hair. They each rubbed their face and arms with the fresh mud of the beast's tail waste and, thus costumed, they made their approach on the herd.

The beasts were sprawled in the grass, leg-tucked and indolent, chewing blankly and lidding their eyes against the hot wind. The fat cow that Good Runner had marked earlier as the leader was again positioned in the front of the group, and the huge bull was once more in the rear. Clearly, the hunters had a choice. They could circle around to the left to attack the cow, which would increase their risk of exposure, or they could attack straight on and hit the bull.

They chose the cow.

Their disguise served them well. Getting down on all fours and concealing their spears behind their bodies, they started their crawl around the herd. One of the bulls turned his head once and looked directly at them with his tiny red-shot eyes. They froze, but the bull looked away sleepily and they continued their approach. The younger cows resting with their calves in the center of the group likewise saw no threat in slowly moving clumps of grass that smelled exactly like themselves.

Thus the hunters reached the flank of the leader cow. Her puny tail flicked mechanically against the heat and the insects. Her jaws worked with a steady grinding rhythm and her giant belly rose and fell contentedly.

The scarred hunter stood up then without a sound and into that bulging flank, just behind the cow's shoulder, he thrust his lance.

The cow let out a roar and her body jerked and for a moment her eyes rolled back in her head. Her front legs shot forward and her rear legs gathered and with a ponderous surge she lifted herself from the ground.

Exactly in front of the cow Good Runner stood. He could have extended his spear and touched her with it, so close was he. The cow lifted her head and gave a fierce bellow. Her eyes flared whitely and thick globs of saliva spurted from her jaws and ran down into the tangled clot of hair below her chin. She threw her head back and peeled her upper lip and laid the tip of her horns against her cape to show her rage.

At that moment Good Runner gave his own scream and thrust his spear deep into the cow's chest, just between her legs.

———

Von saw the movement above him to his left, the orange cap and the chalky startled face and the orange vest and then the whole presence of Bike Kimball's body rising out of the ridge line, hesitant and bewildered, glancing alternately at him and at the buffalo. For a moment their eyes met.

As if that meeting were a signal, Bike slammed his rifle into his shoulder and sighted at the bull and pulled the trigger.

The shot was an explosion, slapping the earth and pounding the air into swollen rings that backed up on themselves and then broke apart. At the far end of that invisible arc of sound the bull stood proud and lofty as before, flaunting his invincibility at the second intruder as he had at the first, as he had so many times before at the encroachment of a brash young bull. He saw the man on the ridge as merely another creature he did not fear, standing oddly upright with a strange sticklike extension to his upper body. The bull heard the terrible sound the stick made and blinked at it but he knew nothing of center-fire ballistics or of projectiles that traveled so fast they couldn't be seen, and the 220-grain soft-point bullet struck him at a speed of 2,400 feet per second just above the black leather of his mouth before he had even finished blinking. It shattered his jaw and ripped out part of his tongue and lodged in the large bone of the left leg just below his shoulder. His rear legs sagged and he staggered backward and then steadied himself. He shook his head and clots of blood and bone from his mouth flew back and caught in the rich brown hair of his neck. He tried to swallow and close his jaws but he could not. He turned downhill slightly just as he heard the sound again and the second Spitzer blew the top half of one horn apart and slammed into his shoulder, deflecting downward and smashing the bone. He lurched to the side and caught himself and tried to locate the creature on the ridge but he couldn't. He pawed at the ground and lowered his head and tried to give a roar to the anger that was building in him but the blood was pouring out of his nostrils now, over the demolished tongue and into the tuft of hair below his chin. He threw back his head and touched the tips of his horns to his hump to show his rage, but the movement dizzied him and he nearly fell. He started to turn back to locate the cows and warn them of the danger that was here and the sound came again and a terrible cutting pain ripped through the top of his head. His eyes filled with a red wetness and he couldn't see. His legs buckled and his head dropped down. For a moment his anger surged into strength and he lifted his head and shook it defiantly down the ridge. But the pain was too great to sustain it, and the fear that he had forgotten for so long came back. His head sagged and he felt the ground slipping away from where he stood and he fell swiftly into an unending blackness.

Bike came running then, his face flushed but still showing the puzzlement. The awful silence had returned to the ridge and Bike's voice was strident and out of proportion as he came bounding up. "Von, I saw it! You had that bull cold and you didn't take the shot!"

Von shook his head. "The waste," he said.

"Seventy-five yards! You could have shut both eyes and dropped him!"

"It shall be unlawful to waste, or permit to be wasted—"

"A trophy bull, man! He'll go two thousand pounds if he'll go two hundred. And you gave him to *me*?"

Von turned away. The dead buffalo looked shrunken now, part of the earth, a stained boulder in the autumn grass. "I can't do it anymore, Bike. I can't kill another animal."

"What are you talking about? You might not get another chance like this. It's a once-only hunt, man. You've got to *fill*!"

"You!" Von shouted, and it seemed as if it were another's anger. "You've got to fill, not me!"

"That's nonsense. You put two hundred dollars down for your permit. You told the state you wanted to take an animal. The state expects—"

"Don't tell me about the state. I don't care about the state."

For the first time, Bike went quiet, looking at the rifle hanging from Von's hand, searching his face. "What's gotten into you? You've never acted like this before. What's the matter?"

"Let it go, Bike."

"What do you mean, let it go? You're a hunter, for God's sake. You waited six years for the permit and you come out here—"

"Is that all we need, just the permit? Does the permit make it right?"

"What do you mean *right*?" and there was some impatience now.

Von shook his head. "Let it be, Bike."

Red Taddish came then, striding up over the crest of the hill and starting down this side, stopping at the bull and then coming on again, the big Colt-Sauer swinging like a scythe from one hand. "Whose kill?" he called.

"Mine," Bike called back.

"It figures," he said, and then he was there beside them, big and splotchy-faced and out of breath. He glanced at the buffalo again and then at Bike. "A once in a lifetime head and you shoot it up like a kid drilling a can with a new .22. I thought you wanted a mount? All you got now is winter meat. Who wants it? Who in hell came for meat?" He shook his head savagely. "Fucking shame, man."

"You'd better get the Blazer," Bike said to him, and his voice was tight. "I'm going to need the winch to get the bull down to the road."

"You're too far from the road. It'll ruin the hide, winching him that far." Red's eyes were raw and cold as he studied the fallen buffalo. "Hell, it's already ruined. Maybe you can make some kind of buffalo rug out of it. Fuck Karen on it in front of the fireplace. Maybe she won't mind the holes. Maybe she can hook her feet in them."

Bike's face drained. "You don't like not being the first to take an animal, do you, Taddish? Or are you afraid you'll miss out altogether?"

Red's face went gray. "I won't miss out, buddy. You can bet your ass on it!" And he stomped off down the slope.

At the bottom of the slope lay a narrow unimproved road that intersected after a few hundred yards with the Bloody Hands Gap road. At the intersection stood the dust-caked orange-and-blue Blazer with the hook and pulley built into the rear topframe, and nestled behind the chromed front bumper the Sidewinder III winch that they had all agreed last summer they would use to haul in the buffalo they were going to take out of hunt area 600.

CHAPTER 13

With the cow buffalo lying dead on her side the short hunter propped open her jaws and Good Runner cut out her tongue with his fleshing knife. He sliced the thick ropish organ in half and the two of them sat in the blood-spattered grass and cut off slices of the tongue and ate them until it was completely devoured. The blood ran warm and red from Good Runner's mouth and trickled down over his chin just as he remembered it.

Her heart pierced by the spear Good Runner had thrust into her chest, the cow was the only beast they slew. It was the only beast they needed. The remainder of the herd ran off a great distance into the grass and the two hunters never looked at them again.

When they had finished eating the tongue, the scarred hunter stuck his short spear between the cow's hind legs and propped them apart and Good Runner cut the hide open from just beneath the beast's waste hole all the way up the belly to the place in the chest where the spear still protruded. He then sliced through the skin over the abdomen and snipped the thin muscle separating the breathing cage from the guts. He cut out the liver and set it aside and then made several cuts along the backbone

214

so that the gut bag could free itself, and when it had slid out onto the ground he cut off a piece of the gut about the length of his body and pressed it through his fingers until he had squeezed its contents out upon the ground. He repeated this action until the piece was completely void of waste and then he tied a knot in one end. Finishing this, he bent down and severed the big tubelike vein leading from the beast's heart. When the blood gushed out he fitted the open end of the piece of gut over the vein until the entire length of gut was filled. He presented it to his companion and then drank from it himself when the other had finished, using his fingers as a kind of valve to pulse the warm red liquid into his mouth. Then he tied the end shut and draped it around his neck.

Next he picked up the liver and cut it precisely down the middle. He laid one piece aside and cut the remaining half into two pieces, one for his companion and one for himself. And again they ate. The meat was a warm spongey honeycomb of flesh and it seemed to Good Runner that with each mouthful of food the strength surged back into his arms and legs.

When they had finished consuming the fragment of liver the two hunters knelt at the side of the beast and cut free two huge sections of hide. Laying the sections on the ground they threw into them the chunks of meat they carved from the cow's body —the strip of pungent fat from along the backbone, chunks from the haunch and the hindquarter, pieces of the stomach and a pink-gray coil of the small gut. When the two pieces of hide were full of meat they wove ribbons of tendon through holes they had cut in the edge, and tied them up, and thus made bundles they could carry.

When they had finished with the bundles, Good Runner knelt at the front of the cow and jerked the spear free and with great care cut her heart from her body. He impaled the heart on the point of the spear and passed it slowly back and forth along the full length of her. The blood from the cow's heart trickled down the shaft of the spear and onto Good Runner's hands, making

215

of them strange orange gifts in the sunlight. He could not burn sweet grasses now but he could sing the chants that would rise up from this place and reach the Beast God. Hearing their songs, the God would know of the hunters' gratitude, and of their courage. He would recognize the strong heart of the cow leader and restore it to her. He would remember her pain, and theirs, and He would let it pass from them forever.

And so they knelt in the trampled grass and sang the chants.

When they had finished, Good Runner fixed the butt of his spear in the earth so the heart of the cow beast could hang there while it waited to return to her body. They drank blood from the gut tube one last time and then gathered up the bundles of hide and left that stained plot of earth and trotted away across the grass.

Red changed his mind and came back to the ridge with the Blazer, but he had only 120 feet of cable in the winch and it wasn't enough to snake Bike's buffalo down the hill and onto the road. He swore and kicked dirt and finally pulled out from the back of the Blazer one of the two coils of ¾-inch rope with the blue threading in it that Von had bought at the Granger Hardware the week their permits came. The second coil Von kept in his Jimmy. Red attached 150 feet of the rope to the cable and even then he had to drive into the meadow and up to the first crease of the slope before they could tie the end of the rope around the buffalo's legs and winch him down to the road.

Once there, Bike trimmed a length of scrub oak branch and propped open the rear legs of the bull and proceeded to eviscerate him. He made a few cuts with his knife and the huge wet discolored pouch of intestines flowed out onto the ground like a glob of lava. He cut the main arteries at the base of the bull's neck and the blood drained out onto the clay in bright red runners. In the meantime, Red was recalling his cable with his hand-held three-position switch and when he had finished he coiled the blue-threaded ¾-inch rope and threw it into the back of the Blazer. By the time he rejoined Bike at the side of the road he was brimming over with complaint. "You're gonna play hell getting that animal out of here, Kimball. It's too big. You'd better go get your saws and quarter up right here where you are."

Bike looked up from his work with some surprise. "That wasn't the deal," he said. "I need to hoist him up on the Blazer."

"Goddamn it, man, use your head!" It was almost a shout. "He'll weigh a fucking ton. How you gonna get him up?"

Bike got to his feet. "With the tackle. That's why we rigged it. That was the plan. We'd gut and bleed in the field and then haul all three animals back to camp and hang them there. They've got to be skinned. And they've got to cool out."

Red shook his head. "Your animal's gonna flip my vehicle over backwards if we try to hoist him. He's too heavy." He walked into the middle of the road and came back. "I'm not going to use the Blazer anymore. I damned near ripped my cable out getting the animal down here."

Bike said tightly, "I can't work on him like this."

Red gave a snort. "The pioneers used to do it, the pure hunters who had nothing but grass and prairie for a hundred miles. That's what you always told us. But you're lucky, you got one of those pure hunters right here to help you." He turned to Von. "Ain't that right, Wallace? You'll help Mr. Game Management manage his game, won't you?"

Von didn't answer and Bike said through his teeth, "I can't leave my animal here in the road."

Red's face flared. "Then I'd say you got a problem. And what you gotta do now is figure out how to solve the sonofabitch!" He stomped off to the Blazer and gunned away down the road at the front end of a long thick tunnel of dust.

At the grassy tree-rimmed camp alongside the Notom highway Karen had finally convinced Dorothy and Sandy that it was time to go look for their husbands, and she was driving slowly east on the Gap road when the Blazer shot over a knoll in front of her and would have struck the Bronco head-on except that she swerved frantically to one side. "For Christ's sake!" she cried, skidding to a stop on the shoulder of the road. "Where does that jackass think he's going?"

"Was he alone?" Sandy demanded, staring after the fleeing Blazer. "I couldn't see. Was Von with him? How about Bike?"

"Maybe something's happened," Dorothy exclaimed. "Maybe there's been an accident."

Karen muttered, "Oh, for Christ's sake!" and she whipped the Bronco around and started after the cloud of dust that was the Blazer.

They had almost caught the cloud when it swung off the Gap road and careened onto a secondary road that led north into a valley between two low hills. Karen followed and after a quarter of a mile she caught the dust and disappeared into it and shot out the other side, but only because of Sandy's inexplicable impulse to glance back at the cloud did she see the Blazer sitting off to the side of the road. She shouted at Karen and Karen skidded fifty yards before she got the Bronco stopped and they all jumped out.

Thinking back on it, they remembered seeing everything in wholes as if they were an audience at a showing of slides where the new one could not begin until the last one ended. The Blazer sat on the shoulder of the road and Red was standing at the right front fender, holding his rifle out in front of him in a sort of jousting position, looking into the meadow. For that moment there was a total absence of movement. There was no wind. A diffuse daylight blurred everything and a strange

218

threatening hush was all about. Within the meadow itself—a treeless rectangle set apart upon the earth like the place on flesh where bandage tape has been—there was a herd of buffalo.

They numbered half a hundred perhaps, at a distance of maybe a hundred yards back from the road. They were moving slowly. There was the black collective mass of them and then, within that, the shaggy bob of individual heads. Huge heads. Monstrous. They were a shock, a sudden disbelief. "My God," Dorothy breathed, breaking the silence. "It's the buffalo!"

Even as she spoke, Red lifted the rifle to his shoulder. With her calf at her side a cow moved stolidly in the van of the herd, her hips tawny and her midbody brown and the pelage of her hump a rich black fur. Through the matted frontlet that overhung her forehead she peered idly at the human clumping along the road. Her face bore that peculiar puckering of her kind, wrinkled just above the nose like a chamois that was wadded up before it dried. Her horns were curiously inadequate for the size of her head. She was hovering and huge and front-heavy, and for that single moment, there with her calf, terribly maternal.

Red Taddish shattered that tableau forever with a blast from the Colt-Sauer.

The calf, head up and staring at the road with that elfin mimicry of the young, took the heavy boattail bullet squarely in the head. It shattered his skull and his brain all in one instant, and the tiny form slumped forward into a heap.

Only Dorothy's scream was there to challenge the booming convulsion of the shot. "No! No!" It was its own explosion, that scream; it trailed the other when the other rocked itself out in time and distance; it became an echo that took on a life of its own. "You . . . killed . . . that . . . baby!" She threw herself at the distance that lay between her and Red, her arms in the air and her hair streaming. "That . . . calf . . . you . . . shot it . . . you killed it . . . killed it . . . you . . . sonofabitch!" and she flung herself at him, flaying, pounding, her face the tic of madness and the eyewells spilling outrage as if it were blood. "You did it you killed that baby I hate you you sonofabitch why aren't you dead I wish you were *dead dead dead*!"

Red reached out with a single hand and placed it against Dorothy's face and shoved her backward into the dirt.

With the fall her screams became sobs and her body twisted in the agony of them. The fierce eyes were closed now, shutting out sight. She rolled onto her side with her fists grinding at her face just as the other two women reached her.

In the meadow the cow had jumped aside at the sound of the shot but now she was back at the limp bag of her calf, nosing it, butting it gently as if in reprimand for having lain down, licking its face in an effort to get it to stand. Red's rifle was at his shoulder again for a second shot and the powerful Magnum bullet struck the lower part of the cow's foreleg and blew it completely off. She tumbled onto her side and then threw her head up and partially righted herself, pawing desperately at the earth with the one front hoof, eyeing the calf and bellowing frantically.

Karen and Sandy got Dorothy to her feet and were brushing dirt from her clothing and trying to get her hands away from her face when the third shot came. The deadly 300-grain bullet tore into the fallen cow's hump and a chunk of flesh and hide flew up as though a bird had made a nest in that snarled wool and then jumped free at the sound of the shot.

Dorothy was on her feet but she couldn't walk and the two women carried her to the Bronco. She was quite small—frail, tiny-boned; they had never realized how truly small she was.

In the meadow the herd was starting to mill about, startled by the rifle shots. The boldest came up and sniffed the cow and the calf and then backed off, puzzled by the smell of blood. Some circled warily and others ambled off and some stared across the meadow at the road and bawled in bewilderment.

Once in the Bronco, Sandy cradled Dorothy in her arms and

Karen turned the vehicle around and started back to their camping park next to the highway.

On a flank of the herd a young bull stood eyeing the flower of dust in the road. He was a big animal but not gigantic, not yet that proud hulking mass that a mature bull can become. His chin hair was matted with spittle and he stood at the edge of the herd like a preoccupied monk whose careless spits hadn't quite cleared his goatee. When Red Taddish shot him his head jerked and his rear legs sagged. He caught himself and took a few steps toward the road, his short tufted tail arched over his rump like a scorpion's. He stopped and swung his head around in an attempt to lick at the pain in his side where the blood was beginning to bubble. He couldn't reach it and it made him angry and he let out a roar that belied his size. At that moment a second bullet whistled through the feeble curtain of his beard and plowed into his throat. His whole body rocked but he did not go down. He struggled for a moment to get his breath and another bullet clipped the top of his skull and powered into his hump. His eyes rolled and froth began to form on his mouth. He moved forward but his walk was suddenly erratic. He couldn't keep his head up and his legs were splaying badly and the hair at his neck dripped blood like an oil pan that has been put on wrong. He fell finally, going down in that leaden awkward way that shot game fall as if grace left their body when the light did, and all their weight was double when they died.

The two women carried Dorothy into the Pace Arrow and put her to bed immediately. She seemed totally stricken. Her hands were cold and her skin was blue-white and she would not speak. Sandy sat beside the bed and stroked her arms. Karen pulled all the shades in the Pace and then went to the kitchen and quietly gathered up all the sacks and packages and cartons of vodka miniatures and took them out in back and smashed them against a boulder. When she came back inside she whis-

221

pered to Sandy, "I've got to go find my husband. I don't know where he is. I need to find him."

"Yes. Von, too. I'm sure they're together."

"Will you be all right? Do you think Dorothy—?"

"You go on. We'll be fine," and after a bit Sandy heard the Bronco start up and move off down the Gap road. The silence that settled in then was eerie, almost menacing; there was only Dorothy's shallow breathing and, indistinct and far away, a sound of thunder.

Karen traveled east on the Gap road nearly two miles and when she came to the second branch road she turned north and spotted the parked Jimmy immediately. Von and Bike were bent over a buffalo carcass on the side of the road and Karen got out of the Bronco and went to them. They both stood up. "We thought we heard shots," Bike said to her.

"You did," and after her long answering silence, Bike said, "Well?"

"Red found the herd. Or part of it. On that first branch road west of here."

"Did he get his animal?"

Karen studied Bike's face. "He got three of them."

Bike's face drained. "*Three?* Three animals *himself?* You got to be kidding."

"He killed a calf. And a cow. We saw that. And as we were leaving he was shooting at a bull."

Bike swore under his breath and Von said, "I told you that guy had cracked." And then he said, looking at Karen, "Where's Dorothy and Sandy? Why aren't they with you?"

Karen took a deep breath and let it out noisily. "Sandy's with Dorothy in the Pace. Dorothy's out of it. Totally. When Red started killing buffalo Dorothy attacked him. She went nuts. Red knocked her down. It was terrible." She paused. "We took her back to the Pace and put her in bed. When I left them Sandy had just about gotten her to sleep."

222

A ball of thunder rolled through the bunching darkness overhead. Von said, "Why don't you two finish up here? I'm going back and see Sandy," and he left them there at the side of the road with the half-butchered buffalo and got into the Jimmy and drove off toward the Notom highway.

When Dorothy was asleep Sandy returned to the El Dorado and was there alone when she heard the Blazer pull up in front of the Pace Arrow. She knew without looking it was the Blazer; she could distinguish each of the vehicles by its sound. The noise of the car door slamming was followed by a silent period and it was then that she went outside and stood on the step and waited. After a few minutes Red came out of the Pace carrying an armful of cheesecloth game bags and a sheath of knives, and when he spotted Sandy on the step of the El Dorado he stopped.

"Is Dorothy still asleep?" she called to him.

"She's asleep."

"She could be dead, you know. If we'd let her run out into the meadow to protect that calf like she started to she *would* be dead." She could feel the loathing well up from her body with every word. "That was a shameful performance out there."

"At least I'm man enough to pull the trigger," Red replied, walking over to her.

"You're not a man, Red Taddish." She practically spit it at him. "You're a little boy who cheats at the games he plays. All the games. Your wife's known it for a long time and now the rest of us know it." She eyed him coldly. "A man hunts the way he lives. He brings the morality of his life to his hunt. You didn't bring much to yours. Just another violation."

Red stepped closer. His face was seared with a kind of frenzy that wouldn't abate and his eyes were hot and uncentered as if they were floating. "Still the Sister Superior, aren't you? Still the little Miss Snooty who thinks it doesn't stink."

Sandy inhaled deeply in her anger and her breasts pushed against the cardigan sweater she was wearing. Red suddenly reached out and shoved her back against the door of the motor home, dropping the sheath of knives and some of the cheese-cloth bags, and then he yanked the door open and pushed her inside. She struck the wall and fell to the floor and he reached down and grabbed her by the hair and jerked her to her feet. She let out a scream and he hit her with his fist, just below the eye. She began to fall but he reached out and caught her. He held her up in front of him and ripped the sweater and the blouse from her body, and then her brassiere. Her breasts ex-ploded nakedly from the cloth and he squeezed them with his hands and rubbed the big full nipples across his mouth. When she tried to pull away he twisted her hair until she screamed with the pain. Keeping one hand in her hair he ripped open the belt of her jeans. "Take them off!" he hissed. She worked them down over her hips and when they were gone he reached down and tore her panties off. He dropped his own jeans and gripped his penis in his hand and showed its dark red hardness to her, and then forced her to her knees and rubbed it back and forth through the blood that masked one whole side of her face. He retrieved one of the flimsy cheesecloth bags from the floor and dropped it down over her head until it completely enclosed her nakedness, and yet seemed to reveal it more, to heighten it. "You're some rack of meat!" he breathed, and pushed her down onto the floor and mounted her, pulling her hips up to him while he pumped them. But after a few thrusts in that position he turned her over onto her hands and knees and entered her from the rear. His hand still gripped her hair and whenever her whimpering got too loud he twisted it. He pushed the mesh game bag up around her shoulders and his breath whistled in his pleasure of her nakedness.

He didn't last long. In the excitement of his impending or-gasm he let go of her hair and clutched her hips in both hands and in the paralysis of ejaculation he slipped out of her and couldn't get back in and he shot his juice all over the cleft of her buttocks. He moaned throatily and his body quivered and when he had finished he pushed her flat on the floor and stood up and buckled his jeans. Then he knelt beside her on the floor and pulled the game bag down over her hips once more. "Sweet," he whispered. "Sweet fuck," and he stood up. "You fell and hit your face," he said, seeing it swollen and discolored. "That's how you tell it. When you get dressed I want you to throw that game bag away. And keep your mouth shut or you won't have any face to explain!"

He turned and left the camper and when he was outside he picked up the fallen bags and the sheath of knives from the ground. Walking to the Blazer he laughed to himself when he realized that during the whole business his cap hadn't even come off.

Von parked the Jimmy and was about to enter the El Dorado when he heard the sound of off-road vehicles behind him on the Notom highway. He turned and saw two Jeeps turn onto the Gap road, the first Dr. Hall's and the second Dr. Garland's. They stopped immediately and called to Von. Had he had any luck? They'd seen absolutely nothing of any buffalo herd, had he?

"We spotted a part of the herd today," Von called back. "They've obviously split up. But the chances are good that they're all here in the area somewhere." He went on to explain that there were two tributary roads leading north off the road they were on now, the first located about a mile east and the second another mile beyond that. "It's your choice," he added. "My party has taken game on both roads. They're in the field now dressing out. You'll probably see them."

Dr. Hall thanked him and suggested that they all get together later that night for a drink. "Our ladies are staying in the motel at Notom," he added, and he started to drive away and then stopped and motioned for Dr. Garland to park his jeep and come with him, which Garland did.

"You're leaving your Cap-shur," Von called to him. "Weren't you going to try and sneak—?"

"Naw," Garland called back. "Maybe another time. But

thanks." The two men waved and drove off, and Von opened the door to the El Dorado and went in.

The short tubby Bountiful dentist turned north at the first road and about a quarter mile in he spotted the three buffalo carcasses in the meadow grass with the big red-haired man bent over them. He remarked to Garland that one of the carcasses looked awfully small. "Almost like a calf."

Garland replied that it couldn't be. "Probably part of the one he's dressing out." He looked into the meadow himself. "But there's definitely two adult carcasses there. Why would he have two?"

"One most likely belongs to that fellow we just spoke to. The poet. He must have gone back to the camper to get some gear and the big fellow stayed with the kill."

Hall laughed. "Good deal, having a friend who'll do your field work for you. I'm sure you'll dress out my buff while I sit here in the Jeep and sip a little brandy."

"What are friends for?" Garland answered with a shrug of his shoulders, but then he grew serious and glanced again into the meadow. "Obviously the herd was here earlier and then moved on. Probably in farther, along this road."

They continued north until, about two miles in, the road reverted back to the crude trail it had started out as. There was a small arena at the end, a sort of cirque made of grass that fanned out of the dead hackberry and the oakbrush, and they stopped and made a couple of forays and then took a stand that lasted about an hour. But nothing showed itself. There was no sound anywhere except a wind blowing out of the gray unrelenting sky, and they turned the Jeep around and headed back.

They were perhaps a quarter mile from the Gap road intersection when they saw the herd.

It surprised them. One moment there were junipers bunched darkly on the lower slope of the ridge and the next moment they broke up into a slow-moving emergence of buffalo. First trees and then animals, and so mixed together at first sighting that it was difficult for the eye to separate them.

Hall stopped the Jeep and the two men jumped out into a shallow ditch on the west side of the road. Once they got stationary they began to see things clearly. The Blazer was still parked on the side of the road where it had been before, and the three animal carcasses still lay mounded in the grass like a disrupted birth. But the red-haired man was nowhere in sight.

Then suddenly, so suddenly there was no immediate reality to it, a bull buffalo galloped into view on their right. He was in the throes of panic. He bucked and twisted and spun first to one side and then the other, finally skidding to a stop in the grass with his tiny front feet planted neatly together. Then he leaped backward into a repetition of those contortions, all the while bellowing in terror.

"What the hell?" Hall cried. "What's that damned bull doing?"

"Look at him. Look at his hump. There's something wrong with it."

"My God, yes, there's something . . . there's something *on* it!"

"Look out, he's seen us! He's coming this way. He's . . . God, he's charging us!"

He was. Head down, rocking insanely, the bull was headed directly for them.

The dentist stood up in the ditch and steadied the .45-70 Government against his shoulder and with great coolness slammed a 405-grain bullet into the charging buffalo. The bull pitched forward onto his knees and then got up and the dentist drilled him with a second slug. The bull dropped straight down and his chin bounced on the ground and he was still.

Upslope, the buffalo herd swung out to one side like a hide-covered gate and fled the field. The two men climbed out of the ditch and ran into the meadow and when they were within two dozen feet of the dead bull they stopped.

"Oh God," the dentist said.

The veterinarian moved forward, walking directly up to the fallen bull. He saw that there was a cover of game bags tied to the bull's hump and that something lay beneath it. He cut the first of the many strands of rope that wound around the bull's neck and body and legs, and then he folded the layer of bags to one side.

What lay beneath was a human body tied to the buffalo's hump, the face bloodless and the hair red and both smeared thickly with dung. The man's eyes were open. Staring. Terrified. Dead.

A short distance away on the Gap road the Kimballs were nearing the intersection, headed back to the camp, when they heard the boom of the two shots from the .45-70 Government. They glanced toward the sound and saw two men run across the distant meadow and jump into a Jeep and race down the road toward them.

Bike wheeled the Bronco onto the road and when they got close to the Jeep he shouted to Karen that he thought it looked like the two hunters from Bountiful, the two doctors. When the vehicles reached each other and skidded to a broadside stop in the middle of the road, Karen threw open her door and got out but neither of the two men in the Jeep followed suit. "Accident!" the man behind the wheel shouted at them. "One of your people! Get help! Get the sheriff! My God!"

Karen whirled to Bike. "You go!" she shouted. "Notom. Phone. State Patrol. Sheriff's office. Something!"

"But what about the meat in the back? What about—?"

"*Fetch*, Bishop! I'll stay with these guys. Now *go!*" She jumped into the Jeep and both vehicles spat dirt at each other racing apart.

But in the Jeep, Karen could get no answers. Shaking and gray-faced, the two hunters could only mumble their bewilderment and stare ahead at the road. The Jeep stopped shortly and they all got out and Karen saw everything pretty much in degrees of disbelief after that. She saw the dead buffalo immediately with the peculiar baglike shapelessness that all dead animals so quickly acquire, and then at some point in her walk up the meadow she realized that the extra lumping of the buffalo's back was not some bizarre displacement of the spine in death but rather a human body wrapped in mesh bags, and that it was Red Taddish. And he was still. Awesomely still. Still in the way that a winter log is more still than the ice it is frozen in.

After that shock she had to look at everything two or three times before she could even attempt to comprehend it, wondering whether the blood spotting the bags was the man's or the animal's, whether the excrement on the man's face was there because he had accidentally rolled in it or whether it had been purposely smeared on him in a defilement she couldn't begin to confront. And had she ever seen an animal fall in just that position?—upright, with its legs drawn under as though it would gather itself at any moment and shake off the accident of its mortality and bound away to join the herd. She wondered too if it was simply a gimmick of the movies or if dead men's eyes could actually be closed by passing a hand over them. Red Taddish's eyes needed to be closed. "Will one of you close his eyes, please?" she said to the two men standing there, and she shuddered.

The taller man's stepping forward to obey her shattered completely the sense of unreality, and everything became a detail. She smelled the biting fecal-urine odor of the two bodies and saw the bullet wound in the top of Red's shoulder close to the neck, with the blood congealing now. She saw that his orange cap was missing and that the rope that bound him to the dead bull was ¾-inch with a blue threading in it. She kept looking at the rope and then without looking at anything additionally, she said, softly, "Oh, Von, for Christ's sake, Von," and it was like a moan, and no one heard her.

An off color caught at the edge of her vision and she glanced toward the bull's rump and saw imbedded high in one immense haunch the shaft of a dart approximately three inches long and about the color of a manila folder. One of the men was saying, "There was something wrong with the bull, we saw that right away." His words were a curious monotone of confusion and dread. "He was acting crazy. He was bucking around in the grass like a wild horse."

"Do you see the dart?" Karen said.

"He was charging us. I had to shoot. I think I shot twice. Maybe three times. I had to do it, he was heading right for us!"

"Do you see the dart?"

"How could I know there was a man on his back? How could he *get* there? Tied *on* like that. My God, how?" The taller man broke in then and said to Karen, "What did you say?"

Karen pointed to the dart in the buffalo's hind leg. "Do you see it? It looks like one of those darts zoo people use. Or veterinarians. You see it on TV documentaries and like that," and the faces of both men turned in a dumb unison and stared at the stricken giant sprawled before them on the ground. Karen said then, forcing it into their awareness, "Isn't one of you a veterinarian? Don't I remember your telling us that in Hanksville or Bullfrog? Isn't it one of you?"

She could have skipped the identity part of the question for she already had an answer. The two men stood there staring at the buffalo's haunch, their faces naked as dough and their eyes riven with a disbelief that was nearly audible. Without obstructing their view of the dead animal in any way, Karen stepped around in front of them and said quietly, "Do you know what I just thought of?" She waited only a moment and then went on. "When the sheriff gets here and starts his investigation he's going to see that dart and right away he's going to start looking for the gun that shoots it. It's bound to be in somebody's Jeep. Isn't it? And then he's obviously going to assume that the bullet that's in the dead *buffalo* is the same kind that's in the dead *man.*" She stopped and shook her head vigorously so they could see it, and then deliberately allowed a tiny bit of incredulity to shade her voice, so they could hear it. "Guys, that's going to be easy for the sheriff. But when you tell him you don't know how the man got on the animal's back . . . That's going to be *hard!*" She let that concern hover there between them like a fanned odor, and then she had questions. "What was it, guys? What was your motive? Was Red after one of your wives? Or was it both of them? Did he count coup on your ladies back at Bullfrog?" She waited, clucking a little in appreciation. "He was a mover, you know. A real cocksman." She put her hands together. "I wonder what your patients back in Bountiful will think about this? Will they be sorry that you stand to lose everything you worked so hard to build up? Or will they be secretly pleased?" She eyed them steadily, and then in her most confidential tone she said, "You know," and she let that leader hang there until they were forced to look at her for the completion, "you know, I've always been very healthy but it isn't impossible in this short time before the law gets here that I could be stricken with an attack of amnesia. Accompanied, of course, by a temporary blindness. And both conditions caused by the shock of all this, you understand. By the time I recover —and I've always been able to recover very quickly from any kind of sickness—that dead man there on the buffalo's back could be lying on the ground where he belongs, and the rope and the bags and the dart and the orange vest could have vanished completely. Been destroyed, so to speak. I mean . . . the man *is* dead, isn't he? You could say *murdered,* tied up like that on the animal and all. And the time and expense of defense lawyers and trials and the notoriety, well, that isn't going to bring him back, is it? Hell, if I were the sheriff it would be a lot easier for me to understand the death of an improperly dressed hunter than it would this little scene we're looking at now. I mean, this is tough, guys. What's the sheriff going to put in his *report?*" She watched the two men play with those thoughts the way you can watch a November wind play with a scrap of paper from a summer picnic, pushing at it, picking it up and running it a ways and then letting it go, lifting again, turning it over and over. . . . "Then there's the hard evidence," Karen said. "The real clincher stuff. Whose bullet is in the dead man's body? What gun did it come from? Is it *my* gun?" and she peered up at them with a terrible innocence. "Guys," she said, letting her shoulders drop helplessly, "I don't even *own* a gun." She stood there, pretending to wait for an answer, until both men began a little shuffle with their feet and wouldn't look at one another, nor at her. "I'm going down and sit in your Jeep now," she announced, "and suffer my attack of illness. If everything goes right I'll be cured by the time the sheriff gets here." She turned to walk away and then turned back. "As hunting accidents go, this one isn't that bad. Hell, just a few years ago down by Pinto Little some asshole blew two kids off their bicycles. Killed them outright. In their own lane. Said he thought they were muleys."

The sunset was brief. It was, after all, November. At about the time the light first began to fail, Bike drove in off the Notom highway followed by a deputy sheriff of Wayne County in a black-and-white Blazer with a big yellow star on each door and on the hood. It in turn was trailed by a paramedic in an Ambocab from Hanksville.

Karen met the tiny convoy at the Gap road intersection and led them to the meadow where the paramedic examined the body and the deputy wrote down the statements he got from Dr. Hall and Dr. Garland, as well as from Karen. Then the deputy and the paramedic placed the body of Red Taddish in a body bag and the moment they zipped it shut was the next to last time Karen Kimball shuddered. The *precise* last time was when they all returned to the parking camp and Von led Sandy out from the El Dorado. Von's eyes were red as if he had been crying but it was Sandy's face that made Karen shudder. It looked like she had colored the entire bowl of one cheek with two or three of the brightest crayons in a box of Number 8 Jumbos. The deputy saw the bruise too. "What happened to you?" he asked Sandy suspiciously, for he was a little on edge. "Has there been another accident?"

"Recoil," Sandy answered, having trouble moving her lips when she spoke the word. Von explained that he'd been teaching his wife to shoot a rifle and the butt piece had jumped and struck her in the face.

"You city people and your guns," the deputy said, but with considerable relief, and after that exchange he spoke to a few of the people individually and then to all of them assembled in a circle around him, including Dorothy. Mostly, he read back parts of his report. It was a kind of review and he asked for additions or revisions if they thought any were needed. His words were grim and officious and he was never once aware that Karen was standing at one end of the gathering when he began his report and at the opposite end, next to Von, when he finished. Von noticed. He saw her coming. When she finally reached him she stared into Sandy's face and then into his as if she were asking a question. Von spoke a single word to her, "Red," and it was the answer.

Still not speaking, Karen reached down and grasped Von's hand and turned it over. The daylight had failed by then but she didn't need it, she merely ran the tips of her fingers across Von's palm to feel for the rope burns.

They were there.

"I'm going to have to ask all of you to follow me into Hanksville," the deputy announced, directing his flashlight onto them. He didn't need the light to see them, it was merely a gesture of self-importance and one that reinforced his authority to make such a request. "In the matter of Robert Taddish of Granger, Utah, I plan to file a report of accidental death, gunshot, with the coroner of Wayne County. I've asked some of you to report yourselves as witnesses and to make yourselves available to testify at a coroner's inquest if one is called. Arrangements will have to be made for disposition of the body as soon as we arrive in Hanskville," and he glanced at Dorothy. "We should be finished with this by noon tomorrow and then you will be free to go."

The formality ebbed a little with the deputy's final words; there was some visible sagging around the circle, an unobtrusive shifting of feet, someone breathed audibly. But then the deputy spoke again. "I must also inform you that I will have to report a permit violation to the Division of Wildlife Resources. As best as I can determine, there are five dead game animals that can be accounted for here. One of them is a calf. According to a Mr.—" and here he directed his flashlight onto the clipboard again—"a Mr. Bikelin Kimball of your party, the taking of a buffalo calf on hunt area 600 is strictly illegal."

CHAPTER 14

They reached the caves late in the afternoon of the second day.
The Great Light sat squarely on the horizon, huge and orange
and rayed with dust, and the Women said later that it seemed
the two hunters came directly out of the Light, that it was like
they had been trapped in it and had escaped, stumbling forward
in that awful heat with their heavy bundles of hide.

They climbed the stone steps of the ledges and staggered
deep inside the caves, into the rearmost chambers where the
coolness and the darkness were. They collapsed onto the soft
fur mats and the Women dumped pouch-lined baskets of sweet
water over their heads; they tried to drink it as it coursed
down their faces, and they slapped noisily at it, and rubbed it
over their bodies. One of the Older brought the sacred horn and
burned dried pods to their victorious return, and to the un-
·known cow beast who had surrendered her gift, and to the tall
hunter who had given up his life. But by the time the pods had
burned themselves out the two hunters were asleep.

When they awoke, the People took them by the hand and led
them to the huge cave of the Ceremonies where a great fire had
been prepared and where a circle of beast skulls watched the
flames with dark hollow eyes. The People burned tufts of bitter
nettle and passed them over the hide bundles the hunters had

235

brought back to them. The hunters opened the bundles and showed the meat to the People. It was crusted with blood now and smelled strongly of the beast from whom it had come, but it was still there in the bundles, all of it. Only when the hunter chief had eaten could the others eat, and only he could distribute meat. The rules were important and must never be broken. The two hunters had eaten the last piece of liver on the run home, as well as the handful of small intestine, but the remainder was here for the People—the chunks of hindquarter, the section of haunch, the rope of muscle they had stripped from the cow's backbone that would be dipped in hot fat now and hung in the cave for several days to dry. It was all here.

When he was awake and fully prepared, Good Runner donned the white skull-and-hide robe and danced the circle of fire for the People, his face blackened with soot and his arms streaked with ocher, shaking the horn rattle and calling to the ghost of their slain companion, the tall hunter, and waving above the flames the touch stick that was made of magic hair. As he danced for them, the People sang their own chants of memory and respect.

Then the feast was made ready. A big chunk of meat was cut up into individual pieces and impaled on roasting sticks. The haunch was wrapped in thistle root and wet husks and placed in a shallow pit under burning coals. Thin strips were sliced from a slab of rump meat and laced upon wet rawhide thongs stretched over a smoky fire. From a tripod straddling a fierce nest of coals hung a large roast skewered with bone needles. Sweet water was there in horn cups. A broth of herbs steamed in a stained stomach pouch. Heady buttons of cactus leaf and the roasted seed nuts of the pine tree lay cupped in a decorated bullrush basket.

Then, with a piece of cooked meat in one hand and a piece of raw fat in the other, Good Runner stood up and took a bite of each and began the feast. When he had eaten several bites the scar-marked hunter sat down beside him on the robe and did the same. Then the People ate.

236

When Good Runner had satisfied himself with the food he returned to his cave with the Woman, and with the Children also. His feet had stopped bleeding and the cramps in his arms and legs gradually went away, and he slept. At one point in the night he awoke and rolled over on the mat and removed the Woman's soft calfhide robe and enjoyed her. When he had finished he lay beside her and put his arms around her and fell asleep. In the dawn he awoke and drank sweet water, and again he slept.

He slept most of the day and in the evening he got up and ate a bowl of pounded fat and tree berries that the Woman fixed for him. Afterward, he went outside and sat on a ledge above the mouth of the cave and watched the Great Light sink into the far hidden well of the earth. Then he returned inside and called the People together and told them they must leave their home here in the caves and return to the land beyond the smoking mountains. Perhaps the beasts had already gone to that land. He hoped so. Certainly he could promise that sweet water could be found there in abundance, and that the Great Light would not burn so fiercely in the sky.

The next day the People assembled their robes and their hides and their weapons and their sacred objects and prepared for the long trip. They ground fresh seeds with the roots and the bulbs that had been soaked in a salt broth, and then stuffed the resulting pulp into dried gourds. They packed the reed baskets with cured meat and covered them with squares of the softest skins. They filled extra pouches with water. They harnessed the dogs to the traveling sleds and packed the sleds full. They loaded the antler racks and the bone cradles and the hide boats, and all of the People did what they knew to be their share of the work.

In the morning when they left the caves there was a white fog rising from the green narrow place where the waters ran. The scarred hunter dropped back to the rear of the band and Good Runner took his customary place in the lead, putting the Great

Light at his back and keeping it there. The fog disappeared
quickly and the Great Light rose up like the angry flames of a
husk and resin fire. A hot wind blew down upon them and as he
led his band directly into it Good Runner sensed that perhaps
the wind was not a temporary thing, but permanent; that it
would not stop when it reached them as he once had thought
but would blow on past across the land, across the ridges of ash
and out onto the endless flats with their burned grasses and
blasted trees, over the very edges of the earth and his time upon
it.

He sensed that it would blow forever.

That evening the rain came, finally. Not snow, but rain, a dis-
mal exasperating petulant rain that didn't have the courage
actually to *fall*; it merely hovered at the corners of things, about
the roofs and in the tops of the trees, drizzling on everything.

In the morning it stopped and Bike Kimball drove to the
Armory and checked his kill in against his permit. He kept the
head, mutilated as it was, believing that a taxidermist he knew
in South Salt Lake could rebuild it to his satisfaction.

By midmorning Von Wallace had admitted to the Wildlife
Resources officials the taking of five animals against only three
permits in the Bloody Hands Gap area the previous day. He
accepted responsibility for all findings of violation that might
be brought, without attempting to explain them. He surrendered his hunting license, and his buffalo permit and tag. He
donated all carcasses left in the area to the Big Game Department, and paid for their disposal.

By twelve noon Dorothy Taddish had completed arrangements for disposition of her husband's body. She expressed
absolute agreement with the coroner's finding of accidental

death, free of gross carelessness or intent, and the coroner offered his heartfelt sympathies to her, adding that hunting accidents were doubly tragic because they usually occurred at times of group fun and high excitement.

Dr. Hall and Dr. Garland were extremely subdued right up to the time of final farewell, when Karen spoke to them somewhat privately and kissed each of them lengthily on the cheek. Some of the dismay that had clung to them seemed to diminish. They went over and shook Dorothy's hand and extended once again their offer of unlimited assistance, financial and otherwise. Tears actually came to Dr. Hall's eyes. "There's adequate insurance and I'll be perfectly all right," Dorothy assured him, holding both his hands in hers. "Please don't blame yourself. Don't dwell on it. Please."

The Granger caravan left Hanksville then and began the long trip home. Bike drove the Pace Arrow and Karen drove the Huntsman. Dorothy rode in the front seat of the El Dorado with Von and Sandy. Sandy's face resembled a pop-art decal and Von's looked exhausted. The day seemed leached out, used up, left behind like a stalk in the wind. "It's so dreary," Dorothy said. There was no anguish in the remark, merely an acceptance. "Winter's almost here. Spring seems so far away." Her eyes flared suddenly and her hands flew to her face. "Oh, God, what do I do now? I've lost my husband."

"Bullshit," Sandy said, and it was so ordinary, so unemotional, that Dorothy parted her hands and looked at Sandy to confirm that she had actually said it.

Sandy didn't return the glance. "You can't lose something you never had," she said, "so the first thing you do now is start being honest about that."

"Oh, Sandy, don't be mean."

Sandy reached over and held Dorothy's hands so she couldn't hide in them again. "You weren't listening, Dorothy. I said you had to be *honest*. You're not going to fool anybody with that poor me crap anymore. All that ever got you was a

239

cheap seat on the inside of a vodka bottle. You don't belong in there. It's too much waste."

Dorothy made an effort to free her hands but it was unsuccessful; they were like bird wings in Sandy's grip. Neither of them spoke. It was as if both of them were waiting, but not for the same thing. After quite a long time Sandy said, "Did you know that Utah has the highest birthrate of any state in the nation?"

Dorothy lifted her head but she didn't speak.

"Would you like to get some of that?" Sandy went on. "Some of that birthrate action?" She waited. "It might be fun." Again she waited. Dorothy was looking at her now. "There's something else Utah has a lot of," Sandy said, "and that's handsome men. I'll bet there'll be a few of them at the new job you're going to go looking for that would just love to spray some of that conception seed on a pretty little chick with crazy eye sockets."

Dorothy said then, softly, a little brokenly, "Oh, Sandy," and she leaned against her, not to hide there or to be held, it wasn't that at all, it was more an acknowledgement, an affirmation. She didn't remove her head from Sandy's shoulder. After a few miles she fell asleep.

Von drove without speaking, without looking at the two women. There was the hum of the tires and the sound of the wind probing at the window seams, a nostalgic chantlike song that tugged at thought and reminiscence like running water did when you watched it too long. He drove through Caineville and Notom and toward the rising ground of the Reef. On both sides of the road the land lay hard and dry and carved. It was not a menacing landscape, he thought, it was merely old. Windswept and vast and old. He thought of the ancient hunters who had crossed here, the ones Sandy had mentioned the first day, the people who had dwelled on the land for a certain period and then passed on. He had a sudden sense of history and of time, the long long way that man had come. "Bike's right about the rules," he said. "We can't make things work without them. I'm sure there have always been rules, since the beginning."

Sandy looked at him. "And the hunting?"

"We have to make up our own mind on that. It's a moral thing and we're moral creatures, not legal. I think it's sort of like the poem. A shadow falls on everything we kill. On all the blood we shed. There's no law that can ever change that."

Sandy reached behind the sleeping Dorothy and placed her hand on Von's shoulder and left it there as he drove.

A blast of wind shook the vehicle and Von watched the red sand blow over the road and out across the land. He knew that a trillion grains of sand had scoured and formed that land. Water had tumbled and swirled and swept all but the hardest rock away to a sea that had dried up eons ago. What was left were the bones of time, the skeleton of what the earth had been. They lay scattered now, buried here, tilted and wedged and naked there, all silent, all worn, all mourned by a wind that had blown forever.

DONALD E. WESTLAKE
Writing as
RICHARD STARK

Classic Crime Novels featuring Parker, the fearless steel-fisted hood who will stop at nothing to get what he wants.

"Super-ingenious, super-lethal...Parker is super-tough."
The New York Times Book Review

THE HUNTER   68627-9/$2.50

Doublecrossed by his wife and left for dead after a heist, Parker plots a relentless trail of revenge that leads him into the New York underworld.

THE MAN WITH THE GETAWAY FACE   68635-X/$2.50

Disguised by plastic surgery, Parker is safe from revenge by the Mob, but his plans for a new heist turn out sour when he learns that his partner's girl is out to cross them both.

THE OUTFIT   68650-3/$2.50

After an attempt on his life, Parker decides to settle the score with the Outfit, and goes after the Big Boss with an iron will and a hot .38.

THE MOURNER   68668-6/$2.50

Blackmailed into robbing a priceless statue, Parker figures he can make the crime pay—but he doesn't count on a double cross, a two-timing blonde, and a lethal luger aimed to kill.

THE SCORE   68858-1/$2.50

When an invitation to a heist turns into a plan to rob an entire town, Parker begins plotting a perfect crime that calls for guts, guns, and a whole lot of luck.

SLAYGROUND   68866-2/$2.50

After a heist goes sour, Parker, pursued by a couple of crooked cops and some local hoods, escapes with the loot into a deserted amusement park where all that matters is staying alive.

Westlake 8-84

VIETNAM

NOVELS WRITTEN BY
MEN WHO WERE THERE

THE BIG V William Pelfrey   67074-7/$2.95
"An excellent novel...Mr. Pelfrey, who spent a year as an infantryman in Vietnam, recreates that experience with an intimacy that makes the difference."
The New York Times Book Review

WAR GAMES James Park Sloan   67835-7/$2.95
Amidst the fierce madness in Vietnam, a young man searches for the inspiration to write the "definitive war novel." "May become the new *Catch 22*." *Library Journal*

AMERICAN BOYS Steven Phillip Smith   67934-5/$3.50
Four boys come to Vietnam for separate reasons, but each must come to terms with what men are and what it takes to face dying. "The best novel I've come across on the war in Vietnam."
Norman Mailer

BARKING DEER Jonathan Rubin   68437-3/$3.50
A team of twelve men is sent to a Montagnard village in the central highlands where the innocent tribesmen become victims of their would-be defenders. "Powerful." *The New York Times Book Review*

COOKS AND BAKERS Robert A. Anderson   87429-6/$2.95
A young marine lieutenant arrives just when the Vietnam War is at its height and becomes caught up in the personal struggle between the courage needed for killing and the shame of killing. An Avon Original. "A tough-minded unblinking report from hell." *Penthouse*

A FEW GOOD MEN Tom Suddick   87270-6/$2.95
Seven marines in a reconnaissance unit tell their individual stories in a novel that strips away the illusions of heroism in a savage and insane war. An Avon Original. "The brutal power of defined anger." *Publishers Weekly*

AVON Paperbacks

VIETNAM

A WORLD OF HURT Bo Hathaway   **69567-7/$3.50**
A powerful, realistic novel of the war in Vietnam, of two
friends from different worlds, fighting for different reasons
in a war where all men died the same.
"War through the eyes of two young soldiers in Vietnam who
emerge from the conflict profoundly changed...A painful
experience, and an ultimately exhilarating one."
Philadelphia Inquirer

DISPATCHES Michael Herr   **68833-6/$3.95**
Months on national hardcover and paperback bestseller lists.
Michael Herr's nonfiction account of his years spent under fire
with the front-line troops in Vietnam.
"The best book I have ever read about war in our time."
John le Carre
"I believe it may be the best personal journal about war,
any war, that any writer has ever accomplished."
Robert Stone (DOG SOLDIERS) *Chicago Tribune*

FOREVER SAD THE HEARTS Patricia L. Walsh   **88518-2/$3.95**
A "moving and explicit" *(Washington Post)* novel of a young
American nurse, at a civilian hospital in Vietnam, who worked with
a small group of dedicated doctors and nurses against desperate
odds to save men, women and children.
"It's a truly wonderful book...I will be thinking about it and
feeling things from it for a long time." Sally Field

NO BUGLES, NO DRUMS Charles Durden   **69260-0/$3.50**
The irony of guarding a pig farm outside Da Nang—The Sing My
Swine Project—supplies the backdrop for a blackly humorous
account of disillusionment, cynicism and coping with survival.
"The funniest, ghastliest military scenes put to paper since
Joseph Heller wrote CATCH-22" *Newsweek*
"From out of Vietnam, a novel with echoes of Mailer, Jones and
Heller." *Houston Chronicle*

AVON Paperbacks